DARK JUSTICE

Nicole A. Bentley
and
Deborah Britt-Hay

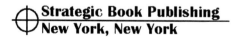 Strategic Book Publishing
New York, New York

Original version Copyright © 1994.
Revised version Copyright © 2008 by Nicole A. Bentley and Deborah Britt-Hay. All rights reserved.

Strategic Book Publishing
An imprint of AEG Publishing Group
845 Third Avenue, 6th Floor – 6016
New York, NY 10022
http://www.strategicbookpublishing.com

ISBN: 978-1-60693-406-7, 1-60693-406-6

Book Design: Bruce Salender

Printed in the United States of America

Acknowledgments

Our deepest thanks to everyone without whose help *Dark Justice* would not have been possible. First, to our families who endured our long hours at the computer and our absence from the dinner table, their patience, support, and tolerance are greatly appreciated.

To Dr. Joseph W. Cox, former president of Southern Oregon University and retired Chancellor of the Oregon State System of Higher Education, who encouraged and supported our writing endeavors.

To Allan Adams, former president of Fawcett Publications, now deceased.

To Dr. Rod Badger, professor emeritus, for his help and advice regarding tetradotoxin.

To Dr. Karen Gunson of the Oregon Crime Lab in Portland, Oregon, who patiently explained how tetradotoxin works and how it can be detected during an autopsy.

To Detective Shirley Peters of the Medford, Oregon, Police Department for her advice regarding the workings of a small-town police department.

To Bryan Workman who supplied critical information about firearms.

And last, but certainly not least, to Mary Linn Roby, a much-published author and one of A-1 Editing Service, LLC's star editors, who critiqued and reviewed the novel with her eagle eye and made it the best that it could be

Without them, this novel would not have been possible

CHAPTER 1

"I'm sorry, Steven," she whispered, "I wish it could have been different."

His eyes, glazed and unfocused, stared up at her, his mind refusing to accept the truth.

"Put the gun away, Meagan, you don't know what ..."

The shot interrupted him.

"I'm sorry," she said again. "You left me no choice."

He lay still, looking boneless and disconnected on the priceless Tabriz carpet as the thunder that had taken him echoed through the room. Blood crept across the rug's midnight-blue field and mingled with its crimson edge.

As the smell of cordite assaulted her nostrils, she began to shake. The sun, which had made a cameo appearance among frowning pewter-colored clouds, hid again, darkening the study. The sudden sound of distant thunder brought terror with it. What insanity had she committed? And what would be the consequences?

But she wasn't crazy. Scared witless, yes. Sick at heart that her life had come to this, yes, but not crazy. Somehow, she had always known it would come to this. Somehow, she had hoped it would not have to.

Steven's hand, extended in a final menacing gesture, seemed

to reach for her. Suddenly, her anger boiled over, and nine years of suppressed anger and hopelessness came tumbling out.

"How does it feel, Steven? How does it feel to be on the receiving end?" she yelled. Her voice faltered and tripped on her vocal cords, daring her to breathe. It could have been her lying here, dead! Why did she not have the guts to do this long time ago?

But finally, it was over.

She breathed deeply to get herself under control. Another spell of dizziness overcame her, and she leaned against Steven's desk for support. Shoving the small .22 semi-automatic pistol into her jacket pocket, she forced herself to gather the thoughts that were ping-ponging around in her head.

She had to get moving. Every minute counted.

Earlier, after parking her car half-a-mile down the road, she had walked to the house and, shoes in hand, had come in through the kitchen and tiptoed into Steven's study. His back to her, he had been standing in front of the picture window, gazing at the pasture that stretched behind their home. Clutching a heavy tennis trophy with her gloved hands, not giving herself a chance to think, she had struck him on the back of the head with all her strength. He had turned as he fell, the disbelief in his eyes replaced by terror when he saw the gun in her other hand.

Her thoughts raced back to last night's terrible scene when finally, incomprehensible as it seemed to her now, she had made her decision.

"Who do you think you are, embarrassing me in front of everyone at dinner by coming on to Jon MacLean like a cheap slut?" he had shouted, pushing her against the bedroom dresser.

But this was not the time for retroactive anger. Precious minutes were racing by, minutes she could ill afford to squander in needless reflections.

Slipping her shoes back on, she retrieved the ejected casing, shoving it in the pocket of her jacket, along with the gun, before sprinting toward the garage where she had hidden a storage box earlier. Taking it to the master bedroom, she flung open her closet's doors and began to scatter clothing from it and from her dresser drawers, all over the floor. Pawing through her jewelry chest, she selected a few pieces of expensive-looking costume jewelry and dropped them into the box, along with the costly camera Steven had given her for Christmas and which she kept on the closet's shelf. She raced upstairs to her office, picked up her laptop computer, ran back to Steven's study, and, averting her eyes from his lifeless body, removed two guns from one of the desk drawers and added them to the box. Going into the kitchen, she unlocked the French doors leading to the brick patio and, taking a large rock from the garden, she broke the glass, sending glittery shards across the kitchen floor. Breathless, she then returned to Steven's study, adrenaline galloping through her system.

Suddenly, she remembered the pistol and shell casing in her pocket and stopped in mid-stride. Going back to her bedroom, she opened the wall safe hidden behind her furs and evening gowns and put both items inside. Why she had bothered to pick up the ejected shell casing she did not know, but somehow it had seemed like the right thing to do.

Her first attempt to close the safe failed because of the shaking of her hands. She tried again—successfully this time —and closed the hidden panel that blended almost perfectly with the wall. As she reached Steven's study again, she stopped to catch her breath.

Although it seemed like hours, the whole thing had taken less than fifteen minutes.

She told herself she must calm down. It would be pretty tough going, but everything would be okay

It had to be.

Had she forgotten anything? She did not believe so. Her mouth was so dry that her tongue felt like parchment glued to her palate. Quickly, she walked back to where her blue BMW was parked, drove it into the garage, and put the box into the trunk. She would dispose of it later.

She was suddenly overcome by a panic attack.

What in God's name had made her think that she could get away with this? The police would be here as soon as she called

CHAPTER 2

"Alix, there's a Dr. Meagan Rathburn on Line Two," Sergeant David Barnes said, turning to look at his boss. "Says she just got home from work and found her old man shot through the head and her house ransacked."

"*Hijo de* … !" Alix caught herself before she could finish the vulgarity and blushed furiously. Even now she could hear her mother's disapproval. *Really, hijita!* Old habits died hard, and she still felt guilty when using language she knew her mother would find objectionable.

She picked up the phone. "Detective Alix Mendez here, Dr. Rathburn. I'm so sorry to hear about your husband. My partner and I will be there in just a few minutes. What's your address?"

She wrote it down as she got to her feet.

"Thank you," the woman said, and Alix could hear the tremolo in the cultured voice. "But hurry, please hurry! Steven's just lying here, dead, shot! And I don't know what to do!"

"We'll be there as soon as we can. Please try to stay calm," Alix told her. "Well, I guess that shoots my plans for a romantic evening with Lloyd down to hell," she said, turning to Dave after hanging up the phone.

He grinned. "You guys have been married, what, three years now? And you still act like honeymooners?"

"Hey, I waited a long time to find the right guy," she said. "But things like robbery and murder have a way of interfering with one's romantic plans. "To think that Lloyd and I were going to ..."

Dave raised his hands, palms out, and grinned. "Never mind, Alix! You might be sorry you discussed your bedroom escapades with me, and I might not respect you in the morning."

Alix Mendez was a statuesque woman who carried her height with considerable panache. Forceful, arresting were the words that her face brought to mind, a face that would have been at home on an antique Spanish *escudo*—an expressive, lived-in face that reflected not only her moods but also a vulnerability often at odds with the image of the self-assured cop she normally projected.

Alix's looks were a roadmap of her colorful ancestry—the magnificent mahogany hair worn in an old-fashioned Gibson Girl topknot, a gift from an Italian grandmother who had left a trail of broken hearts; the imperious nose, high cheekbones, and deep-set amber eyes from a Moorish ancestor who had conquered Spain in the eighth century; and the willful mouth of her namesake and great-great-great-great-grandmother, Countess Alix de Marigny, who had barely escaped the French Revolution and sought refuge in England.

Four years ago, Alix had become not only Red Pine's first Hispanic policewoman but also its chief of detectives. Although only in her mid-thirties, she had risen through the ranks thanks to a combination of ambition, hard work, tenacity, and an uncompromising set of ethics. Rumor had it that her accomplishments were the result of her gender and ethnicity, but she had thumbed her nose at her detractors—her track record was ample proof that being a Latina woman in an Anglo male world had nothing to do with her success, and as far as she was concerned, those who thought otherwise could go straight to hell. Pushing herself to the limit, she had moved up from recruit to lieutenant in record time, perhaps in an effort to justify the chasm her career choice had created between her and her parents several years ago.

Red Pine, the small community nestled at the foot of the

Siskiyou Mountains in the Pacific Northwest, was home now. Its laid-back lifestyle, eclectic residents, and pristine scenery had been instrumental in her decision to spurn larger cities and a bigger salary—a decision she had never regretted. However, on days like today, she was rudely reminded that life in Red Pine was not really that different and that murder happened here as it did everywhere else.

But not as often.

"Louise, get the CSU and Dr. Gardner over there pronto," she told her secretary, handing her the Rathburns' address.

"What gives, boss?"

"Robbery and murder, from the sound of it."

She glanced up and did a double take. Louise, who doubled as dispatcher and had been with the department for more than twenty years, wore a multi-hued ankle-length skirt reminiscent of the 1920s, a matching turban, and a scarf, which she had draped around her neck with considerable flair.

"Who're you supposed to be today?" Alix asked cautiously.

"Isidora Duncan, who else?"

"Of course. Silly me! But don't you go getting that scarf caught in your typewriter. I would have a hell of a time explaining it on an accident report."

"The problem is moot, Alix," Louise said primly, "considering we haven't used them since the chief bought us those nice new computers."

"Yes, I forgot," Alix said wearily, ignoring Louise's grin. "Or at least I'm trying to." Her secretary loved computers and had quickly become proficient while Alix had a hate-hate relationship with the devices. "So what happened to my old Underwood?" she added plaintively.

"I think the chief offered it to the Smithsonian, but they politely declined, so he gave it to the Salvation Army," Louise replied, waving as Alix made her departure.

The two detectives' arrival at the Rathburn home coincided with that of the Crime Scene Unit. Finding the door open, they let themselves in and found an ashen-faced Meagan standing in the corner of the study and far from her husband's body, which was sprawled on the floor by his desk.

Dr. Joe Gardner, the long-suffering county medical examiner, trotted into the room and knelt next to the body. Gardner was in his early sixties and had the body of a teardrop, a craggy face, and the alert gray eyes of a field mouse on the make.

Flashing her badge, Alix introduced Dave Barnes. After looking at the body, she led Meagan, who was shaking so hard that she could hardly walk, into the living room where she sat down next to her on one of the two sofas whose leather felt as soft as the nose of a newborn colt. Dave solicitously placed an afghan, which was draped on the back of the sofa, around the young widow's shoulders.

"Tell me what happened from the time you got home, Dr. Rathburn," she said, watching the woman next to her shred the tissue she was holding into minuscule paper balls that peppered the skirt of her white wool suit.

Meagan looked up at her, tears running down her face. "I teach criminology at the university," she explained. "My last class ended at two o'clock. After that, I attended a lecture for a visiting professor and then I drove home. When I got here, I saw Steven's car in the garage, so I came in and called out to him. He didn't answer, and I saw that the French door's glass was shattered. That's when I realized something was very wrong," she added in a tremulous voice.

She paused to dab at her eyes. "As soon as I opened the door of the study, I saw him lying on the carpet. I saw the hole in his head. I saw blood everywhere. I was terrified, wondering if the killer might still be around, but I heard nothing so I called you right away. Steven teaches ... taught political science," she added with a catch in her voice.

Alix was unable to tell whether Meagan's sob was an expression of nervousness or grief.

"But why didn't you call an ambulance right away?" Alix asked. "He might have still been alive."

"There was ... there was nothing I could do. He was dead, I was sure of it, and there was nothing I could do! Oh, my God!" Meagan took another shuddering breath, then struggled to compose herself. "I checked for a pulse. There was none."

Alix eyed her warily. Meagan's eyes were huge and unfocused in her bloodless face and her distress seemed genuine, yet the detective experienced a feeling of malaise. Something was screwy here, but what? She wished she could put her finger on it.

"Can I call someone to stay with you?" she asked gently.

"No one! No! I don't need anyone! Just leave me alone! I can't believe this has happened!" Meagan shouted, her voice now bordering on hysteria.

She was not at all the sort of person Alix had expected. The young professor wore a beautifully cut suit that Alix's expert eye identified as a Chanel creation. She was tiny, as fragile and delicate as a Dresden figurine. Her strawberry blond hair framed a perfect oval face, and heavy lashes that shadowed huge slanted green eyes gave her a seductive odalisque look. She had the milky complexion of a natural redhead and a small straight nose dotted with tiny freckles and exuded a smoldering sensuality of which she seemed totally unaware. A picture of her in seventeenth-century court dress, dancing the minuet at Versailles on the arm of the Sun King, popped into Alix's head. The young woman's beauty was surrounded by an aura of innocence and vulnerability that Alix felt sure would appeal to every male's protective instincts.

It was strange, though. Usually, she felt a certain affinity for people who had suffered the sort of shock Meagan had experienced, but now, even though there was every reason in the world to feel sympathy, she felt nothing but a faint repugnance, which made no sense at all. Perhaps she was tired of all this death, of the ugliness and brutality she saw daily.

"Mind if I look around?" Alix asked.

"No, not at all," Meagan told her as she walked toward the window facing the pasture where Steven had stood just moments earlier.

Alix rose and began going through the house. On the first floor, she saw a master bedroom, bath, living room, and a study—now the scene of intense police activity—the library, a kitchen and laundry room, and a small bathroom. Two guest bedrooms, each with its own bath, and a small study that Meagan apparently used as her office comprised the upstairs.

As she entered the master bedroom, a flash of red caught Alix's eye. Lying on one of the chairs was a flimsy camisole, the type of cheap, sexy underwear featured in some mail-order catalogs, its bodice torn. Alix frowned, unable to reconcile the tawdry garment with the elegant woman downstairs.

Upon returning to the living room, she found Meagan staring out the window, arms crossed, lost in thought. "Dr. Rathburn, do you mind sitting down? I'm sorry to have to ask you this but can anyone confirm your whereabouts this afternoon?" Alix asked as both women resumed their seats on the sofa.

Meagan nodded wearily as she dabbed at her eyes with a fresh tissue. "After I finished with office hours, I went to the lecture and reception around three thirty. Many of my colleagues, including the university president, were there." She gave Alix a thin smile. "It's okay, Detective, I know that the spouse is always the obvious suspect."

"Then you also know that these are routine questions," Alix replied. "Any idea as to who'd want to kill your husband?"

"None," Meagan said, shaking her head. "He was well liked, an excellent professor, very active in the community. Robbery's got to be the only explanation."

But is it, Alix wondered. "Any idea what's missing?" she asked.

Meagan reached for the glass of water Dave Barnes had thoughtfully brought her and thanked him with a weak smile. "No, but I haven't had a chance to look around to find out. I'm sure you realize it was the last thing on my mind when I found Steven …"

Tears again misted the thick eyelashes. She looked around for a box of tissues and seemed startled when she found none.

Alix offered her a Kleenex from her purse. "I'd like a list of the missing items as soon as you can," she said gently.

Meagan nodded again as she reached for the Kleenex. Alix glanced at the large, perfect solitaire sparkling on the other woman's right hand. "You keep much jewelry at home?"

"Just this ring. It's been in my family for years. The rest is in a safe deposit box at the bank."

Alix walked over to the living room window and saw Dave Barnes bending over as he checked for tire tracks and footprints. "What time did your husband normally get home?"

Meagan was silent for a moment, her hands torturing the hem of her skirt. "It varied. Sometimes he'd go into town to run errands after office hours or ride his bike. He would often correct papers until I came home, usually around four-thirty. And sometimes we'd meet in town for dinner. Our routines varied, so I guess the only regularity about our schedules was its irregularity."

Alix looked thoughtful. This would make it difficult for anyone to know for sure when either Steven or Meagan might be home. "Did he normally park his car in the garage?" she asked.

"No. He usually left it in the driveway in case he had to go out again."

"Do you and your husband own any guns?"

"Yes, a .38 police special and a .357 Magnum. Steven kept them in one of his desk drawers in the study. For protection, he said. I told him that he shouldn't keep guns in the house, and I was right. What good did they do him today?"

"Were they registered?"

"Yes."

"Did he also own a .22?"

Meagan frowned. "I don't think so, no."

"Do you mind looking to see if the guns are still there?"

Meagan rose and went to the study, followed by Alix. She averted her eyes from Steven's body, opened a drawer, and drew in a sigh. "They're gone."

Her already-pale face blanched. "Oh, God! I just remembered! I've got to call Steven's parents. How am I going to tell them about this? I wonder if Jon MacLean could come over," she said softly, almost to herself.

Alix looked up. "Dr. MacLean in the Psych Department?"

"Yes. Steven and I met him and his girlfriend, Margot Cavanaugh, when we came to Red Pine. We became good friends, and they really helped us get acquainted on campus." Although her speech seemed more collected, her delivery was still mechanical and stilted.

"Jon and I worked together on many cases," Alix said. "I'd be glad to call him for you."

"Thank you," Meagan replied, her eyes downcast.

Quite a woman, Dr. Rathburn, Alix thought. Such control! I'd be a screaming maniac if it were Lloyd lying dead on the floor. But, she reminded herself, people did react to grief differently.

Dr. Gardner took her aside. "I'll have an autopsy report for you as soon as I can. Cause of death was the shot to the head, and from the tattooing on his skin and the size of the entry wound, it looks like a .22 fired at almost point-blank range. The bullet probably hit bone. It didn't exit."

"Time of death?"

The old ME shrugged. "Rigor mortis hasn't set in yet. No evidence of lividity. I'd say, less than four hours."

"Any other injuries?"

He nodded. "A bruise on the back of the head. Blunt instrument of some sort, maybe one of those trophies. You'll know more when the lab goes over them. The skin wasn't broken, so I suspect the blow was meant only to stun him."

Alix thanked him pensively, wondering why the intruder had not bludgeoned Rathburn to death when he already had a weapon on hand to do the job, whatever it was. Why hit him over the head and then shoot him?

She eyed Detective Hank Brown who was dusting for fingerprints while Jim Harrison ran the evidence vacuum. Because of the department's size, Jim also doubled as photographer.

Alix picked up the phone and dialed a number she knew well. "Jon," she said when he came on the line, "Alix here. A friend of yours, Steven Rathburn, was shot and killed a while ago. Looks like robbery. His wife's asking for you."

"Steven? Jesus, Alix!" Jon exclaimed after a short, stunned pause. "I'll be right over. Any idea who did it?"

"Not yet."

"Poor Meagan! How's she holding up?"

"Well, she looks like she could use a friendly shoulder."

"Please tell her I'm on my way," he told her.

Alix hung up. "Jon will be here as soon as he can, " she said to Meagan as she continued making notes in her small notebook.

"Thank you," Meagan answered mechanically. Suddenly the life seemed to have gone out of her.

Dave Barnes came back into the living room. "The tire marks belong to the two cars in the garage, Alix. Nothing else. Any sign of a weapon in here?"

"No, and no shell casing either. Maybe the killer used a revolver, but then why bother to retrieve it?"

Dave gave her a your-guess-is-as-good-as-mine shrug, and less than fifteen minutes later, Jon MacLean entered the room. He was a handsome, slender man with a body honed by years of martial arts training. A thin white scar on his left cheek and startling blue eyes in a tanned face gave him the look of a buccaneer of yore.

After acknowledging Alix with a smile and a wave, he went to Meagan who was still sitting on the sofa, looking vacantly into space. He bent his tall frame to kiss her cheek, and his lapis eyes shimmered with compassion. "I'm so sorry about Steven, Meg. I came as soon as I could. Are you okay?"

She gazed up at him and gave him a slight nod, her face streaked with tears, her head tilted to one side, a charming mannerism she seemed to perform unconsciously and without guile as she accepted his kiss.

He peered into her face. "Are you sure?" he asked with concern. "You don't look all right to me. Why don't you give me your doctor's phone number and let me call him so he can give you something?"

Meagan lifted both hands, palms out, in an impatient gesture. "No! I'm okay, really. Why does everyone keep asking me if I'm okay? Everything's all right! It's got to be all right!" Her self-control seemed to slip away, and her voice held a tinge of hysteria.

Jon and Alix exchanged a startled look.

"Sorry," Meagan said, quickly recovering. She passed a wary

hand over her brow. "I didn't mean to be rude, but this whole thing is like a terrible nightmare."

She turned toward Alix. "I apologize, Detective. I don't know what came over me."

"It's okay, " Alix replied. "It's normal under the circumstances."

Now what was that all about, she wondered? A puzzled expression darkened Meagan's face as she slowly shook her head. "I don't get it, Jon. Why kill Steven? Why not just take whatever they wanted and leave?"

"Meagan, there are a lot of weirdos out there," he said, his arm encircling her shoulder. "Some kill without provocation and most don't need a reason. You guys are perfect targets for a robbery out here, isolated as you are. Steven probably walked in on a burglar, things got out of hand, and the guy shot him so Steven couldn't identify him."

He turned toward Alix. "What do you think?"

"Too soon to tell," she said evasively. "I'll talk to the neighbors in case they saw or heard something. But you're right, Jon, this house's isolation provides a great target for would-be burglars."

"My immediate neighbors work," Meagan told Alix. "Paul Johnson is a colleague of mine, and his wife works in the district attorney's office as a legal secretary, so I doubt they were home and able to hear anything."

Alix nodded. "I'll talk to them. You're sure I can't call someone to stay with you?"

"Thank you, no. I'll be fine. You're very kind, and I'm sorry if I sounded rude and ungrateful."

Alix was still unable to shake her discomfort. Everything seemed on the up and up—a homeowner walks in on a thief, the intruder shoots him, the person dies. It happened every day all over the country. So what was her problem? Damn if she knew.

Doc Gardner motioned to the paramedics to load the body on the stretcher and take it to the waiting ambulance. Alix saw Meagan avert her eyes as the attendants placed Steven's body on the gurney and zipped it in a body bag. Unlike others Alix had observed who wanted to take a last look at their loved one, Meagan made no attempt to do so. Indeed, an expression very much like relief seemed to cross the widow's face.

Jon gave her hand a slight squeeze. "Why don't I make us all some tea? It'll make you feel better," he said, apparently misunderstanding her reaction as he saw her shudder.

Meagan tried to compose herself and gave him a weak smile. "Spoken like a true Brit. Tea as a cure for everything."

The tea made, Jon offered some to Alix who declined with a slight shake of her head. She had seen the expression on Meagan's face as the gurney had brushed past her. What was it? Fear? Revulsion? Perhaps guilt? Meagan's green eyes had revealed nothing.

Jon gently ushered Meagan to the sofa. She sat down and cradled her cup with both hands as if to absorb its warmth. After Dr. Gardner had left, Alix got to her feet. Her notes crowded several pages of her notebook.

"I'm sure I'll have more questions, Dr. Rathburn, but they can wait till later. I assume you have no plans to leave town?"

Meagan shook her head. "We're in the middle of spring term. I wouldn't think of leaving my students in the lurch, especially without telling you."

Alix thought she detected a tinge of sarcasm in the widow's voice but shrugged it off as a product of her often over-active imagination. She still could not put a name to what was nagging at her. Maybe she'd talk to Jon about it when she had something more concrete to go on. From their past association, she knew that his point of view could often put a different spin on a case. His dispassionate, logical way of looking at situations provided balance to the gut-reaction impulsiveness that sometimes clouded her judgment.

* * *

After everyone had left, Meagan sagged with relief. It had been easier than she thought. Certainly, it looked like the police had bought the robbery motive. She had two things going for her—her alibi was rock solid, and nobody knew about her and Steven.

But the woman detective was a sharp cookie. Those amber eyes of hers missed little. It would be a grave mistake to underestimate her.

Going into Steven's study, she stared with revulsion at the blood staining the fringe of the Persian rug, a grisly reminder of what had once been her husband.

Her husband.

Dr. Steven James Rathburn. Prominent university professor. Sought-after lecturer. A pillar of the community. And, from all appearances, a loving spouse.

Steven.

Rage roiled up from her stomach and crept into her throat. For years she had hid the truth, walked on eggshells, hated herself for her weakness and self-imposed taboos.

And then there had been last night.

Her marriage had gone hideously wrong almost from the beginning, and the happy times had become only distant memories. Steven had quickly changed, becoming first verbally, then physically abusive, although his remorse afterwards was always overwhelming.

"I'm sorry I lost my temper, but it's your fault for provoking me," he would always say. "It's up to you to learn what makes me angry."

Like a fool, she had believed him, and for a while, the good times would overcome the bad ones. But he never failed to put her down and his verbal cruelty had been almost worse than the physical abuse. When she was asked to present a paper at a prestigious seminar in Rome, he said that she had been invited only because of his reputation and when, shortly after their wedding, she had bought a beautiful green gown that complimented her eyes, he had asked her why she had wasted their money on "that piece of crap."

She had returned the dress and tried to hide her tears, asking herself why she put up with him. But she knew. She knew.

Nine years ago, she had been a brilliant criminology student at UC Berkeley. While working on her master's degree, she had signed up for one of Steven's classes and fallen hopelessly in love. His charm, his sleek athlete's body, his caressing brown eyes and winning smile had blinded her to the warning signs like fog shrouding a jagged coastline.

Just when she was beginning to think that her interest was one-sided, he had come up to her one day after class and had asked her out to lunch. After that, he had wooed her relentlessly for several months with extravagant bouquets and small gifts, seemingly content just to make her smile. After her graduation summa cum laude, they were married in a wedding given by her mother and stepfather at their Atherton home. They then flew to Maine to meet Steven's parents who had missed the wedding because of his mother's illness.

"I'm sorry they couldn't come, Steven," she told him. "Having them at our wedding would have made a perfect day even more special."

"Forget it, Meagan," he said curtly. "Mother's prone to that sort of thing."

He had not elaborated, and the look on his face had precluded any questions. It was not until later when she met Joan Rathburn, a sparrow of a woman who always agreed with her husband, that she found out what "that sort of thing" was. Frank Rathburn, a carbon copy of Steven, brooked no disagreement regarding his opinions, and he had opinions on just about everything. Meagan, sensing an odd tension between the couple, had politely inquired about Joan's illness and had been startled by the naked fear in the woman's eyes.

Upon their return to California, they had had their first argument, and the intensity of Steven's anger had made her cringe. "Goddammit, Meagan," he had yelled, "Don't second guess everything I do or say. I'm your husband, remember? I'll decide what's best for us."

Afterward, as they readied for bed, he had asked her to perform certain sexual acts, and when she found she could not force herself to comply, he had hit her hard, splitting her lip and sending her reeling across the room. "You're my wife and you'll do whatever I tell you. Got that?"

Terrified, she had brought the swelling down with ice and concealed the discoloration with makeup. She had even forgiven him when, filled with what he claimed was remorse, he bought her a beautiful gold bracelet encrusted with emeralds in an exclusive San Francisco jewelry store as a peace offering.

"I'm so sorry, babe," he had told her. "It must have been the wine, and you looked so sexy in that new nightgown. I lost my head. I swear I'll never do it again."

But it was yet another empty promise. Anything and everything seemed to provoke Steven's trigger-like temper. He was clever, though, never hitting her where it showed, but her stomach, arms, back, and thighs were always covered with bruises. She could not remember when she had last worn a short-sleeve blouse or felt the sun on her body. Worse, she knew that the neighbors, especially old Mrs. Collingwood next door, suspected what was going on.

Steven called her fat even though she wore a size-six dress; stupid although she was better read than he; lazy despite the fact that she managed to keep the house spotless while also working on her PhD.

Then one summer, they went to the Greek Islands and, for one short week, the magic was back. They swam, made love, and ate *baklava* and *domates yemiste*—wonderful tomatoes stuffed with herbs, rice, and meat—and danced in the moonlight. She dared to hope again, only to see her hopes shattered when they returned home and the cycle of abuse resumed.

One day, when she had gone to the emergency room using an alias after a particularly violent episode, the doctor had looked at her suspiciously.

"What happened, Mrs. Herion?" he asked. "How did you get these injuries?"

"I tripped on the rug and fell." She gave him a shy, embarrassed smile, but she knew he was not fooled.

There was doubt in his voice as he asked her other questions, which she skillfully dodged. She knew that he knew she was lying, and because he was kind, she had timidly started to reach for the help she thought he was offering, only to feel him withdraw, clearly reluctant to get involved in a family situation. "I wish I could do more for you, Mrs. Herion," he had said, "but all I can say is, watch your step."

It had been a pointed warning.

On another occasion, she had confided in Jeanne Davis, an old college friend, over lunch. Jeanne had laughed. "You're kidding, Meagan, right? Steven wouldn't do that! You must've done something to make him mad."

Meagan had gotten to her feet and left without a word, convinced of her culpability and certain that seeking help was useless. And so, ignored, betrayed, and filled with hopelessness, she had gone on as before until, after moving to Red Pine, she realized that Steven was cheating on her. She had smelled the perfume on his clothing, found the lipstick on his handkerchief, and read the phone numbers hastily scribed on matchbooks.

One night, he found her emptying the pockets of his navy blazer in order to send it to the cleaners. He had shouted at her to leave his clothes alone, sending her reeling across the room with a vicious shove and telling her that he was sick of her spying on him.

Soon she did not care. At least he was discreet, frequenting places where chances of running into someone they knew were slim and taking his escapades to other towns to protect his own reputation. However, after discovering his indiscretions, she had moved into one of the guest bedrooms and refused to share their bed in a rare show of defiance. It was what had triggered his rage last night when he had brutally raped and beaten her as he pressed the .22 pistol he kept in the drawer of his night table to her temple.

"Next time you deny me, I'll kill you, bitch! I mean it! Now put on this red camisole and act like the whore you are!"

Afterward, she had locked herself in the bathroom and spent the rest of the night in mindless panic while he yelled obscenities through the door.

She had thought of leaving him on many occasions. Most women in her situation would have, she knew. And wasn't it what she told the women she counseled? Of course, they did not have Idrys Sanborne for a mother, a woman who would never understand or forgive. How could she leave Steven without letting the whole world know the truth and exposing her shame? No one in her family had ever divorced, and for that reason, and because of Idrys's inevitable anger and disapproval, she just could not do it.

But who was she kidding, she told herself at times when she was being totally honest with herself. She could not leave if she wanted to. She was such a pathetic coward! Time and time again, she made excuses for her weakness and cowardice.

Last night, however, she had reached the end of her rope and made her decision. Physically, emotionally, she could no longer take the abuse, trapped in a bizarre, high-noon duel of sorts from which only one could survive. She had seen her own death in Steven's eyes and in the gun he had pointed at her.

And she very much wanted to live.

* * *

Meagan was a criminologist, an educated, intelligent woman. Yet she was well aware that she had not acted like most women faced with a life-threatening situation. Instead, she had reacted in the manner her mother had drilled into her since she was a tiny child, focused only in protecting her family's name and reputation at any cost.

She could still hear her mother's soft, southern accent. "You must always think of appearances, Meagan. You have to protect our family name, our reputation, even if it means lying. This family doesn't air its private affairs in public."

"But, Mama, you always told me lying was a sin."

"I'm talking about the family," Idrys had replied sternly. "The Sanbornes have never been involved in a scandal. See to it that they never are."

Meagan's father, her distinguished, charming father whom she had loved despite everything, was dead, and she had no siblings, no relatives, no close friends to confide in. Her mother was all she had, and Meagan could not risk her wrath. So she had planned her husband's murder. To make her abuse public and have her personal reputation fodder for cocktail-party gossip simply was not an option.

Even if she were strong enough to defy her mother and leave Steven, she knew he would not rest until he tracked her down and made her pay. And after that hellish night, she had focused only on what she planned to do, her pain and terror finally giving way to hatred and despair and a steely resolve.

* * *

A sudden realization jolted her back to the present. She was free! But her euphoria was short lived. Freedom would not last unless she kept up the charade by calling Steven's parents and her family and playing the part of the bereaved wife. She was a good actress. Had she not played a part for the world for the last nine years, and today for the police?

Hopefully, she had convinced Alix of her innocence, but she had probably made some mistakes, like picking up the spent shell. Yet it was not damning, and apparently, Alix had thought little of it. But what about her reaction when the gurney carrying Steven's body had brushed past her, or her angry outburst in response to Jon's caring questions?

Twice now, the stress had caused her to drop her guard. She must never make such mistakes again.

But she was only a criminologist, for God's sake, not a career criminal! She had no first-hand experience at murder. What she did have, however, was an alibi. And Alix, no matter how clever, would be hard pressed to uncover a motive.

She suddenly felt calmer but without warning, exhaustion overcame her, perhaps caused by the persistent cold and chills that had been plaguing her for weeks now.

But now, she could put the nightmare behind her and go on with her life.

CHAPTER 3

"What's going on with the investigation?" Jon asked as they sat in Alix's cozy living room and watched a blazing fire burning brightly in the brick fireplace. The aroma of her favorite coffee from the highlands of Nicaragua wafted through the room.

"Not a hell of a lot," she replied, looking ill at ease as she sweetened her coffee with condensed milk. "I've got some ideas, but I'm not ready to discuss them with you."

"Why not?" he asked, looking offended.

"Because they're just vague thoughts and suppositions, and I don't want to commit myself just yet." She leaned forward, elbows on her knees as she gazed into the fire. "Jon, you've known the Rathburns since they came to Red Pine. What can you tell me about them?"

"Well, they came from the Bay Area about four years ago after they both got teaching jobs here. Margot and I befriended them and helped them become part of the academic life. They seemed crazy about each other. He was always stroking her hair or patting her arm, and she hung on to his every word. You know, that sort of thing. And being popular and attractive, they soon became an integral part of the community. Everyone thought the world of them."

"Anything else?"

"I soon realized what a terrific professor Meagan is," Jon went on. "She's devoted to her students, especially Paige Chatfield, a student she's grooming for graduate school. She's also involved in all kinds of committees and co-facilitates a group for battered women. Steve was good in his field, but he didn't come close to having his wife's fire in the classroom or her dedication to causes she believes in."

He smiled and reached for his cup. "I often wondered if he wasn't a little jealous of Meagan's popularity. And being married to someone as attractive as she is might cause any man to feel threatened."

"You suppose there's another man? It would give her a hell of a motive to kill her husband," she said, eyebrows raised.

"If there is, I sure don't know about it, and in a town the size of Red Pine, keeping that sort of thing a secret would be like hiding an elephant in your living room. And why would she want to kill Steven, for heavens' sake? They were devoted to each other!"

Alix gave a Gallic shrug. "Well, I'll check on it anyway. How about another woman?" she asked, avoiding his question. "Did Rathburn have a problem keeping his pants zipped?"

Jon shook his head. "Can't say I ever heard any rumors to that effect."

"Well, I'll check on that, too. And another thing," she added.

He gave her a questioning look.

"They've apparently been married for quite a while. How come no kids?"

"I don't know. Too busy with their careers, I guess," Jon replied. "Anyway, the subject never came up, and I never asked."

"Always the diplomat. I wish I could be as tactful."

"Forget it, Alix. It would be totally out of character."

"You're trying to tell me I'm a nosy bitch who can't mind her own business?"

"You're a detective, my friend. You're *supposed* to be a nosy bitch who can't mind her own business."

"Thanks, *amigo*!"

He laughed. "Hey, you asked! I'll tell you this, though. I saw Meagan at the park once. She was watching a young mother with

27

her toddler, and her expression was one of sheer yearning. I think that's why she feels so close to Paige. I'm sure she thinks of her as the daughter she never had."

"Well, it's none of my business," Alix told him. "And I don't think it's germane to my investigation anyway. But where does their money come from, Jon? I can't believe that professors' salaries are generous enough to pay for their kind of lifestyle, including that gorgeous collection of Meso-American art, her designer wardrobe, and that enormous solitaire she wears."

"I think Meagan inherited some sort of trust fund from her father, and she mentioned once that the ring had been in her family forever," Jon replied. He leaned back in his chair and put his arms behind his head. "One thing has been bothering me, though."

"What?"

"She's been acting out of sorts lately. She lacks her usual get-up-and-go and she looks like she's lost a lot of weight."

Alix was silent for a while. "There's something very strange about this case, Jon, but damned if I know what." Like many cops, she had learned to trust her gut feeling and had developed a special sixth sense that seldom failed her.

"Did you talk to the neighbors?" Jon asked

"Yes, and got zip. They were both at work, but even if they had been home, chances are they couldn't see or hear much. That house is pretty secluded, but I suppose privacy was the Rathburns' reason for buying the place. If robbery was the motive, it's isolation makes it a perfect target for anyone who knew they both worked and that they had a few bucks. And that .22-caliber pistol would barely be heard from the driveway, let alone a quarter of a mile away."

He eyed her warily. "You said *if* it was a robbery. What else could it be?"

"I don't know yet. It's one of the ideas I've been nibbling on."

She found it difficult to tell him of her gnawing suspicion that there was more to the case than met the eye. There had been something about Meagan that morning, something not quite right. She had been shaken, but not as a new widow would have been. It was akin to hearing a single wrong note in a symphony. And for now, at least, she could not explain it herself.

He shrugged. "Okay, I'll buy that for the time being. So what was stolen?"

"The usual stuff that can be sold for quick cash—costume jewelry that the thief might have assumed to be real, a camera, a laptop computer, two handguns, that sort of thing. But the burglar ignored the pre-Columbian figurines. I'm guessing he was not familiar with Mesoamerican art and thought they were just ugly souvenirs from some tourist trap."

"I know for a fact that they're not," Jon said, grinning. "I tried to buy some of them for my collection, but they wouldn't hear of it. It's too bad. I'd kill for those Mochicas! Sorry," he added, seeing her expression, "Wrong choice of words."

"I saw something strange in the master bedroom, Jon," she said.

"Really? A secret closet with whips and chains, tall boots, and lots of leather outfits?" he quipped.

Usually, Alix was ready to laugh at Jon's jokes, but not today. This was too serious to laugh about.

"No, but there was this cheap camisole lying on a chair. You know, the kind you can buy from a mail-order catalog. It wasn't even silk and looked like it might belong in a hooker's room rather than in the elegant bedroom of two academicians."

"Who's to say what games people play in the bedroom? Maybe Steven bought it for her."

"Maybe," Alix said uncertainly. "Still ..." She dismissed the rest of her sentence with a wave of her hand.

"Where's Lloyd?" Jon asked.

"Working on his book in the study."

Alix had met her husband, her senior by sixteen years, while investigating the murder of his wife, Dorothy, the victim of a serial killer. The charming 1920s Tudor house, which had been Lloyd's home and where he and Alix now lived, had been a challenge to Alix who had ultimately imprinted it with her own cachet by incorporating all her treasures as part of the décor. The result was eclectic and startling. Exquisite netsukes and a Satsuma tea set, brought around the Horn by Alix's great-grandfather, cuddled atop an eighteenth-century sideboard. Persian and Chinese carpets, gifts from her parents, and Tiffany, Webb, and Waterford cut glass blended in as if they had always lived side by side. The result was a tasteful mixture of coziness and elegance.

Alix rose and started to pace, her trademark sign of her thought process at work. Being a big woman, and often ungainly, she caught her foot on one of the table's legs and barely avoided a fall. "*Mierda!*" she said with feeling as she went on tracing a path around the room.

"So I assume your guys are out on the street tracking the stolen stuff down?" Jon said, tactfully ignoring her mishap.

"Barnes and Belford are checking all the pawnshops within a hundred-mile radius."

She stopped pacing long enough to stir the fire with a poker, sending a nosegay of sparks up the chimney.

"But even if it was robbery, it's hard to believe it was the work of a common burglar. I mean, most of these guys aren't brain surgeons, Jon, and they usually leave some clues. Yet we found no tire tracks, no odd fingerprints, nothing. So how did the thief carry the stuff away? By burro? And it, at least, would have left hoofprints! And no fingerprints? Come on! How many burglars take the time to wipe them off unless it's a Park Avenue job? This burglary's so clean it's positively sanitized. There are too many unanswered questions, and I feel as uncomfortable about this case as if I'd tried to squeeze into a size-four dress."

She sat down, absently petting Zeus, her Doberman, who looked up at her adoringly. "And something else," she continued, kissing the top of the big dog's head.

"What?" Jon asked, trying to follow her quantum leaps of thought.

"The weapon. A .22 isn't a normal street gun. Sure, it's lethal at the range it was fired, but punks normally prefer the bang and flash of Clint Eastwood-type firearms."

Anger darkened her face and her amber eyes turned jet black. "You know how I feel about murder, Jon. It's the ultimate theft. It's not only the victim who loses, but society as a whole."

Jon nodded. Indeed, senseless murder was Alix's *bête noire,* one of the few weaknesses that at times obscured her judgment.

When their friendship was still in the budding stage, Alix had told him about her first partner, senselessly murdered years ago by street punks seeking their special brand of weekend thrills. They had shot him down because it felt good, not because he posed a threat, since they had already disarmed him. The killers had never been caught, and Alix, young and inexperienced, had blamed herself for failing to prevent his death. She had carried the guilt for years, unable to forget the huge wound in her partner's chest, the blood that stained her hands, or his begging look as he had died in her arms.

Suddenly, Zeus looked up and wagged his stubby tail as Lloyd appeared, followed by Mack, his Scottish terrier. Lloyd O'Rourke, a retired political science professor, had been hard at work on final revisions to his book on the Civil War. The book was due in three weeks, and Lloyd had been burning the midnight oil to meet his publisher's deadline.

He was a handsome man whose brown hair was starting to gray at the temples. Gentle hazel eyes sparkled with intelligence behind thick glasses. He wore brown corduroy pants, a plaid shirt, and an old jacket with leather elbow patches and looked like the stereotype of the absent-minded professor that he truly was. The unlit pipe clenched between his teeth did nothing to dispel the cliché.

"Hi, honey," he said, bending to kiss her, "Have you seen my glasses?"

Alix and Jon suppressed a smile as she, trying to keep a straight face, said, "You're wearing them, Lloyd."

"Oh, so I am. What are you two up to? Have you solved the murder yet?"

"Give me a break," his wife said affectionately. "The case is only a couple of days old. He thinks I'm Superwoman," she added, turning to Jon, "and that I can solve a case just like that." She snapped her fingers.

"That's because I know you can," her husband said. "I've seen you in action, remember?"

She smiled. "Thanks for that, *querido.* Your confidence does great things for my ego."

"Making any headway?"

"Not a hell of a lot," she said, shaking her head. "Everybody, including our friend here, swears that Steven Rathburn was a combination of Sir Lancelot and Mother Teresa."

Lloyd frowned. "Then something's wrong. Nobody's that perfect."

The phone rang. Alix answered it, and a warm smile lit up her face. "*Mamacita!* What a surprise. How're you and *papá?*"

"*Bien, hijita,* but we miss you. When are you and Lloyd coming down for a visit?" her mother asked.

Alix sighed. "Not for a while, I'm afraid. I'm smack in the middle of a murder case, so I don't know when I can get away."

"It's been so long since we've seen you," Doña Rosa said plaintively.

"I know, *mamá,* but you know how it is."

"*Sí,* only too well," her mother replied.

Alix smiled inwardly. They had been through this before. Rosa was as aware of her daughter's infatuation with her career as she was of her husband's dislike for Alix's chosen profession.

"How's *papá?*" Alix asked.

"Oh, you know, the usual. Busy with the ranch and with the Foundation," Doña Rosa said, making reference to the Alejandro Mendez Foundation, which had been the brainchild of Alix's great-grandfather.

"What's new with everybody?"

"Let me see. Your cousin, Aurora, just married an Alitalia pilot."

"I thought she'd married that French race car driver, Pierre somebody."

"No, that's Rosario, your Aunt Fidelia's daughter."

"*Madre de Dios*! How am I supposed to remember all this," Alix said plaintively. "I'm glad you're keeping track of everybody so that I don't embarrass myself at family reunions."

"Your mother?" Lloyd asked after she hung up.

"Yes, they want us to come down for a visit."

"That would be great," Lloyd said. "Perhaps you could take a leave of absence from work, and maybe we can take a cruise, too."

Alix gave him a quizzical look. Now what was that all about? Lloyd detested cruise ships and had never brought up the subject before.

"Lloyd, I have a murder case on my hands. I can't very well drop everything and go cruising the seven seas," she told him.

"But maybe you'll make short rift of this case, and then we can go somewhere for a couple of weeks," Lloyd persisted.

"Thanks for the vote of confidence, dearest, but somehow, I don't think it's going to happen."

"Is something bothering you?" he asked gently, looking at her tense face.

She shot Jon a quick look. "A few things."

"How is it going with your parents?" Jon asked.

"Better, but we still have a long way to go."

Alix thought briefly about her often-rocky relationship with her father, Oscar Mendez. Her parents, socially prominent and doggedly traditional, had hoped for a more suitable career for their only child, and she remembered their dismay when she had fallen in love with law enforcement, creating a painful rift between parents and daughter that had lasted for years.

"To this day, my father hates everything about my career, although Mother came around long time ago," she said. "Yet he seems to be getting used to the idea, although I know he'll never approve totally. But marrying Lloyd helped," she mused, her face softening as she looked at her husband. "They think he's the only man in the world who can keep me under control."

"Little do they know," Jon said, getting to his feet. "I tried for years before Lloyd came on the scene! Well, I'd better go and pick up Margot. We're supposed to go to a reception at the president's home tonight."

"Give her our love," Alix said. "Say, how about dinner Saturday night? You have my word Lloyd won't go near the kitchen so you have no excuse to beg off," she added, giving her husband a roguish grin.

"Hey!" Lloyd protested, "I may be a failure in the kitchen, but in other rooms in the house …" He wiggled his eyebrows suggestively and kissed his bunched fingertips.

"You'll get no argument from me. And look at Pépin le Bref," she said, making reference to King Charlemagne's diminutive father. "He was vertically challenged, but I hear he was dynamite in the bedroom!"

"But that was in the eighth century! Jon exclaimed.

"So what? Some things never change," Alix countered.

"This conversation's getting pretty racy," Jon told her, laughing. "I'd better leave before you two incriminate yourselves in front of a witness. And dinner Saturday sounds great. I'll bring my green chicken enchiladas. You two can fix a salad, and Margot can make one of her famous desserts. I'll ring you tomorrow to confirm."

Those green enchiladas of yours are death on my waistline," Alix said, sighing. "I gain three pounds every time I look at them. And speaking of Margot, how are things going with you guys?"

"The same, I guess," Jon said, shrugging. "I mention marriage, she puts me off, and it often causes a bit of a tiff. I don't get it," he added. "She says she loves me, yet she won't give me a commitment."

"Be patient, 'migo. Marriage is serious business. Margot will marry you when she's ready, and I suspect you wouldn't want it any other way."

Jon shook Lloyd's hand, kissed Alix on the cheek, and left, but her unease about the case and her refusal to discuss it with him gnawed at him.

* * *

On his way to pick up Margot, Jon thought about Steve Rathburns' murder and his conversation with Alix.

During the course of a kidnap-murder investigation, the two had met and they had become close friends. They shared the same interests and background, and their friendship now fitted them like well-loved old slippers. Working on many other cases together, they had also developed a rewarding professional relationship, which was why Alix's refusal to discuss her theory with him tonight was an irritant he could not dismiss lightly. By the time he reached Margot's apartment, he tried to put it out of his mind and focus on the evening ahead.

Margot came to the door and pecked him on the cheek, looking terrific in a teal silk crepe dress that flattered her creamy skin and raven hair. A gold belt encircled her tiny waist, and except for a pair of beautiful pearl and gold earrings, she wore no jewelry. She was short, shapely, and spunky, and her green eyes flecked with gold sparkled when she saw him. He held her close, kissing her soft mouth, nuzzling her neck, and inhaling the familiar scent of Caron's *Fleurs de Rocailles*, a flowery scent that suited her perfectly.

As she disappeared into the bedroom to get her coat, Jon looked around the apartment with the same feeling of pleasure he always experienced.

Eclectic artwork enhanced its undeniable modesty. Soft shades of mauves, blues, and off-white imparted a sense of elegance and restfulness. A white sofa decorated with blue and mauve pillows faced a beautiful ebony Oriental coffee table, and prints in unusual frames decorated the walls. On the bookshelves, law books cozied up to texts on art, finance, ballet, and literature, and lush ferns and blooming houseplants were everywhere.

Margot reappeared, carrying her coat. "Did you see Meagan today?" she asked. "How's she doing? What a terrible thing to happen! I can't imagine how's she is handling it!"

"I saw her yesterday for a few minutes. She looked kind of numb, but that's normal, of course. I'm glad she's planning to take a few weeks off," Jon told her.

"I feel terrible for her, Jon. The two of them seemed so happy. I'll stop by in a day or two to see how she's getting along. Any word about the funeral service?"

"Tomorrow afternoon at three," he said, helping her into her coat. "I'll pick you up."

They had met when he had run into her at a grocery store—literally—and he had helped her retrieve the spilled contents of her shopping bags. She had told him of the many part-time and summer jobs she had worked in order to put herself through college and law school. She was now a rising star in the district attorney's office, and they had discussed marriage. But, although Jon knew she loved him, he also knew that marrying a lord's son scared her to death. He also knew that she hid her lack of self-esteem beneath a façade of toughness and self-reliance and that she would have swallowed ground glass rather than admit it.

* * *

"Looks like a nice crowd," Jon said ten minutes later as they pulled into the circular driveway. As soon as they entered the house, they found that the tragedy was on everyone's lips.

"Isn't this Rathburn murder dreadful?" Alistair Brooks, one of Jon's colleagues, exclaimed. "It's a sad state of affairs when a guy isn't safe in his own home in a town like Red Pine! Do the police have any leads or do they intend to sit around drinking coffee while we all cower in our homes?"

As the evening progressed, Jon was disheartened to find that this was the general drift of what everyone had to say. He knew that it was not that they distrusted Alix's ability to find the killer, but understandably, they were upset and nervous. Plus the fact that everyone knew Meagan and Steven—which was not to say that the latter had had been universally liked. And Jon also knew that there had been something about them as a couple that had put people off, but they would have been hard-pressed to say what that something was. Despite his friendship with Meagan, Jon himself had sensed it.

It was to his considerable relief that he and Margot left an hour later. For once, he could hardly wait to drop her at her door, sensing that it was not an opportunity for them to be alone. Instead, it was a time for questions to which, sadly, he had no answers as yet.

He went home without asking for a nightcap, Alix's malaise still huddling in a corner of his mind like a malevolent spider as he sipped a brandy while listening to a vintage recording of Alex

Moore's *Boogie in the Barrel.*

He finally acknowledged that he was indeed miffed. What was so different about this case that she felt so reticent to discuss it with him as they had done so often in the past?

He went to bed and after considerable tossing and turning, he finally drifted off. His sleep was uneasy, his dreams populated by faceless bodies brandishing small water pistols.

* * *

"What's wrong, my dear?" Lloyd asked after Jon had left, gently rubbing a thumb over the frown line that seemed to have taken permanent residence on his wife's forehead.

She shrugged and spread her hands, knocking over her coffee cup. "I don't know. I have this odd feeling that Steven Rathburn's death and his wife's reactions were a *mise en scène,* a display put on for my benefit."

"Really? What does Jon think?"

"I didn't discuss it with him. Especially since I don't have an iota of proof."

"I see. So you suspect the wife."

"You guessed?" she said, giving him a surprised look.

"Easy. In all the mystery novels, the spouse is always the obvious suspect."

"I'll make a detective out of you yet," she told him. "In all fairness, though, I have nothing to go on except my gut feeling, but what it's telling me is making me very uncomfortable."

"Such as?"

"I'm not sure. The woman's reactions were correct, and so were her answers. She does have an airtight alibi and no apparent motive, but something didn't jive. It's like when part of the orchestra's playing in the wrong key and you can't figure out which instrument is screwing up, know what I mean?"

"Yes, I think so," Lloyd replied, looking thoughtful.

"I didn't tell Jon because Dr. Rathburn isn't just his colleague; she's also his friend, and I knew how he would react. But something's not kosher, Lloyd. I feel it in my gut and I'm going to find out what it is."

"Well, in the meantime, what do you say we go upstairs and I'll show you my etchings, he said, stroking her long auburn hair and holding her close.

"Very corny, *querido,* but whatever you've got to show me, I'm dying to see it," she replied, grinning lasciviously.

Taking him by the hand, she led him toward the bedroom.

CHAPTER 4

Meagan did a slow turn as she scrutinized the living room. The heavy furniture and dark drapes that Steven had favored had to go. Right after the murder, she had given a fleeting thought about selling the house, but despite the fact that he had died here, she loved this property with its stately oaks and liquidambars and the kidney-shaped pond where geese came to winter every year and which the wildlife used as their watering hole. This house was her sanctuary now, a place where she could have the privacy and quiet times she needed. As for redecorating, she knew that she should wait a while so as not to stir up any suspicion that she was not the grieving widow she pretended to be.

Appearances. They ruled her whole life.

One thing for sure, though. She needed to get rid of everything that reminded her of Steven. Later, she could redecorate to suit only herself, using the soft pastel shades she loved, filling the house with plants. Steven had hated houseplants, claiming they were too messy. Wanting to please him and keep the peace, she had given in to his demands. No plants. No pets. No close friends. And no children, she thought bitterly, because Steven hated kids.

Tears filled her eyes, and she seethed with long-suppressed anger and resentment.

She toured the house, seeing it through new eyes because

now, she could do anything she wanted. Steven had dominated everything once, but now …

Going to the bedroom, she began to think of the change a new color scheme would bring to it, perhaps teal and peach, her favorite colors.

But suddenly, a cloud hiding the sun darkened the bedroom. She shivered, and without warning, her thoughts flashed back to the big, sunny bedroom of her childhood filled with dolls and teddy bears, and later, posters of her favorite movie stars. At night, however, it had turned into a chamber of horrors as she held her breath, listening for her father's footsteps on the stairs. And he would come in without knocking, without speaking, and each time she prayed that he would just hug her or tell her a bedtime story, only to see her hopes shattered and replaced by fear, hurt, and shame.

"Daddy, no, please," she would say, trying to push him away. Please stop, I don't want to do this. I'm afraid."

But he never listened and later, he would tell her, "You're my little girl, Meagan. You don't have to be afraid. You're special. This is our own secret, and you must never tell."

And so she learned to dissemble, to pretend it was happening to someone else and that there were two little girls in the room, the one on the canopy bed going through the unspeakable horror, and the other floating free like the iridescent butterflies she loved to watch in the garden.

The abuse had continued until her father's death from a heart attack, which had coincided with her graduation from high school. No one had known or bothered to find out, not her teachers, not even her mother who was supposed to protect her and who had ignored her and called her a liar. She had been eight when she had hesitantly approached Idrys and spoken in veiled terms about what was happening.

"How can you say things like that about your own father?" her mother had demanded, looking at her as though she were dirt stuck to the bottom of one of her dainty high-heel shoes. It's one thing to have imagination, but this is vicious! Are you trying to ruin our family's reputation? Keep this up, and your father and I will have no choice but to send you to boarding school. The little sisters will know how to deal with you. You won't repeat these lies to anyone if you know what's good for you. You have no idea what it would do to your father and me."

When she was thirteen, she had tried again. This time, her mother had only given her a cold look left the room without a word. The icy contempt in her eyes and her final dismissal of her daughter's plight had hurt Meagan even more than the previous cruel words. Idrys had remarried soon after her husband's death, and since Meagan herself had married upon her graduation, she and her stepfather were almost strangers.

Now the rage that had consumed her after Steven's murder closed in on her again.

No more. No more. NO MORE!

She hugged herself and sat on the edge of the bed, slowly rocking, mindlessly rubbing her arms.

No one would ever hurt her again. She would no longer allow it.

Energized by her anger, she went to the bathroom and threw Steven's toiletries into a box, stripping the room of any remnants of his presence. Going back into the bedroom, she removed his shoes, pants, coats, and shirts from the closet and tossed them into large boxes, working feverishly, almost mindlessly.

Her fury spent, she turned on the bathtub's faucets and slipped into a warm bath perfumed with lavender-scented oil. Eyes closed, her favorite Mozart symphony, the *Jupiter*, playing softly in the background, she reveled in the sensual feeling of the water as the jets swirled around her. When the last stirring movement came to an end, she examined the bruises on her body. They were raw and still very painful, but they would soon fade and eventually disappear.

She wondered about the invisible bruises on her soul. Would they vanish as quickly? Would she ever feel whole like a normal woman? And what did a normal woman feel like, anyway?

And then, without warning, deep, wracking sobs shook her as she mourned the loss of her innocence, the betrayal of those she had trusted, and her own perceived inability to reach for help. She sat for a moment, wondering about what she would do now, about what turn her life might take. But then she felt her strength return, along with a new purpose. She would become the woman she always wanted to be—free, strong, in charge of her own destiny.

She was alive. She was going to make it! She looked back on her tears as an expression of weakness.

She would never cry again.

As she climbed out of the tub, she sensed that she had reached an important milestone in her life. She slipped on a flesh-colored silk nightgown with its matching peignoir, purchased long ago and hidden in her lingerie drawer. She had waited for an opportunity to wear them, although which opportunity that might be, she had never been certain, but she knew now that this was the time she had waited for.

Tonight, she was wearing them for herself.

Later, in bed, she sipped a glass of cold mineral water and watched a rerun of *Casablanca*. And just before slipping into an uneasy sleep, she made a silent vow to rid herself of the demons that had haunted her for so long. But there was still the ambivalence, the mixed feelings with which she wrestled, the horror of what she had done just beginning to sink in despite her efforts to push it away. Even while enjoying her new sense of freedom, she wondered what the future held. Would she ever be truly free to love someone again? Sometimes she felt that all that pain has crippled her forever.

For the first time in years, her sleep was finally dreamless and undisturbed.

CHAPTER 5

Meagan knew that it was important for the women to see her at the Women's Center on a regular basis, but she still experienced considerable trepidation as she walked into the room with Kelly Ford, her co-facilitator. Some of the women in the room had heard about Steven and came up to her, offering their condolences. Much to her relief, no one seemed surprised to see her.

Many of the women had children. Others were still children themselves. Some were homemakers without earning skills and others were educated professionals, but all were united in their special sisterhood of hopelessness and despair.

Meagan thought about Vivian O'Neill's words upon her arrival at the Center when she had shared with the other women the incident that had triggered her call to the Crisis Help Line. Vivian was a good example of the type of women the Center had been set up to help. Her husband, Paul, an accountant, had come home from a partner's meeting. When Vivian told him she was leaving, they had had a violent argument, and he had accidentally struck their child, three-year-old Jasmin. Vivian was used to Paul's abuse, but seeing her daughter caught in the middle had created a huge amount of guilt. She had barely slept that night, and when Paul left the next morning, she had summoned her courage and moved out.

Meagan looked around and saw three new women, one of them a tall, fair-haired girl in her mid-twenties with haunting brown eyes who, with Kelly Ford's quiet encouragement, stepped up to the podium and began to speak.

"My name's Daphne," she said, brushing back a strand of hair.

Meagan could see that she was nervous but determined, and she found herself willing her to go on, to tell everyone the truth, to "out" the man who was abusing her. Because someone was, she was sure of it. That telltale bruise on Daphne's jaw spoke volumes.

"Two years ago, I moved in with this man," the young woman went on. "He's … he's so handsome. Black hair, beautiful blue eyes! He looks like a movie star. I know that sounds silly and it probably is, but I was so proud when he noticed me."

How typical, Meagan thought, clenching and unclenching her hands. This lovely girl was actually thankful that some man had paid attention to her. Well, it had turned out to be the wrong sort of attention, had it not?

She thought of Steven and bile rose in her throat. Daphne's story was the usual tragic one. That man had broken her arm, her leg, her nose …

"Finally, I realized that if I didn't help myself, if I didn't leave, he'd kill me," Meagan heard Daphne say. "And that we all have to do whatever it takes to stop being victims."

And that's where I came in, Meagan told herself. If it had not been for her, there would be no place for this child to go. Because emotionally, Daphne was a child, and Meagan had made it her mission to help these emotionally crippled women because she had been unable to help herself.

She shuddered. If only these women knew how she had bought her own freedom …

Meagan wondered who the poor girl might be who was now the focus of the attentions of Daphne's boyfriend, for surely there would be one. Whoever she was, she needed to be warned, but how? She did not even know who the man in question was.

Her fears were confirmed when Daphne went on.

"I've got a job and I'm going to school now, and I've gotten my self-respect back. I swore to myself that no one would ever hurt me again. I hear he's got a new girlfriend, a college student," she added, "and I wish I could warn her. But if he found out, he'd kill me. He holds a position of authority, so I don't dare speak his name, let alone tell that girl what he's like."

Some of the women wept openly when Daphne finished, and Meagan knew that it was because each, in her own way, was working toward the same goal, some making steady progress and others only in fits and starts. And she also knew that there were those who were still in denial, thinking that perhaps things were not so bad after all and considering themselves the luckier ones. It was with this group that Meagan experienced the greatest frustration and for whom she felt the greatest concern. Yet was it not like looking in a mirror?

Many times, she had tried to understand the dichotomy of the successful professor counseling battered women—drilling into them that being a victim was not their fault but that they still needed to do something about the abuse—and the abused wife who failed to heed her own advice.

She glanced around the room. Fresh paint and a few inexpensive watercolors had transformed the room into a welcoming area where the women could temporarily forget their troubles. Round tables and chairs were clustered in informal groupings. Crisp homemade curtains framed the large picture windows, allowing the sun's rays to stream in, and fragrant bouquets of the first lilacs of the season brightened each table. Meagan was pleased at those small touches. It was obvious that someone was trying to make a difference.

"Have you seen Eileen?" Meagan asked Kelly when the presentations were over. "I heard about a part-time job that's made to order for her, something she can do at home."

"No," Kelly said. "That's strange. She's always here."

Kelly Ford, a short, chunky brunette with beautiful gray eyes who held a PhD in social work had befriended Meagan soon after the Rathburns' arrival in Red Pine. Because of their mutual involvement with the support group, they had become friends. The two men, however, had disliked each immediately and therefore, the two couples had never socialized.

"I'm so sorry about Steven," Kelly said. "I wasn't sure you'd come today, but you were right to want to be here. Now it's the women's turn to be supportive of you. Please let me know if there's anything Larry or I can do to help. In fact, why don't you stay with us for a while?"

"Thanks, Kelly, but I'll fine," Meagan said, hugging her. "Steven's parents are supposed to arrive this afternoon and my mother's flying in tonight. I won't be alone."

"When's the service?"

"Tomorrow at three at St. Paul's Episcopal Church."

"Any news from the police?"

Meagan shook her head. "Not yet."

"Well, let's hope they have a suspect in custody soon," Kelly said, slipping into her all-weather London Fog. "And remember what I said. If you need to talk to someone and you don't feel like being alone, come stay with us. Or I'll come and stay with you. I know Larry won't mind."

"I promise I will, Kelly," Meagan replied. "But right now, I need some time to myself."

Somehow, however, during the drive home, she found herself unable to put Eileen Murdoch out of her mind. Eileen was a shy twenty-two year-old woman with two young children. Her husband, a truck driver, was on the road a great deal and when he was home, he terrorized her and the children. She had left him once, only to go back when he promised things would change, but they had not, and Eileen had started to attend the meetings again. Over the past few months, she and Meagan had become close, and Meagan sensed that Eileen was working up her courage to leave her husband again, this time for good.

She felt a stab of concern, almost a premonition. But if she called, Eileen's husband might answer. And when he was home, he did not want to share Eileen with anyone else, even another woman. Meagan knew that this was typical of abusers to try to isolate their victims.

On impulse, she decided to drive by the Murdoch home to see

if the big rig Rich drove was parked out front. Pulling over to the side of the road, she rummaged through her briefcase for the little notebook that held the women's names, addresses, and phone numbers, carefully recorded in the special privacy code she had devised.

Meagan frowned when she saw Rich Murdoch's blue and white rig parked in front of a small frame house in a middle-class neighborhood. The street, flanked by large maple trees now barren of leaves, was deserted except for a skinny red dog with picket-fence ribs wandering in the street, sniffing at garbage cans. A child's red tricycle lay abandoned on its side in the driveway near an old blue Ford Fairlane. A big calico cat lay on the porch, pretending to be asleep while covertly watching the robins frolicking on the lawn.

He was home! Meagan would have to try later but in the meantime, she had a lot to do in order to get ready for the arrival of her mother and Steven's parents. It would be, she knew, difficult to keep up the façade of the grieving wife for the next few days. Yet, distasteful as it was, it had to be done. She smiled bitterly.

Appearances. Again. Always.

They seemed to rule her entire life. Would she ever be able to shake free of them?

* * *

Eileen Murdoch cringed as her husband towered over her, sullen and weary after his eighteen-hour drive back from southern California. The uppers he had taken to stay awake and the whiskey he had used to chase them had done nothing to brighten his disposition. Tired and hungry, he was itching for a fight and just looking for an opportunity.

"Where the hell's my breakfast?" he demanded.

Eileen rushed to get his pancakes, sausage patties, and coffee ready. Rich was a big man with a powerful physique, good looking in a coarse sort of way. His mood was darker than usual when she put the plate in front of him. He took a few bites and then, without warning, he swept plate and cup off the table. Fourteen-month-old Kevin, sitting in his high chair and terrified by the noise, began to howl.

"You expect me to eat this shit?" Rich said, getting to his feet. "The patties are burned, the pancakes are soggy, and the coffee's cold. I've been on the road for almost twenty hours straight tryin' to earn a livin' for you and the kids and fightin' my way home through a snow storm, and this is the way you repay me, you ungrateful cow? And can't you keep this damned brat quiet? How d'ya expect me to get any sleep?"

"I'm sorry, Rich, I'll put him down for a nap," she said, recoiling.

"You do that. And where's the hell is Mike? He's never around when I'm home!"

"He's at school 'til two," she said quietly. "Let me fix you something else."

"Don't bother," he grunted. "I'd rather go out and spend my hard-earned money at the diner rather than eat the slop you serve me. And just look at you," he went on. "Can't you wear something else besides those old pants, and do somethin' with your hair? You're a mess, woman!"

As she attempted to squeeze past him to clean up the floor, she slipped on the spilled food and fell heavily against him. He exploded with rage and threw her against the breakfast table with all his strength.

"Come on, you dumb broad," he growled, nudging her with his foot as she slid to the floor. "Get up! It was just a shove, for crissake!"

Eileen didn't move. Blood seeped from her temple, and her face was ashen. Rich bent to pick her up, but something in the way her body lay made him reach for her pulse instead.

"Jesus Christ," he muttered. "The damn bitch is dead."

Ignoring the screaming child, and thanking his lucky star that his oldest son was in school, Murdoch sat down on the sofa to think about what he was going to tell the police.

CHAPTER 6

The spring weather, which had remained clear for a few days, had become blustery again. The precinct's switchboard was atypically quiet as Alix reviewed the reports on Steven Rathburns' murder for the hundredth time. She had just spoken with Meagan who, no doubt knowing it was expected of her, had called to inquire about the progress of the investigation.

Alix reached for another folder and caught her bracelet on the telephone cord. As she pulled her wrist to free herself, one of the bracelet's gold charms came off. "Damn, damn, and triple damn!" she exploded.

She got down on her hands and knees but, startled by Jon's voice calling her name, she managed to bang her head on the bottom of her desk.

"What are you doing poking around under your desk?" he said, clearly amused. "New form of police investigation?"

"I'm in no mood for your doubtful humor, pal," Alix answered. "I've just lost my charm."

"Not from where I'm standing," he said gallantly. "In fact, this is the most charming sight I've seen all day."

She glared at him. "*Puerco!* You're just a male chauvinist pig! Lloyd gave me a little gold unicorn charm for my bracelet for our first anniversary. It's my favorite, and I've got to find it."

"Here, let me help you," he said, looking contrite. They both crawled about on the floor until he let out a cry of triumph and rose, clutching the charm in his hand. "Here's the critter, Alix, safe and sound."

"*Gracias, amigo,*" she said, beaming as she got to her feet. "You've finally made yourself useful."

"Sounds suspiciously like a left-handed compliment," he told her, smiling. "Say, how's the case coming?"

She sat down again, motioning him to the chair across her desk, and grimaced. "It's not," she admitted. "I've got nothing but dead-ends," she told him, her yellow eyes darkening in frustration. Pulling a few hairpins from her desk drawer, she stuck them in her mouth and proceeded to repair her disheveled locks as Jon watched with amusement.

"What in the hell are you grinning at? Have I grown a third boob or something?" she said archly.

"I was just thinking how it happens that a tough cop like you worries about the condition of her hair."

"If that's supposed to be another sexist remark ..."

"You know better than that, Alix. I happen to think it's rather whimsical that a policewoman isn't afraid to be feminine. Male officers don't have that flexibility."

Disarmed, she gave him a warm smile. The remark was typically Jon. He was right. Like Lloyd, Jon was one of the least sexist men she knew.

She threw a folder in the out basket, searched through the piles of papers on her desk, and picked up the Rathburn file again.

"Can you believe this?" she demanded. "No one saw anything. It's like the whole world went deaf and blind when Rathburn was killed. Yet the place's so secluded that I don't know why I am surprised. Makes no sense. And assuming that there *was* a burglar, what he did with the loot? Fence it in Somalia?"

Sighing, she looked around her office, a tiny cubicle littered with precariously stacked files that threatened to tumble at the slightest provocation. The walls were covered with pictures of her parents on the hacienda's patio, wedding shots of Lloyd and herself with their two dogs, and photographs of Jon and Margot. Prior to her arrival, and as an accommodation to her title, her office had been repainted in the obligatory mustard-green color she just knew government agencies purchased by the barrel. Yet at the time she'd been grateful for the fresh paint job, regardless of its color. Today, however, it did little to improve her disposition.

Sheets of rain slanted by the wind did a spirited Irish jig on her window. "Damn this rain," she went on, peering out the window. "Won't summer ever come? And how long is it going to take before I get a lead!"

"Did anything come out from the search of the pawnshops?" Jon asked.

"Absolutely zilch," she replied, her tone reflecting her frustration.

"Maybe the burglar's playing it safe and waiting for things to cool off before getting rid of the stuff," Jon suggested.

"Maybe, but I still don't believe there *was* a burglar."

He gave her a speculative look. "You hinted at that before, Alix. What are you getting at?"

Alix bit her lip. "In your opinion, Jon, is Meagan Rathburn capable of killing her husband?" she said finally.

He looked at her, mouth agape. "That's absurd!" he exclaimed. "Where on earth would you get an idea like that? Meagan not only has an alibi, she has absolutely no reason to kill her husband!"

"Perhaps, but the whole thing's too neat, too pat. No fingerprints, no tire tracks. Doc couldn't tell if the killer used a .22 revolver or a semiautomatic because the damned bullet hit bone and was badly flattened, so the absence of a casing means nothing. I don't know, Jon," she said, shaking her head, "something about the whole thing bothers me."

"My God, you *aren't* kidding! You do suspect Meagan!"

Alix nodded. "I did check out her alibi, of course, and yes, she was in her office until three o'clock. And yes, she was at a lecture and a reception during the time Doc says her husband could have been murdered. And yes, I do suspect her. But I knew you'd react the way you just did, which is why I didn't tell you earlier when you came to our house."

"But Alix, it's ludicrous!"

She knew that Jon would be difficult to convince as far as Meagan was concerned. After all, he had been one of her few close friends for a good many years. From what he had told her about his relationship with the couple, Alix did not understand what he had seen in her, not until now. And now it was a question of murder.

"Okay, think about it this way, Jon," she told him. "It wouldn't have taken her more than five minutes to drive home; ten, fifteen at the most to do the deed; and five to get back. I know because I drove the distance and timed it. And I believe she has the smarts to pull it off."

"You're barking up the wrong tree, babe," he countered, shaking his head. "I'd stake my life on it."

"You may be right, my friend, but I've been in this business too long to ignore my gut feeling. Problem is, I can't prove it."

"Did anyone see her leave the university during the critical time?" Jon asked.

"Not yet," Alix said dolefully, "but I'm working on it."

Her thoughts flashed back to her conversation with the department secretary, a stern, no-nonsense woman by the name of Jacqueline Russell. Ms. Russell had been first startled, then visibly upset by her question.

"It's impossible, Detective!" she had told Alix. "Dr. Rathburn holds office hours between three and four every afternoon, and she's religious about being there for her students. Had she left, I would have seen her since she would have to go right past my office. And she would have left a note on her door. Besides, I saw her at the reception after the lecture."

"Do you always check the doors of every faculty member to see if he or she posts a note to indicate an absence?"

The secretary hesitated. "Of course not, but I'll tell you this. Dr. Rathburn isn't the type to just up and leave without telling somebody."

"Does she keep her door open or closed during office hours?"

"It's usually open, but she closes it when a student comes in."

"So theoretically, she could have left her office, closed her door, and left without you noticing?"

"Yes, I suppose so," the secretary said grudgingly. "But I'm sure she didn't leave."

"And she could have gone by your office without you seeing her if you were, say, at the copy machine or in the ladies' room?" Alix persisted.

"I guess so, yes. But I'm still sure she didn't leave."

Because of Ms. Russell's reticence, Alix decided not mention that interview to Jon, preferring to keep the information to herself for the time being.

Sensing she was holding something back, he leaned forward to catch her eye. "You're not really serious about Meagan, are you?"

How typical of him to want to believe that someone other than Meagan might have done it, Alix thought. He was so good at denial. He always wanted his world to be tranquil and peaceful. Not that she could blame him. She wished hers was, too, but wishing didn't make it so.

"I'm dead serious, *amigo*," she said quietly. "She gave all the right answers, showed the proper grief, but her responses seemed mechanical, rehearsed. And remember the look on her face when they took her husband's body away? I'd give a month's salary to know what it meant. And what about that weird statement? Let's see …"

She quickly reached for her small spiral notebook and read aloud, "'Everything's all right. It's got to be all right now.' Now what do you suppose that meant?"

He shook his head. "Alix, Meagan's got no motive, no reason to kill Steven, and without a motive, you've got nothing."

"I know," she said impatiently. "That's the problem. From all accounts, he was well respected by his peers, devoted to his wife, liked by everyone, and on and on ad nauseam. As Lloyd says, nobody's that perfect."

A whimsical smile stretched her wide mouth. "Strange, isn't it? Just because someone dies, he or she automatically qualifies for sainthood. Why is it that saying something negative about a deceased is a no-no, even if it's true? There's got to be something, something no one wants to discuss. Something no one knows about."

"But do you have any other suspects other than Meagan?" Jon asked.

It was hopeless! What *was* it with him? She certainly had to give him an "A" for effort about refusing to accept Meagan's possible guilt. What would it take to convince him? A video of her doing the deed?

"Not yet, but I confirmed what you told me," she replied, toying with her pen. "Money certainly isn't the motive because Meagan's mother is loaded—real estate, gold, blue-chip stocks, mutual funds, all inherited from Meagan's father, who also left his daughter a substantial trust fund. It's obvious from all the goodies in the house that the Rathburns weren't collecting returnable cans to make ends meet. So money probably isn't be the motive, but something else is. It has to be. And what about that damned red camisole? It seemed so out of place, Jon. I wonder if the Rathburns were into kinky sex games or role playing? Or did some babe visit Steven when the lady of the house was gone? It's all very odd."

Rising, she began to pace, managing somehow to bump into her desk as she rounded its corner. Grimacing, she rubbed her hip. "What does that leave, Jon? Love? Hate? Jealousy? Lust? Revenge? Anger? So far, none of the above seems to apply."

"Why this obsession with her guilt?" Jon asked impatiently.

"It isn't an obsession," she said hotly. "It's my sixth sense at work, and it isn't often wrong. And if I didn't listen to it, I wouldn't be doing my job. You know very well that police work is one-third tedious, plodding work, one-third luck, and one-third gut feeling. Jon," she continued, "there's a very good chance your colleague is out there thinking she's gotten away with murder. And I don't mind telling you that I don't like it. No, I don't like it one bit and I'm going to prove I'm right."

He shook his head, exasperated now. "Alix, you and I have worked together for a long time, but this time you're dead wrong.

Meagan couldn't have done it. She's too kind, too gentle to hurt anyone. You ought to see her with her students and with the women in her support group, how she hurts for every one of them. This is beginning to sound personal, my friend, and not at all like you. Is your ego on the line or something?"

Just as he said it, he knew it had been the wrong thing to say as he saw her expression become stormy and her amber eyes turn black.

"I'm going to ignore that remark, Jon," she said coldly. "This isn't a vendetta, and it's got nothing to do with ego. I don't *want* Meagan Rathburn to be the murderer. Despite my suspicions, I sense a hidden pain in that woman that has nothing to do with her husband's murder. What it is, what caused it, I don't know, but she has a haunted look about her and I feel oddly sorry for her, although I wish I knew why. I'm not out to get her just because I need to solve the case, for Christ's sake! You know me better than that!"

"I'm sorry, Alix," he said, looking repentant. "You didn't deserve that remark. I know you'll get the real killer, my friend, but I also know that Meagan isn't that person."

She shot him a forgiving look. "Thanks for your confidence, but why don't I feel better?"

"Because you always want to catch the bad guy and you want it right now. Despite your talents and other-wordly sixth sense, you're still the most impatient person I know. You're a perfectionist, Alix. You're smart and you're the best cop I've ever had the privilege of working with. You'll get your killer, you usually do."

She grinned, torn between her frustration at his refusal to consider Meagan's guilt, and her pleasure at his confidence in her abilities. "Impatient, huh?"

"Terribly."

"But smart, too?"

"Very."

"A perfectionist?"

"Of the worst kind."

"You sound like Lloyd. Why do I always feel outnumbered

by the two of you?" she said, smiling now.

"Because we're both right and we both love you."

She nodded, disarmed now. "It's mutual, *amigo*. We're still on for dinner tomorrow night?"

"Absolutely. I'm bringing a surprise dish: *poc chúc*, barbecued pork in orange sauce. It's a specialty from the Yucatán. You'll love it."

"Mmm, you're making my mouth water. Be a good boy now and go away before I get sidetracked by culinary delights. I've got work to do."

"Okay, okay! As my students say, 'I'm outta here.'"

"I think I like your old 'cheerio' better," she said. "Classier."

"I'm almost forgot," he said as he rose to leave. "What did the autopsy turn up?"

"Nothing new. Rathburn was shot at almost-point-blank range. The bruise at the back of his head was caused by something blunt, maybe one of the tennis trophies in the study, although the lab found no fingerprints on any of them. Time of death was between two and six, give or take. And Rathburn didn't struggle with his killer. But you already know all that. Oh, he also had a Danish and a cup of coffee shortly before he was killed."

"Now there's a major clue for you! The .22 still bothers you?" he asked.

"Yes, but it's a common enough gun. There're thousands of them that can be bought for next to nothing and disposed of like middle-aged wives."

"Which doesn't help things. I think I'll stop in to check on Meagan to see how she's getting along."

He gave her a devilish smile as he paused at the door. "Parting is as painful as a swift kick in the pants."

"I don't think Shakespeare put it quite that way," Alix told him, suppressing a smile.

The door had no sooner closed behind him than her intercom buzzed. "Alix, a man just called 911," Louise told her. "He's pretty upset. He says his name's Richard Murdoch and that his wife fell and hit her head on the kitchen table. He thinks she's dead. The paramedics are on their way. Jim Harrison's the officer on call. He thought you might want Dr. Gardner notified."

Great, one more thing she did not need today! Why couldn't things run smoothly without interruptions for a change, especially now that she needed to focus on the Rathburn murder?

"Why should Dr. Gardner be notified?" she asked Louise. "Sounds like an accident to me."

"Because it looks like Mrs. Murdoch might have been battered and Jim thought maybe she died as a result of a beating."

Oh, wonderful, a battered wife now! Just when Alix brought herself to the point where it was possible that she could face anything, something always happened to remind her that there was no limit to man's inhumanity to man. Wife beating was common, she knew, and unfortunately, it was more common than anyone wanted to think. Although how a man who professed to love a woman could lay his hands on her was beyond understanding. Lloyd might be discontent with her at times, frustrated because of her devotion to her work, her long hours, the interrupted dinners, but never, under any circumstances, would he ever think of striking her.

Alix wrote the address down and asked Louise to locate Dave Barnes. Today, Louise wore a fringed leather vest over a saffron-colored blouse and a skirt that hung to her moccasined feet. A beaded headband encircled her Brillo-pad gray hair.

"Let me guess. Pocahontas." Alix said, chuckling.

Swinging her purse over her shoulder, she proceeded down the hall at double time, literally bumping into Dave Barnes on her way out.

"Damn! Shawn Connors again," she said, sniffing the air. "This place smells like a pool parlor. I thought the chief had designated this a smoke-free precinct and asked everybody to smoke outside."

"Everyone does except Connors," Dave replied, looking miffed. "That guy doesn't think the rules apply to him and Louise's pissed because she's allergic to cigarette smoke and is threatening to quit."

"I knew we'd be sorry we hired him," Alix said, sighing. "There's something about him I can't stand. And only this morning I had a complaint from someone claiming that he harasses the Mexican field workers. I plan to have a little chat with the gentleman immediately before we get slapped with a lawsuit."

"That should do it," Dave said cheerfully. "We all know about your little chats, don't we?"

* * *

When they arrived at the Murdoch home, they found the front door ajar. A man Alix assumed to be Murdoch was sitting on a worn upholstered sofa, cradling his head in his hands. A baby, sucking him thumb and whimpering, lay in a cluttered playpen. In the kitchen, a woman was sprawled on the kitchen floor, arms akimbo, head resting in a puddle of blood.

Dr. Gardner was kneeling beside the body. "She's gone, Alix."

She turned toward the husband. "Mr. Murdoch, Detectives Mendez and Barnes. Can you tell me what happened?"

"I'm a truck driver. I've been on the road since one this mornin'," he said. Got caught up in a snow storm up on the pass and didn't get home 'til about nine-thirty. I was pretty beat, but Eileen, my wife, fixed breakfast for me, so I was gonna eat it and grab some shuteye, but as I was talkin' to her, my elbow caught my plate and my whole breakfast went flyin' on the floor. She got up to clean up the mess, slipped and fell, and hit her head pretty hard on the corner of the table."

He paused and ran his hand through his thick, curly hair. "I kept thinkin', what if little Mike—that's my oldest son, he's at school right now—comes home and finds his ma like this? So I shook her some and tried to get her up but when I couldn't, I called 911."

His voice was mechanical, and Alix noted that is was totally devoid of the emotion one might expect. Although she was all too accustomed to blood and gore, it was particularly painful to her when someone young and pretty like this woman died before her time. The blood seeping into the neck of her sweatshirt had started to crust. And there were bruises on her face and neck, not all of them fresh.

She made a note in her notebook and quietly said to Dr. Gardner, "I'd like to know if she has injuries consistent with abuse."

He turned the body over, looked at Eileen's torso, back, and legs, and gave Alix an almost-imperceptible nod. "Seems you're right, but I'll give you a complete report as soon as I can."

Turning to Dave, she said, "I want you and Harrison to canvass the neighborhood, see if anyone heard anything between, say, nine-thirty and eleven. Screaming, fighting, anything to indicat the Murdochs had a ... disagreement. And while you're at it, find out if anyone heard anything on other occasions. You know, the usual."

She left the kitchen and returned to the living room where Murdoch, having deposited the now-sleeping infant in the playpen, was staring into the distance. "Did your wife have relatives, Mr. Murdoch?" Alix asked. "If so, I'd like their names and addresses."

He shook his head. "Eileen's pa died a few years back. Her ma used to live in Seattle, but she and Eileen weren't talkin'. I don't know where she lives now."

"What's her name?"

"Evelyn Austin. Why you wanna know?"

"Just routine," Alix said. She knew she was stretching the truth, hoping that Eileen's mother would confirm her suspicions, although the fact that she and her daughter were estranged didn't bode well. "We'll probably have more questions later, Mr. Murdoch," she added. "Were you planning to go back on the road in the next few days?"

"No, ma'am. I'll call my boss and see if I can get some time off. I've got vacation time comin', and I need to figure out what to do with them kids. My mother lives in Portland. I'll see if she can come down andd take 'em with her."

He was too calm about all this, she thought. Even granting that men did not often react to violent death with as much emotion as Meagan had, there was something unnatural about the way Murdoch seemed to accept what had happened, not even showing any concern over the fact that he most certainly would lose his children as well.

The ambulance left with Eileen's body. "What's this?" Dave exclaimed as they followed the ambulance in her car. "We're not bringing him in? It's obvious he abused her and may have even killed her!"

"Bring him in for what? You know better than that, Dave," she said sternly. "We can't prove that he beat her to death, and it could've happened just the way he said. And we still can't prove he killed her unless someone heard them argue this morning. And even then, we have nothing concrete. Let's wait for Doc's report and see if he comes up with something. Right now, we've got to accept the fact that we have nothing to go on when it comes to bringing charges."

"Yes, I know all that, Alix," he said dispiritedly, "but it's not right for him to go scot-free. And now those two little kids are left without a mom."

A thin man with a cadaverous face, hooded black eyes, and a lugubrious expression, Dave loved children. He and his wife, Pat, had tried for years to have kids of their own and were in the process of adopting a Korean orphan. Upon Alix's arrival in Red Pine, the two detectives had become close, and Alix held a special spot in her heart for Dave who had saved her life during the arrest of the serial killer who had murdered Lloyd's wife.

She put her hand on his arm. "Unfortunately, that's the way our system works. I know it's the shits, Dave. It's unfair and far from perfect, but it works most of the time. You're a seasoned cop. You know that."

"Yes, I do know that, but is justice served, Alix? That's the question."

She had wondered the same thing herself many times, knowing that that the justice system often let down the most vulnerable members of society.

As soon as she got back to the office, she called Jon and told him about the Murdoch case.

"That's awful, Alix! You think the husband did it?"

"Possibly, but unless Doc comes up with something concrete,

we can't prove it. Say, I know that Meagan Rathburn facilitates a battered women's group. Could you ask her if Eileen Murdoch was in that group? It's a shot in the dark, but it might be a start. My guys are canvassing the neighborhood to find out if the Murdochs were fighting when he said she fell. Since you said you were going to see Dr. Rathburn, I thought maybe you wouldn't mind asking."

Jon would do a good job of that. During the years that they had worked together, she had come to depend on him more than even Lloyd could understand. She found herself wondering how Jon would feel if she were to leave her job, only to find that she could not go on with the thought. Perhaps she'd think about it later. And again, maybe not. There was one thing about murder. It gave you the best excuse possible to put everything else out of your mind.

"No problem. I'll let you know what I find out," he told her.

"Thanks, Jon, see you tomorrow night."

CHAPTER 7

The funeral was everything Meagan had feared. The open casket Steven's father had insisted on, the sweet scent of too many flowers, the overheated church, everything had conspired to make her feel light-headed and nauseated. The minister, who had not known Steven, had nonetheless talked about his virtues during an interminable eulogy, apparently spurred on by the look of approval on the face of Steven's father.

Meagan's mind drifted as she thought about Eileen Murdoch, who she still had been unable to reach, and about Paige, her protegée, who seemed so distracted in class lately. As she tried to put such thoughts on autopilot, she forced herself to remember the friends, colleagues, and well-wishers who were a bramble of nameless faces. Steven's father had planned a lavish reception following the funeral, personally making the arrangements with a local caterer and boasting about the number of mourners in attendance. Meagan, who had not been consulted, had objected to the size of the affair at first but had finally given in.

"You can't deny a reception to parents who've lost their only child, Meagan," her mother had said in her most honeyed southern tones. "And it isn't seemly to send people away without feeding them."

The hours before she could finally be alone stretched before her like distant horizons, never to be reached, but finally it was over and she was thrilled that her mother and Steven's parents were leaving the following day.

She had to be patient. Only one more day, she thought, just one more day.

She needed desperately to put Steven out of her mind and return to her students, her women's group, the comfortable routine within which she felt safe. Torn between the aftermath of the murder, with which she was still wrestling, and the need to pretend life would be business as usual, she wanted to put the nightmare behind her and try to go on with her life. Accustomed as she was to loneliness, the sudden influx of company was a distraction, an irritant, and the need to be alone to reflect on her future was like a physical craving.

She slowly climbed the steps to her bedroom, thinking about the many women in need, women to whom, because of her own ordeal, she felt so intimately connected. Meagan was fiercely loyal to them. All the women in the group looked up to her, trusted her, and had always provided her with emotional satisfaction. In fact, sometimes she wondered if she needed them more than they needed her.

It was a relief to shed the black dress she had worn to the funeral. It had felt hot and scratchy in church, sticking to her like a second skin, and her veil had made her feel claustrophobic. As she changed into a black cashmere top and silk pants, she once again thought about how ironic it was that she should counsel battered women and yet be unable to seek help for herself. Would she ever break through her self-erected barriers and reach for professional help? Would she be able to learn to talk to friends like Jon who would respect her confidence? But, try as she might, she could see no way out. The need for secrecy had been too deeply ingrained for too many years.

"Are you up there, Meagan? Why don't you try to take a nap?"

Her mother's voice rose up the staircase. Idrys Sanborne's faked concern grated on Meagan's nerves. She tried hard to be appreciative, while at the same time seething with retroactive resentment at her mother's refusal to acknowledge and deal with the abuse she had been subject to as a girl. Why had she failed to help when Meagan needed her? Why had she not believed her, protected her? She could not have been blind to what had been going on. Was it perhaps that acknowledging the truth would have been too painful? Or had she been jealous of her husband's attentions toward Meagan? Now that Steven was dead, it was amazing how so many things were suddenly becoming clear.

Meagan was also puzzled by her mother's insensitivity about the state of her marriage. She could not have failed to know that something was very wrong between Meagan and Steven. She was a mother, so was she not supposed to sense these things? Meagan wondered whether Idrys would have cared, had she known about her dismal marriage. Although she might not consciously admit it, deep down she blamed her mother as much as she blamed Steven for his murder.

It was her mother's fault, Meagan thought furiously. Idrys had not given a damn about her daughter's well-being, or her marriage, or anything else then, and she did not give a damn about her now. Her concern was put on, fake, like everything else she did. Meagan knew that her fate, her future life, depended only on herself, because she knew best how to protect herself from those who might harm her.

Her head was pounding and her thoughts became jumbled. Just one more day and they would all leave. One more day. The words rang through her head, over and over again like a *leitmotif.* One more day. It was all she could think about.

The shrill ringing of the telephone interrupted her thoughts.

Kelly Ford sounded distraught. "I know this has been a terrible day for you, Meagan, but I heard the news when I returned from the reception, and I knew ..."

"What news, Kelly?" Meagan interrupted her, speaking more sharply than she had intended.

"It's Eileen. She's dead."

Meagan sat down hard on her bed, the breath knocked out of her. Kelly's voice suddenly seemed to come from far away. "What are you talking about?" she asked feebly.

"A friend of Eileen's, someone called Heather, called me a few minutes ago. She went by Eileen's house and saw the ambulance and the police. Apparently, it was an accident. She fell in her kitchen and hit her head or something, but Meagan, I have to wonder if it was really an accident," Kelly added, lowering her voice.

A hot ball of bile crept up from the pit of Meagan's stomach and into her throat. She had just buried the man who had abused her for years, and now one of the women in her group to whom she had felt so close was dead. It was too much, just too much to take in. She felt her headache intensify, and she closed her eyes and tried hard to think.

"I called to ask if there was anything I could do without mentioning my connection with the group," Kelly went on. "I said that I was a friend of Eileen's and wanted to help, but her husband told me to mind my own business, said he didn't need any help, and hung up on me. What a jerk! Those poor little kids! The youngest is just a baby."

"Have they arrested him?" Meagan asked, forcing herself to sound calm and professional.

"I don't think so, but I'm sure there'll be an investigation. Why should they take his word that it was an accident? Her body will show signs of abuse, and if I have to, I'll go to the police myself and tell them she was in our group. I'd love to hang that bastard!"

"That wouldn't do any good," Meagan told her. "You know as well as I do that they'll question him but they'll arrest him only if they can prove her death was directly related to a beating."

"I know, I know, but I guess I'm losing faith in our justice system. It stinks, Meagan!" The bitterness in Kelly's voice echoed Meagan's own.

"I agree, Kelly," she said. "Let me see what I can find out and I promise I'll call you. I still can't believe it. Eileen, dead! I …" She stopped as hot tears ran down her cheeks, but she forced herself to speak again. "Thanks for letting me know," she added.

She hung up, sick at heart, but seconds later gut-twisting rage overcame her feelings of loss. Why hadn't Eileen stayed away from her husband? God knew she had tried to warn her! She had loved and nurtured Eileen, had watched her make slow but steady progress. And now that bastard had killed her. Accident or not, he had beat her to death. She just knew it. Irrational as it seemed, she *knew* Eileen Murdoch's death had not been caused by a fall, but of course, proving it was another matter. She would talk to Jon and try to get some information.

Sweet, dear Eileen! Meagan's thoughts flashed back to the day when she had walked into the meeting room after her first attempt to leave her abuser, so frail, so vulnerable, her self-esteem in shreds. She had worked hard at regaining her confidence, but she still loved her husband and, like others before her, she had gone back to him to try one more time. Eileen might have stood a chance, had she not been robbed of it. What a waste, what a rotten, miserable waste!

Meagan started to pace like a caged tiger, striking her left hand with her clenched right fist, green eyes flashing with helpless frustration. She knew that the police would do nothing and that it would be up to her to find a way to bring justice to Eileen, but how?

She felt herself overcome by impotence, anger, and despair.

And then something inside her snapped.

She couldn't breathe. She had to get out of this house!

Rushing down the stairs past her startled mother, Meagan snatched her car keys from the hallway table and ran out of the house without taking the time to grab a coat. All she could think about was Eileen and the other women in her group, all victims waiting to happen. She drove for what seemed like hours. When a red light turned green, she was too lost in thought to drive on until someone honked angrily. Then, startled into awareness, she looked up to see the spires of St. Mark's Catholic Church looming before her.

Something inside her told her to park her car and go in.

The church was cool and almost deserted, except for two elderly women who were leaving as she entered the sanctuary. At the opposite end of the nave, a janitor mopped the floor. Votive candles burned under a picture of the Sacred Heart. The church smelled of incense, dying flowers, and candle wax.

She knelt in a pew as a priest came out of the sacristy and disappeared again, apparently thinking she was absorbed in prayers.

But she could not pray. Instead, her mind seemed to splinter into pieces, scattering everywhere in her brain. She could not think. She could not focus. All she felt was rage and helplessness and fury, which she felt unable to overcome. Her head began to throb again, blurring her eyesight.

But suddenly, as the throbbing eased for a brief moment, a plan started to crystallize in a series of firework-like flashes and bursts. It was wildly dangerous and the pitfalls were daunting, but if she could work out the kinks, how sweet the revenge! She would become Eileen's champion while vindicating herself and all the others as she struck back at the men who made their lives such hell. The police had to work within the framework of the law while she, on the other hand, need not be bound by such constraints. And Eileen's husband would pay. She would see to it that he suffered, just as Eileen had.

She remembered Kelly's statement about her lack of faith in the justice system and smiled bitterly. Kelly would think her insane for even considering such a crazy plot. She would try to talk her out of it. She might even go to the police. But Kelly would never know. Meagan had become an expert at keeping secrets, and her plan would remain hidden in the private recesses of her mind.

There was so much to do now!

Excitement replaced fury. She had the luxury of time to plan her scheme, refine it until it was as foolproof as any plan could be. Modesty aside, she knew she was smart, organized, and most of all, patient. These qualities would serve her well during the most incredible endeavor of her life. And if she made some mistakes in the process, well, she was only human. But she had to do something. She owed Eileen that much.

Crossing herself, she left the church, feeling revitalized. She had a sense of purpose now.

God must have brought her here today for a reason, and now she would carry out the mission He had set out for her.

And for her, the mission had already begun.

* * *

The four friends sat in the dining room, feeling comfortably replete after consuming with considerable élan Jon's enchiladas and pork dish, a salad of respectable proportions, and the crèpes, light as dandelion tops and filled with strawberry jam—Margot's contribution.

Alix rose to get coffee and Kahlùa and soon returned with an enormous tray.

"What's the matter, Alix?" Jon asked her. "And don't tell me it's nothing. You've been distracted all evening."

"I'm fine," she said. "Just thinking about the investigation, I guess."

"Can't you forget business for just one night?"

"That was a great meal, guys," Margot said, breaking in before Alix had a chance to reply. "Any volunteers to run around the block with me to burn off all these calories?"

"And court a heart attack?" Lloyd groaned. "Why don't you do like the rest of us, enjoy the fire and pretend you just had Slim Fast for dinner?"

"A depressing thought," Alix said, "and an insult to Jon's fine cooking."

"Aha!" Jon exclaimed. "Now she's trying to be nice after practically throwing me out of her office yesterday."

"Behave yourselves, you two. Or is this all make-believe so I don't get jealous?" Lloyd teased.

"You forget, *querido*," Alix replied. "I had a crack at Jon long before you came along."

The chuckles around the room told her she had scored a point. Lloyd shook his head, a pained look on his face. "You just had to remind me, didn't you? Don't you know that old fellows like me get their feelings hurt easily?"

Alix groaned. "Oh, puleez! Not the 'old fellow' routine again."

"Listen up, all of you," Jon said. "I have something important to discuss. I've been thinking about a vacation for sometime, and I wonder what you'd all think about going to the Yucatán for a couple of weeks in September, maybe do a bit of snorkeling at Isla Mujeres, and relax in the sun. With Alix along, the language won't be a problem. So what do you all say?"

A dreamy look crossed Alix's face. "Sounds wonderful," she said, "but first, I've got to catch me a killer."

"September isn't a problem for me," Margot said, "I'd love to go, so count me in."

"Lloyd?" Jon asked. "How about you?"

"Count me in, too! My book's off to the publisher in a couple of weeks, and I'll be free as a bird."

Jon beamed. "Terrific. It's going to be a vacation to remember."

Lloyd brought out a map of Mexico, and they plotted the spots they might want to visit with yellow markers.

"Hey, we could fly out of Los Angeles," Alix said. "This would give us a chance to stop on the way down and see my folks."

She lay back in her chair, looking fondly at her husband and friends. It felt good being among those she loved. And yet the murder, and her suspicions surrounding it, weighed heavily on her mind. Pleasant as the evening was, she was finding it difficult to relax and enjoy herself.

As they said their goodbyes, Jon turned to Alix. "I saw Meagan today," he said in a low voice. "She said that Eileen Murdoch was in her support group and had apparently moved out a few months ago. She went to a shelter, but recently returned home, so I guess this confirms your suspicions. Did Mrs. Murdoch ever report her husband to the police?"

"There are no reports of patrol cars going to that address," Alix told him. "The neighbors said they didn't hear anything on the morning in question, but they did say they'd heard fighting and screaming on other occasions. What was Dr. Rathburns' reaction?"

"She was devastated, of course. The first thing she asked was if the husband was a suspect. I evaded the question since I knew you wouldn't want me to discuss it."

Jon had done his best. Alix knew that. If she had reached a dead end, there was nothing she could do about it. But as she and Lloyd prepared for bed, she asked herself how long she would be able to cope with the frustrations of her life as a cop. And she knew that, although he had never mentioned it, Lloyd wondered, too.

CHAPTER 8

Meagan looked at her reflection in the mirror, her expression inscrutable as she styled the long, brown wig she had purchased into an upswept hairdo and secured it with heavy jeweled pins, letting wispy strands frame her face. Pleased at what she saw, she pivoted in front of the mirror, admiring the results. The wig added inches to her small stature, and she was amazed at how natural it looked. It was as if she had been a brunette all her life. The important thing was that she looked so completely different. And the wig went well with her new brown contact lenses.

Next she tried on the short blond wig, which gave her yet another look, both innocent and vulnerable. And then she carefully inserted a pair of blue contact lenses and looked at herself again. She then tried the brown ones. The inexpensive clothes she had bought, some flashy, others plain, were all light-years away from the stylish designer clothes she normally wore and made her feel like a new person. But she was a new person, she reminded herself. Her plan would work, she was sure of it because she had the best of motives—a burning desire for justice.

She brought out two more boxes containing shoes and boots with three-inch heels that would help create the illusion of a taller woman.

They reminded her of the times when, at age six, she had

climbed up to the family attic to play dress up. There had been old trunks and suitcases brimming with treasures—hats from the thirties and forties with feathers and veils, fox scarves with heads whose small beady eyes seemed to follow her around the room, lace and taffeta gowns with beautiful pearl and sequin appliqués. And shoes! Such wonderful shoes! Some with tall, thin heels, others with chunky ones, all far too big for her small feet but such fun to wobble around in.

Her father had admired her as she paraded in front of him in all her finery, her mother's brightest lipstick askew on her small face. "You look just beautiful, Meagan," he had said. "A little lady."

But this was not like playing dress up. This was deadly serious business. She smiled bitterly at the play on words.

She practiced walking around in the thigh-high, blood-red tube dress with the long fitted sleeves and the matching red shoes with stiletto heels that she had come to think of as her hooker's clothes. She soon no longer felt like she might fall on her face. But the biggest surprise was the difference in the way she felt. Wearing the new clothes and shoes, she not only looked sexy but *felt* sexy, daring, available.

Two weeks had passed since Eileen's death. Her conversation with Jon and his guarded response had confirmed her suspicions. Something was definitely wrong, and she no longer needed proof that Rich had played a major part in his wife's demise, either on purpose or by accident. Frankly, she didn't give a damn which. Since the police hadn't arrested him, she could only conclude that they had failed to prove his guilt, if they had even tried. The important thing was that now it was payback time, a time for retribution, a time for justice. She would find out where he went, what he did, what watering holes he frequented.

Picking him up would be easy. She knew from the counseling sessions with Eileen that Rich had cheated on her, which would make the chase even more rewarding.

But doubt suddenly washed over her, and she was overcome by blind panic and an unexpected attack of anxiety.

What if he saw through her and suspected what she was doing?

But she couldn't let negative thoughts stop her now. There was only one focus in her life now, and that was to avenge Eileen's death.

She went to the locked safe hidden behind her evening dresses where Steven's murder weapon was still hidden and took out a map of Red Pine and the small notebook in which she planned to record Rich Murdoch's every move. From now on, she would be his shadow, but he would never know she was there ... until it was too late.

She fondled the .22 caliber semi-automatic pistol she had used to end her own ordeal, remembering with a sense of irony that it had been a gift from Steven shortly after they had moved into this house and which, for some unknown reason, he had never registered. Although she had been reluctant at first, he had insisted that she learn to use it because of the isolation of their home and the rise in suburban crime. As a result of many practice sessions at the firing range, she had become proficient.

Using this gun again was out of the question, but she knew there were ways of obtaining another firearm with no questions asked. Being a novice at the business of murder, she had wondered what to do with it, but the more she thought about it, the more convinced she became that she must get rid of it and get another gun for the job ahead. Keeping Steven's murder weapon had been really stupid so she'd dump it in the river as soon as possible and find another one small enough to fit in her purse. And this time, after Rich Murdoch was dead, she'd get rid of it without delay.

She was learning.

Buying a firearm at a gun show or shop was out—she could not afford to leave tracks. She thought for a long time until she remembered Mario, a young man who had faced a drug charge of which he was innocent. Meagan had convinced an attorney friend just starting out on his own to help him. She knew Mario would help her get the gun.

But first she needed an excuse, one that wouldn't arouse his suspicions, but then again, he might not ask. After all, he owed her. His family would have gone hungry if it hadn't been for her, and he knew it. Of course, there was always a risk, but it was a small one and she just had to take that chance.

That was it then. A shiver ran through her as she again thought of Eileen whose fate could have been her own. Now, despite her self-confidence, she would have to summon all her inner resources to pull off what was to come. Steven's abuse had gone unpunished until she had finally found the courage to put a stop to it forever, and she could do no less for her dead friend. Murdoch had abused his last woman, and she was the one who would see to it that his fate was sealed.

* * *

"So we were right," Alix told Dr. Gardner as she leaned back in her leather chair. "Eileen Murdoch *was* battered."

"Repeatedly and brutally so. Broken bones and internal injuries over a long period of time. Bruises all over her body, plus the fresh ones on her hip and ribs. But what she died of was a *contre-coup* brain injury, which is consistent with a fall as opposed to a blow administered by someone. Question is, did she slip and fall or was she pushed? Unfortunately, I can't tell you that, Alix. I'd like to say that her death was a direct result of a beating, but it could have happened just the way her husband said."

She sighed. "Hell, Doc, I'd hoped …"

"To put him away for either murder or manslaughter," he said, finishing her sentence. "But I'm afraid my testimony wouldn't help, even if he used her regularly as a punching bag."

"Yes, I know. Jon says Mrs. Murdoch attended a support group that Meagan Rathburn facilitated and that she had left her husband once before."

"Poor woman! So young and pretty, and with two little kids!"

"I tracked her mother down," Alix said. "She still lives in Seattle, but she and Eileen haven't spoken in years. She hasn't even met Eileen's kids, and from what I gathered, she doesn't care to. She didn't know about the abuse, but she wasn't surprised and said that she suspected something like that might happen the first time Eileen brought him home. That's why she tried to talk her out of it, but Eileen wouldn't listen and it created a wedge between them."

"How sad," the old doctor said. "So what's going to happen to the children?"

"From what Murdoch said, his mother's going to take them home to live with her. He says he's on the road all the time and can't take care of them."

"Sounds like a copout to me. If he really wanted to keep those kids with him, he'd find a way. Any luck with the neighbors?" the old ME asked.

"They heard screaming and fighting on several occasions, but not on the morning in question. The baby apparently cried a lot, but that doesn't prove anything."

She bit her lip. It was difficult to talk about this without disclosing how frustrated she was.

"Where's the justice I work so hard for, Doc?" she said dejectedly. "What's the point of doing what I do when the good guys always lose out?"

"They don't always, Alix, it just seems that way sometimes."

Alix hung up feeling angry, disheartened, and like she was spinning her wheels. And, recalling similar frustrations while tracking down the killer of Lloyd's wife, she experienced an uncomfortable sensation of déjà vu. Back then, she had fallen prey to serious depression and self-doubt that had almost cost her the case, her beloved career, her self-esteem, even her friends.

She shook her head.

She would not go through that again.

* * *

Rich Murdoch was jubilant. His story had apparently fooled the cops. Even involuntary manslaughter would have meant prison, and he shuddered at the thought. They might suspect something, but they sure couldn't prove it, even after seeing Eileen's bruises. He was off the hook, and his mother had taken the kids home. Now he could do whatever he wanted without Eileen whining about his escapades. Lots of women appreciated what he had to offer and would do anything he asked.

Maybe he'd call Fatso, his old buddy who had just been laid off at the mill. Here was someone who had plenty of time on his hands.

"What do you say we go to the King's Arms tonight?" he asked Fatso.

"But Rich, with Eileen dead like that and all …"

"Oh, for God's sake, man, lighten up, will ya? Life goes on, right? Hell, I'm the one left with things that need doin'. I'm entitled to a little fun, ain't I? There's dirty laundry and dishes everywhere and there ain't no one around to do it. Eileen sure left me in a fix, dyin' on me like that. And I miss my boys, too, but how in hell am I supposed to take care of them kids?"

"You've got time off, Rich. Why don't you go see them at your ma's?"

Rich's eyes fell on a picture of Eileen and the children taken last year, and his eyes suddenly filled with tears, but the nostalgia was short lived. What in hell was the matter with him? He felt stupid, sitting here crying like some asshole. Why should it matter to him if Eileen was dead? She'd been a bad lay anyway, and all she could think about was them kids.

"Yeah, yeah, I'll think about it," he told Fatso. "In the meantime, the house stinks, and I got to fix myself somethin' to eat or go out. Damn Eileen to hell! How could she do this to me?"

Eileen had become a royal pain in the ass in the last couple of months, making phone calls when she thought he wasn't listening, threatening to leave him like she'd done before. She had no idea that he had been listening on the extension when she called the Crisis Help Line. So what if he slapped her around once in a while. What was the big deal? His dad had done the same thing whenever his old lady got smart with him, and nobody had thought anything of it.

Well, he'd made Eileen pay. And she had learned the hard way that no one messed with Rich Murdoch. Broads did not leave him. He left them.

His boss had given him compassionate leave, so he did not

have to go back to work for a while. Great! He'd go out tonight and have a good time. Who could blame him after losing his wife?

"Can't go out tonight, Rich," Fatso said. "I've been called in for work at the all-night convenience store. Money's short these days, what with the layoffs at the mill and all, and the rent's due in a week. How about me and you goin' bowlin' tomorrow, though?"

"Well, okay, suit yourself, buddy, it's your loss. See you tomorrow," Rich said crossly.

That settled it. He would go to the King's Arms and see if Amber Norton was there. She sure was some tasty dish in that short outfit with the low neckline that Harry, the owner, made the waitresses wear. Didn't leave much to the imagination. He'd had his eye on her for a long time, and she had made it plain enough she had the hots for him, the way she wiggled that cute little ass and flashed those big tits of hers. Word was out that she liked the rough stuff, too, and he got excited just thinking about it.

He took a shower, dressed in his best Levis and new Pendleton shirt, and pulled on his favorite black Tony Lama boots. After shaving and splashing plenty of *Brut* on his face, he strutted out of the house whistling *The Yellow Rose of Texas* off key, and on the way out, he snatched his fleeced-lined Levi jacket off the hook in the hallway.

As he stopped at the door to look up at the sky, he breathed in the musty scent of wet ground as the first drops of more rain the weatherman had predicted this morning misted his face.

He didn't see the small black Toyota with the muddied license plates parked half a block down the street or the brunette with the upswept hairdo sitting behind the wheel.

* * *

Since Eileen's death several weeks ago, Meagan had taken her time, following Murdoch's every move and charting his daily routine. By now, she knew his schedule as well as she knew her own, but she wanted to leave nothing to chance before making her move.

And now, a couple of weeks after Eileen's death, she made it.

She dressed with care for her evening's performance. After a substantial dinner to counteract the effect of the beers she knew she would have to drink, she bathed and dabbed on some perfume. The hot, exciting fragrance complemented the sexy red tube dress that ended at mid-thigh and fitted her like a second skin, revealing every curve.

The brunette wig was next. She twisted the long fall on top of her head, letting a few curly strands frame her face. Then she inserted the brown contact lenses and put on two-inch dangling rhinestone earrings. Slipping on the red shoes with their four-inch heels, she looked at herself approvingly in the full-length mirror. The woman looking back at her was tall, seductive, definitely on the prowl—perfect for the scenario she had in mind.

But suddenly, she stopped. There was still time to forget the whole thing and go on with her life. The investigation into Steven's death would linger and falter and finally die a natural death, and she would be home free and …

No! There was still Eileen, her death unavenged, quickly forgotten by a murdering husband and an uncaring society. She could not stop. Not now. She needed to pull herself together and quit acting like a selfish bitch. There was more than just herself to consider now.

Meagan squared her shoulders and let out a deep breath and permitted herself a tiny, grim smile as she left her bedroom. Reaching into the hallway closet, she pulled out her camel hair coat. The wind was howling and the rain had started up again, hitting the living room windows in intermittent drum-roll bursts. She started to open the door before realizing that the elegant coat would not fit the rest of her outfit and settled instead for the cheap raincoat coat she had bought when shopping for her special clothes.

Her new pistol, a .25 Beretta, joined a silk scarf and a pair of thin surgical gloves in her purse. The small gun had felt good when she had tried it out at the shooting range, and she had hit the bull's eye every time. Of course, at the distance she intended to use it, proficiency was irrelevant. As she had guessed, Mario Hernandez had been glad to help, acknowledging her request without curiosity and delivering the gun without questions. He was doing well, holding a steady job, paying off his lawyer, even saving a little money. His family was eating, and he was grateful. She felt safe, knowing that he wouldn't associate giving her the gun with the murder of an unknown truck driver.

During the weeks she had stalked Murdoch, she had often followed him to the King's Arms Tavern where he went every Saturday night with unfailing regularity. Tonight, she wanted him to get there first and have a few beers before she made her appearance.

* * *

She arrived at the tavern around eleven. It was a popular meeting place for loggers and truck drivers on their nights out, an old postal relay station which had been converted into an imitation English pub by its owner, Henry Simmons, and that dated back to the 1800s.

Henry, however, had gotten somewhat carried away with his decor. Great elk and deer heads with full sets of antlers adorned the smoky walls fashioned from the original timbers—the only authentic remnants of the historical structure—with the addition of pseudo-shields bearing coat-of-arms, fake crossbows, and even an armor propped up in the corner. The whole garish effect was tempered by a beautiful golden oak bar and original tables and chairs rescued from a turn-of-the-century San Francisco establishment. The wood floors were covered with sawdust, and a small dance floor with a jukebox in an adjacent room beckoned those wanting to combine a bit of dancing with beer drinking. Inexpensive drinks, generous sandwiches, and friendly waitresses contributed to the tavern's popularity. But gone were the days of the "tupenny nutting" when friendly wenches obliged the gents in the back room and women customers were barred. Nowadays, the wenches were coeds waitressing to defray college expenses or secretaries working an extra job to pay for their kids' braces, and the women customers often outnumbered the men.

The King's Arms Tavern was always mobbed on Friday and Saturday nights, and when Meagan arrived, dense cigarette smoke, the clinking of frosted beer glasses, and the raucous laughter of thirsty throats assaulted her. A fire burned and crackled in the huge corner fireplace where several recent arrivals stood, warming their hands. Four pool tables and benches were set up in another room for those preferring to play or cheer on their favorite players. The clicking of pool balls blended with high-decibel conversations, excited shouting, and the rollicking boogie-woogie sound of the old piano manned by Terrence Green in the tavern's main room.

Word was that Terry was around eighty-two, but no one knew for sure. One thing was for certain: no one could massage the black-and-whites like old Terry. Short and wiry, washed-out blue eyes sparkling merrily behind steel-rimmed glasses, Terrence Green was an institution at the King's Arms.

A strapping six-foot logger with a leathery complexion betraying years of outdoor work, the sleeves of his checkered work shirt rolled up over massive arms decorated with tattoos, stood next to the piano, trying to clap his hands in time with the music and sing along. Unfortunately, he had downed enough drinks to make it difficult to carry the tune. But despite the fact that he was singing off-key, he was having himself a grand old time.

Meagan spotted Rich Murdoch sitting at the bar, his arm possessively draped around the shoulders of a young blonde waitress. He leaned over to whisper something in her ear while dipping a hand in the top of her well-filled blouse as they both laughed uproariously until the bartender shot her a warning look. Giving him an apologetic half-smile, she picked up her heavy tray and began serving a group of customers who greeted her with appreciative shouts.

Meagan took off her raincoat and folded it, placing it on top of her zippered purse, a few stools away from Rich Murdoch, climbing up on a stool and making sure that, in the process, her already short skirt hiked up almost to her panty line, a maneuver that did not go unnoticed by Rich. She fished a cigarette from her purse and ordered a beer from the bartender. Harry, instantly solicitous, produced a lighter even before she had placed the cigarette in her mouth while putting a cold beer in front of her in one fluid motion.

She was well aware of her impact she was having on Murdoch whose Adam's apple was doing elevator maneuvers as he ogled her although she studiously ignored him until, unable to contain himself any longer, he slid his beer over and took the vacant stool on her left.

"Hi, I'm Rich," he said, giving her a lascivious grin as he peered down her cleavage. "You gotta be new around here. I've never seen you before. Believe me, I'd remember. What's your name, gorgeous?"

Turning, she gave him a lazy, sexy smile full of promise and a flirty glance from under her long lashes.

"Name's Jennifer," she drawled in the throaty boudoir voice she had practiced. "Mah friends call me Jen. I just moved to Red Pine las' week from Tenn'see."

"Wow!" he exclaimed. "A southern belle! Let's see what we can to make you feel at home, Jen. How 'bout a dance?"

"Love to … Rich, was it?"

"Yes, ma'am. What you do for a livin', Jen?"

"I'm a waitress lookin' for work," Meagan told him, making sure her left thigh brushed his right leg. I was hopin' there'd be an openin' here. Maybe you know the owner and can help me out? I'd be mighty grateful."

"Hey, Harry's a good friend of mine," he said. "He's the owner and bartender. That's him over there. Tell you what, Jen, I'll put in a good word for you and all if I can have a dance. What do you say?"

She took his arm as he led her to the dance floor, strutting like a peacock. It was clear that he thought he had landed himself this gorgeous hunk of woman, one that would probably do anything he wanted if he helped her get a job. Maybe even before. Meagan was certain that, if she seemed friendly enough, he would make a pass as soon as possible.

Rich was surprisingly graceful for a man his size and moved

with innate rhythm. After the dance, they returned to the bar and had a few more beers. By now, a miffed Amber had gone on to greener pastures and was sitting on one of the loggers' lap while awaiting her next order of drinks.

At around one-thirty, when many of the regulars had left, Meagan reached for her raincoat and purse, nodded her thanks to Harry, and started to walk toward the door.

"Hey, where're ya goin'?" Rich exclaimed. "You ain't leavin' yet, are ya? Come on, babe, the night's still young. How 'bout we go somewhere a little more private? You know, somewhere quiet where we can get better acquainted. Couldn't even hear myself think in there with that jukebox blarin'. Whadda ya say?"

She looked at him as they walked out the tavern door together. She couldn't stand the smell of his aftershave or the feel of his hand on her elbow, but she knew that she had to make him believe otherwise. The very sight of him repulsed her, but she forced herself to choke down the bile that rose in her throat and go on with the charade.

"Why don't we go to my house?" Rich suggested, staggering slightly. "We could get real cozy and nobody'll bother us. What do you say, huh? Here's my pickup right here. Won't take us long to get where we're goin'," he said, steering her toward where his pickup was parked.

"Hey, that's great, Rich, but don't you have a roommate or something?" Meagan asked.

"Nah! My wife's dead, and my kids live with my mother."

They now stood outside the tavern near his pickup truck. What a creep he was! His wife was barely in the ground and here he was, already looking for a good time with apparently no regard for the memory of the woman he had killed. Getting laid was the only thing on his mind. He was a scum of the worst kind.

"Sorry to hear that," she said. She slowly licked his upper lip with the tip of her tongue and noticed from the bulk in his jeans that she had achieved the desired result.

She shivered with disgust as she kissed him, but in the end, it would be worth it. He would soon realize who had the power. He thought he was pretty smart, but she was much smarter than he was, and he was about to know that he'd met his match.

"Maybe I'd better not," she told him. "I gotta be fresh tomorrow mornin' so I can look for a job, and it's gettin' pretty late, Rich."

She made a feeble attempt to pull away.

"Aw, come on, don't be such a cockteaser, Jen," he said, sounding irritated. "Don't worry about the job, okay? If I ask Harry to hire you, you're as good as hired. I'll talk with him tomorrow, I promise. Now come on, let's go," he added, pulling on her arm.

"Well, maybe just for a little while," she murmured.

"Here we go," he said, opening the truck's door for her, clearly eager to get her in the truck before she could change her mind. "Get right up there and …

"I'd rather follow you in my car, okay, Rich?" Meagan interrupted. "Then I can go on to my place without makin' you drive back here. And besides, I'd rather not leave my car here."

"You do that, honey," he replied, shrugging. "You just follow me now, hear?"

"Don't worry, lover," she said, managing a smile with some difficulty. "I'll be glued to your back bumper."

When they arrived at his house ten minutes later, Meagan parked her rented Toyota behind his pickup, selecting a dark spot near trees and shrubs, away from street lights. He unlocked the door, letting her in first, and then, without turning the lights on, grabbed her by the waist and kissed her hungrily.

"Hey, you're hot, ain't you?" she said, trying to laugh while fighting back the nausea that was creeping into her throat. "Don't turn the lights on, okay? It's better dark like this, more romantic and all."

"You sexy broad!" he said huskily. "You're sure an excitin' little bitch!"

"You're pretty excitin' yourself," Meagan replied, rubbing his crotch. "Where's your bathroom, big boy?"

"To your right. And the bedroom is right next to it," he said suggestively as he reached for her again. She forced herself to fake a giggle and grabbed her purse, nimbly stepping aside and backing into the bathroom, which was lit only by a small night-light. He followed her and before she could safely step inside, he pulled the red tube dress down.

"Jesus!" he whispered when he saw that she was naked underneath. "Come to me, baby, and I'll show you a real good time."

Somehow she managed to shut the bathroom door against him as she stepped nimbly inside while giving him a coquettish wave. "You just wait a minute, you hear? I'll be right out."

"Hurry it up, will ya?" he grumbled. "A man can only stand so much. I'll be in the bedroom waiting for ya."

"I sure hope so," Meagan sang airily, taking a pair of surgical gloves out of her purse and slipping them on. The gun was already loaded and ready to fire. When she came out of the bathroom, it was covered with a hand towel and she wore only her red shoes, dangling earrings, and a grim expression.

Rich was sitting on the edge of the bed, naked. "Whatcha doin', Jen?" he exclaimed. "Move it, will ya? Why're you just standin' there, for crissake? Let's get this show on the road!"

This was the moment Meagan had been waiting for, the moment when he saw her for what she really was instead of some tramp who had wandered into his life looking for a good time. Not some mindless bimbo eager for whatever goodies he could hand out. She had come for revenge, and he would know it before he died.

"Turn on the light, Rich. I want you to see everything," she ordered. Gone were the honeyed drawl and the seductive purring. Her tone was icy and shimmered with exquisite anger.

As soon as the light came on, she dropped the towel, revealing the Beretta. Rich stared at the gun with uncomprehending eyes.

"Jesus, what's going on here?" he shouted. "What is this, a holdup?"

"You'd like to know, wouldn't you, you sorry son of a bitch!" Meagan hissed. "Well, I'm going to humor you. It's payback time, you scumbag! How does it feel to be defenseless? How does it feel to know what Eileen must have felt each time you beat her up?"

"Eileen? You knew Eileen? Who the hell are you?" he said in a strangled voice.

"She was in my support group," Meagan told him grimly. "I got her to move out of this house, and she was ready to make a new life for herself and the kids. But somehow you talked her into coming back. And when she did, you killed her."

"It was an accident," he whimpered.

She loved the expression on his face and that moment of realization made it all worthwhile. The power! He knew who had the power now. She could see the terror in his eyes. His face sagged as if he was about to break into tears. Perfect! It was just as she had hoped and planned for. She reveled in the abject look of terror in his eyes.

"Accident or not, I don't give a damn, Rich," Meagan told him, shaking her head and letting the wig's brown hair tumble down around her shoulders. "She's still dead, and you killed her."

It was almost time. She felt a rush of exhilaration as she trained the gun on his forehead, wanting to savor the moment, the control she was exerting on a man for the first time in her life. What a great feeling it was!

"I know the police can't prove it," she continued, "so you think you got away with it. Well, I've got news for you, buster! You may have fooled them, but you sure didn't fool me. Now I'm here to make you pay and make sure you never hurt another woman again!"

Her voice held him captive as she spat the words at him, watching him grovel at her feet. She smiled as she smelled the acrid smell of his sweat and fear. "Eileen used to tell me how you'd hit little Mike because he cried when he was teething and had a fever. You probably enjoyed kicking him around too, didn't you? Well, it's the end of the line for you, Rich, and if you believe in anything, I suggest you say a quick prayer now because it's the last chance you'll get."

She saw him trying to rise, but he stopped in his tracks as soon as he looked at her. She knew from his expression that he now realized he should not doubt her sincerity. Not for a minute.

"Don't, you bastard!" she spat at him. "Don't you dare move, or I'll blow your head off right now! And don't try to pull a fast one because I'm an expert shot. I'll start with your kneecaps and work my way up to your balls, then to your stomach, and let you die here, slowly and painfully. From what I hear, it's not a pleasant way to go."

She watched him as he sat very still, looking at her, seemingly unable to control his shaking, and she laughed when she saw urine run down his legs and pool on the floor.

"Now, listen," he pleaded. "You've got to listen! You got this all wrong! Eileen, she was always whinin', always naggin'. Then she was goin' to leave me. You understand that, don't you? I mean, what can a guy do if he can't be boss in his own home?"

"So you beat her into staying? Terrified her and the kids? Is that what it took for you to feel like a great big macho man? Who do you think you're kidding, you piece of shit? I know what Eileen's life with you was like because I've been there."

She motioned with the gun. "Now off the bed! On your knees! Your pathetic life is about to come to an end, so let's see if you can leave this world with some dignity. And I hope that wherever you're going when I'm through with you, it's not where Eileen is. She deserves some peace from you. Now! On your knees!" she repeated.

Alternately mumbling and crying, he fell to his knees, his arms shielding his head.

"Please, you can't do this! You'll never get away with it! Please!"

What a wonderful feeling to see him begging her now. What an exciting, wonderful feeling to know that she held all the cards, that she could make him grovel as he had done with Eileen!

"What's the matter? Scared, are you?" she mocked him. "But just a minute ago, you couldn't wait to jump my bones! What made you change your mind? Is it this itsy bitsy gun? Is that what's keeping you from getting it up, Richy boy?"

Ignoring his babbling, Meagan slowly circled him a few times, imprinting his face, his trembling voice, his mindless terror, in her mind as she remembered her father molesting her, Steven's threats and abuse, her pain, her despair. And Eileen's fear as she talked about Rich. She imagined it all in a rush, all the women who had been ridiculed, beaten, humiliated, forced to commit acts that made them little more than animals.

No more! Never again!

It was time—judgment day for Rich Murdoch.

Picking up a pillow, she placed the gun against it and shot him twice behind the left ear. The muffled shots made no more noise than a popping cork as he fell. His body jerked a couple of times, and then he was still. Blood ran from the corner of his mouth, the two holes, looking like a single shot, piercing his thick neck.

It was over.

How different it had been with Steven! And how much easier it had been this time to rid the world of another abuser! Tonight her hands had been rock steady and the revenge sweet as she watched Rich beg and plead and crawl on the floor as she herself had done many times, and as she was sure Eileen must have, too.

The aftermath of her deed suddenly set in, and she felt a wave of dizziness overcome her, but she knew this was not the time for weakness. Dropping the pillow, she quickly put the gun back in her purse and rushed into the bathroom to splash some cold water on her face. Cupping her hands, she took a couple of drinks and, after steadying herself on the counter and breathing deeply, she felt herself come to life again.

Fueled by the urgency of the situation, she raced around the house, wiping fingerprints from every surface she had touched before donning the gloves. She picked her red dress up off the floor and pulled it back on, ignoring the two shells from the Beretta. It wouldn't matter if they were found because she intended to get rid of the gun even before Rich's body was found.

After one last look around to make sure she had forgotten nothing, she put on her raincoat and covered her head with her silk scarf. Outside, the street was deserted and silent save for the occasional barking of a dog and the steady drip of the rain on the concrete sidewalk. One lone light burned in a house a few doors away.

Meagan was about to leave the safety of the porch and walk

toward her car when she heard voices and saw a couple walking arm in arm toward her, laughing and joking as they headed for a white Buick parked at the curb just ahead of Rich's truck. She quickly ducked back into the cover of the porch, her heart beating so hard she felt sure the couple could hear it. But they had not seen her, nor did they suspect her presence, as they got in their car and drove away.

Meagan heard nothing but the faint sound of a car engine about a block away, and as soon as the couple departed, she took a deep breath and briskly walked to her Toyota. She was relieved to see that its license plates were still muddied and unreadable. Refraining from turning on her headlights until she was half a block away from the Murdoch home, she drove slowly away, staying well within the posted speed limit.

Upon arriving home, she took a bath so hot that her delicate skin turned bright red as she scrubbed and scrubbed in an attempt to wash off all remnants of Rich Murdoch's hands on her.

She felt ... how did she feel? Exhilarated, yes, but much more. She was filled with a sense of power while also experiencing a strange sadness, and she asked herself why. She had vindicated Eileen, humiliated Rich, and finally, she had killed him. But something was missing. Why was she still hurting so? Shouldn't the killing have eased the pain?

She looked deeper inside herself and felt no guilt, only glee at having accomplished her mission. Killing Rich had been far easier than shooting Steven, but she had not faced the fact that killing for revenge was an aberration. Her focus on avenging Eileen had blinded her to its true horror.

As she stepped out of the tub and looked at herself in the mirror, she experienced an epiphany.

And then the blinding realization hit her full force.

Murderer! She was nothing but a cold-blooded murderer!

A mirthless smile stretched her lips and soon turned into uncontrollable, hysterical laughter.

She had stepped over the line, knowingly this time.

Tonight, for the second time, she had switched places with the batterer.

CHAPTER 9

The ringing of the phone brought Alix out of the shower on the run. She heard Lloyd answer it, but by the time she had wrapped a towel around her dripping hair and put on her robe, he had already left.

About fifteen minutes later, the phone rang again.

"Alix, we have a problem," Dave Barnes said. His baritone voice held an urgent note. "I called you a while ago and left a message with Lloyd, but I guess he didn't tell you."

"No, he didn't," Alix said, frowning. "He probably forgot."

That's odd. Not at all like Lloyd to forget something like this.

"So what's going on, Dave?"

"Rich Murdoch was killed execution style, either late last night or early this morning," Dave told her. "One of his buddies, a guy by the name of Scott Pruitt, found him. Says he tried to phone Murdoch several times and then finally went to the house. The door was unlocked, so he let himself in. Murdock was lying naked on the bedroom floor, shot twice in the head."

"So the crime scene has been contaminated," she mused.

"'Fraid so, but at least, shook up as he was, the guy still had the good sense to call us right away. The CSU team's already there, and Doc Gardner's on his way. I told Pruitt to just sit tight and not touch anything."

Nothing was ever simple, Alix thought. Pruitt's story was that he had walked in and found his friend's body. Maybe it was true, maybe not. The trouble was that they'd have to take his word for it until they could prove otherwise.

When Alix reached the Murdoch home, Dave was waiting for her, as were the television crews and the press.

"Oh, no!" she moaned. "It's vulture-feeding time. And there's that obnoxious Joel Nehring. What have I ever done to you, God? That guy brings out the absolute worst in me. Just seeing him makes me want to pluck his beige hair out one at a time."

"Now, Alix! You know darn well we don't have time to indulge in these small personal pleasures," Dave told her, grinning. "Besides, you promised the chief ..."

"Yes, yes, I know! You all remind me often enough that I've got to try to get along with those people. The department's public image and all that ..."

Her sigh could have put out a small brush fire. As the press surrounded her, she said, "Sorry, folks, I don't have anything to tell you at the moment. As you can see, I just got here."

A short man with an acne-peppered face and clothes that defied description stuck a microphone in her face. Joel Nehring had the look of a fat puppy experiencing her first heat, and Alix was overcome by an irresistible urge to hit him with a rolled newspaper.

"Any theories as to what's going on here?" he asked, giving her his most ingratiating smile.

"Since I don't have a crystal ball, I have none at this time, Mr. Nehring," she said frostily. "I know as little as you do and I don't deal in suppositions. Please call my office this afternoon. I may have more to tell you then."

Ignoring the group's wails of protest, she and Dave went into the house. Alix couldn't help but notice the stark contrast between the spotless home Eileen Murdoch had kept and its present condition. Dust balls were everywhere. Dirty dishes filled the sink and littered the counters of what had once been an immaculate kitchen. Gone was the pleasant lemon scent of furniture polish, replaced by the smell of old cigarettes, trash, and dirty laundry.

Rich Murdoch lay on his stomach, naked, eyes open and staring. Two closely spaced shots marred the back of his neck. There was very little blood. A pillow, which had disgorged its stuffing, lay on the floor next to his head.

"Mafia style shooting, hey, Doc?" Alix asked the old ME who was bending over the body. "Small-caliber gun, shot through a pillow to muffle the sound?"

"That's what it looks like," he told her. "Very efficient. If the first bullet didn't kill him instantly, the second surely did."

"What else do we have?"

"Well, looks like he's been dead at least eight hours. Fixed lividity and rigor mortis are present, but I'll have more for you after the autopsy. Your guys have already picked up the shells and retrieved the bullets. They went right through him. Looks like a .25 caliber pistol."

"Let's check out the neighborhood," Alix said, turning to Dave, "and see if anyone heard or saw anything. Get a couple of the guys on it right away, will you? Hey, Jim, you got the shells?" she asked Jim Harrison.

Jim was short, thin, and had the sad eyes of a bloodhound, "Yeah, here they are," he told Alix. "Both .25 caliber. Interesting, huh? Someone sure wanted to make certain they didn't fumble this job. Reminds me of mob executions."

So he had noticed it too. She wondered what it all meant. Mob executions in Red Pine? What was the world coming to?

Rich Murdoch's friend was spread out in an armchair in the living room looking like a beached whale. He had small eyes, closely spaced and the color of mud, and sparse blond hair. He wore an oversize white tee shirt that sported large perspiration stains, and faded blue sweat pants that had seen better days.

Alix took out her small notebook. "Mr. Pruitt? Detectives Mendez and Barnes," she said. "Are you okay?"

He nodded feebly. "Yeah, just shook up, that's all."

Well, she could certainly understand that it wasn't everyday someone walked in on a corpse, especially that of a friend, but, nervousness aside, she hoped he could contribute something to the investigation.

"What happened since you last spoke with Mr. Murdoch?" she asked.

"Well, me and him, we were supposed to go bowlin'. He got some time off because his old lady ... well, she died coupla weeks ago. He wasn't supposed to go back to work 'til next Monday, so we thought we'd bowl a coupla of games, have a coupla beers, maybe meet some br ... ladies."

He paused for a few seconds, probably to gather his thoughts. "I called him to say I was comin' over," he continued, "but Rich didn't answer. So I came over to see if maybe he was outside workin' in the garage or somethin'."

He wiped his moon face with a dirty handkerchief, and Alix saw that his color was beginning to return to normal.

"When I got here," he went on, "there was no answer, so I tried the front door. It wasn't locked, which was real strange 'cause Rich, he was almost paranoid about lockin' doors. So I jus' went in and called out. When he didn't answer, I looked around and found him in the bedroom."

"Any idea who might have wanted to kill him?" Alix asked.

"I jus' don't know nobody who'd do a thing like that, ma'am," Pruitt replied. "I mean, he had a hell of a temper and a big mouth and all that, and he irked quite a few guys over the years. But me and him, we go way back. Growed up together, went to grammar school and high school together."

"Anything else?" Alix asked.

Would this guy have anything productive to contribute? Not likely, from what he was telling her so far.

"Well, there was these guys we played cards with who didn't like Rich much," Murdoch said, "but I can't think of nobody who'd want to kill him. I mean, if people went around killin' everybody with a bad temper and a big mouth, there'd hardly be nobody left!"

"Did Mr. Murdoch gamble?"

"You think maybe he borrowed money from loan sharks, couldn't pay it back, and they iced him? Like in the movies?" he asked with barely concealed excitement.

"Just wondering," Alix told him.

It wouldn't be the first time that a seemingly innocent card game had escalated into violence over a few bucks. Some players took their card games pretty seriously. Perhaps a sore loser had decided to get even.

He shook his head again. "We played poker quite a bit—me, him, and some other guys, once or twice a month when he was home, ya know, but he wasn't what you'd call a gambler. He just didn't make that kinda money and he was always short before payday. I used to bail him out before I lost my job."

"What did he spend his money on?"

"Oh, ya know, the usual. A camcorder. A new rifle—he liked to go huntin'—things for his pickup. Stuff like that. And he liked the ladies."

"You mentioned his temper. Did he ever get into fights?"

"Sometimes. But all I know is there's guys out there who don't like Rich, but not enough to kill him, ya know."

"How about the ladies? Did he have girlfriends?"

"Oh, yeah! Old Rich, he liked the ladies. Married, divorced, single, made him no never mind. Took 'em out even before his old lady died. He sure liked the ladies," he repeated, "and they liked him right back." From the wistful note in his voice, Alix guessed Fatso envied Murdoch's success with women.

"Do you know of any particular married lady whose husband might have caught up with him?" she asked, "Or a jealous boyfriend?"

He seemed to hesitate for a split second, then shook his head. "No, can't say that I do."

Alix noticed the pause and shot Dave a glance. He made a note in his own notebook.

"Thanks, Mr. Pruitt. Please leave your phone number and address with Detective Barnes in case we have more questions for you, okay?"

Pruitt nodded and rose to leave.

After he was gone, Alix turned toward Dave. "Those poor children, orphaned so young!" she said. "First their mother, and now their dad." The look in her eyes spoke volumes as the memory of her long-dead partner's two small children flashed through her mind.

Back in the bedroom, she found her fingerprint technician dusting for prints while the medical examiner stood, watching the ambulance attendants zip Murdoch's body into a body bag.

"How're you doing, Hank?" she asked.

"Fine. I've still got a bit of ground to cover here. Got some good prints, but can't tell yet who they belong to."

"Concentrate on the bedroom, will you? Maybe the evidence vacuum will pick up something important. Go through this place with a fine-toothed comb. We're going to need all the help we can get here, guys. I don't want any screw-ups."

Dr. Gardner walked out with the ambulance attendants. "You'll have my report as soon as I can get it to you," he told Alix.

She nodded absentmindedly, tugging at an errand strand of hair. "I wonder if Murdoch was with a woman and her husband or lover surprised them and killed him before he had a chance to throw something on. That would explain why he was naked," she told Dave.

"Doc," she said, turning to Dr. Gardner, "I'd like to know if he had intercourse before he died."

"Of course," he said, following the gurney out of the room. "You know that's part of the autopsy."

"If he was with a woman, he must have let her in," Dave said. "Remember what Pruitt said? That Murdoch was paranoid about locking doors? Maybe they came in together and had a fight. Maybe he tried to rough her up and she killed him and took off. That would explain why the house wasn't broken into. But if he didn't know who was at the door, he probably would've pulled on some pants first or something."

Alix looked around. "Let's see if we can retrace Murdoch's steps," she suggested just as Pruitt appeared in the doorway, shifting his weight from side to side in a rocking motion.

"I thought you'd gone, Mr. Pruitt," Alix told him, "but I'm glad you're still here. Let me ask you something before you leave. Where did Mr. Murdoch go when he was home? A favorite bar, restaurant, pool hall, you know, that sort of thing? With whom did he pal around other than yourself? And what about the women you mentioned?"

She wondered how much she could believe this man and decided that he was probably pretty trustworthy since he didn't seem to be the type, or have the imagination, to make things up.

"Well, me and him often went to the King's Arms Tavern on the old highway," he replied. You know, the place just at the edge of town? Done up like an English pub? Food's pretty good. Rich wanted to go there last night. Said he was off for a few days and asked me to come along, but I was workin'. I've been out of work, and it was a chance for me to pick up a coupla extra bucks."

Alix nodded and motioned him to go on with a wave of her hand. Could someone at the tavern remember anything? She knew that it would be the next logical step to check it out.

"Rich really didn't have no friends 'cept me," Pruitt went on, "and maybe old Henry who owns the tavern. And there was no special girlfriend. Like I said, he liked to play the field."

"Can you give me some names?"

"Well, there was Amber Norton. She's a waitress at the tavern. They kinda messed around every time we went there, ya know, kidded around, danced, had a good time. The others I don't know 'cept by first names. Rich talked a lot about his women, but he didn't mention no last names."

He paused for a while, then said, "Detective?"

"Yes?" Alix replied. "Did you remember something else?"

"Well no, not really. I jus' wanted to say somethin', ya know, jus' for the record. Rich, he wasn't perfect, ya know? He beat up on his old lady pretty regular and cheated on her and all. But me and him, we've been friends for quite a spell. And he had a pretty rough time when he was growin' up. His old man drank and beat up on the family pretty regular, so Rich was over at my house a lot when we was both kids. He didn't have nobody to look up to, no role model, know what I mean? And he loved his little kids and his wife in his own way, though he had a funny way of showin' it. And he worked pretty hard to make a livin' for them, so what I'm tryin' to say is, nobody's perfect, right?"

He turned crimson as he turned on his heels and left.

Alix was touched by the fat man's loyalty. No, no one was all bad, and Pruitt's clumsy attempts to explain his friend's actions had, if not excused Rich Murdoch, at least shed some light on his behavior. And he was cooperative, even if he wasn't the sharpest instrument in the toolbox—she would count her blessings any way she could.

From the look in Lloyd's eyes the other night when she had left in the middle of dinner to go back to the precinct, if there was any way she could make it appear that her work was easing up, she would do it, and cooperative interviewees were a start.

She was withdrawn and silent during the drive to the King's Arms Tavern. "Dave," she said finally. "If Murdoch brought a woman home, why did she kill him? And if a husband or boyfriend surprised them in bed, why didn't he kill the woman, too?"

Dave pursed his lips. "I don't know, but I'm inclined to agree that a woman's involved."

"And that the shooting happened as a result of her being there?"

"Could be. Maybe she came home with him, and he wanted to play rough and she said 'no go.' Or maybe it was a woman he'd dumped for another, and the dumpee objected. Pruitt said Rich played the field."

"I see you caught that pause when I asked Pruitt who Murdoch was running around with."

"Sure did, and I made a note to check it out. From what Pruitt said, Murdoch wasn't particular about the women's marital status. Sounds like they were all fair game, and there were quite a lot of them."

"Well, from the dead man's rather abundant attributes, I'd be willing to bet that he didn't suffer from lack of female companionship."

"Alix! You peeked! And you, a married woman!"

She grinned. "Married, Dave, not dead. Besides, it's hard to overlook the obvious." She quickly became serious again. "We've got a lot of maybes and suppositions. Oh, and one more thing. I want to know if the victim had a rap sheet."

"And I'm sure you're about to tell me to get going on it."

She gave him a sheepish grin. He knew her well. Working with someone like Dave was a joy. They always seemed to be in synch, anticipating each other's thoughts. She felt fortunate indeed to have him as a partner and a friend.

* * *

Henry Simmons was about to open the tavern for the late-afternoon crowd when the two detectives arrived. Since it was still early, the parking lot was empty and the tavern was cool, dark, and deserted. After Alix introduced herself and Dave, Henry invited them to sit down and asked a shapely young blonde girl to bring them soft drinks.

"Was Rich Murdoch here last night, Mr. Simmons?" Alix asked.

Henry was a corpulent man with a bulbous nose and a face with the broken capillaries normally associated with a heavy drinker, but his bulk masked quick reflexes and a powerful physique. He brooked no nonsense in his establishment, so those willing to abide by the rules were welcome. Troublemakers were not. A retired Marine, he acted not only as his own bartender but also as his own bouncer.

"Why, yes," he said, lighting a cigarette and offering the pack to the two detectives, who shook their heads. "He came in around ten, ten thirty, something like that. Why do you ask? Is he in some kind of trouble?"

"The worst kind," Dave said. "He's dead. Murdered last night."

"Murdered? Holy smoke! Who did it?"

"That's what we're here to find out, Mr. Simmons. Was he here alone?"

"He came in by himself, if that's what you mean, but he wasn't alone for long. First he and Amber—that's the gal who brought you your drinks—were kinda playing up to each other, as usual. But then a woman came in, and Rich fell all over himself and never gave Amber a second look. She was pissed off about it, I can tell you that."

"Who was the woman? Did you know her?"

"Never seen her before. Not one of my regulars. Good-looking gal, dark hair, brown eyes. Five six or seven, give or take. Slim. Curvy in all the right places." His hands outlined a woman's figure. ""She wore dangling sparkly earrings and a red dress. You know, one of those tight-fitting things."

"A tube dress?" Alix asked.

"Yeah, I guess that's what they're called. Great body. The dress didn't leave much to the imagination. I think I heard her say her name was Jen and that she'd just moved up from Tennessee."

"Was she alone?"

"Yeah."

"Did they leave together?"

"Can't say for sure. They got up to leave at about the same time, but I don't know if he took her home or not. Knowing Rich, it's a pretty safe bet he didn't pass up the opportunity if it was offered. It was past one thirty, and I wanted to close up, so I didn't pay much attention. Everybody had pretty much gone by then except for a few couples, and they left about fifteen minutes after Rich and the gal in red took off."

"Did anyone else leave about the same time?" Alix asked.

Henry shook his head. "No, just them."

"Did they seem to be arguing when they left?"

"Oh no, not at all! They were as cozy as two peas in a pod," Simmons said, grinning.

"And you're sure you've never seen the woman before?"

"Positive, I'd remember the body, if not the face. She was quite a dish."

"I'd like you to help the police artist with a composite," Alix told him. "She might be the last person who saw Murdoch alive. Are you willing to come down to the station?"

"Sure thing. I'll be there first thing tomorrow morning if that's all right." His eyes narrowed. "You think she killed him?"

"I don't know, Mr. Simmons, but we need to check every-thing out," Alix replied. "And I'd appreciate anything else you can remember. In the meantime, if you see her again, please call me right away. Here's my card."

He nodded. "No problem. Always glad to help the police."

It sure was nice when potential witnesses were happy to co-operate. So far, she had been lucky with Pruitt and Simmons, but sometimes she ran into recalcitrant individuals who refused to assist the police or pretended not to remember in order to avoid getting involved.

"I'd like to talk to Amber now, Mr. Simmons," Alix told him. "By the way, do you know if she and Murdoch dated?"

"I'm not sure whether or not they 'dated.' They messed around a bit when Amber was working. They joked and kidded during her breaks. I have a rule of sorts about waitresses not dating customers, but if they're gonna to do it, they're gonna to do it, and there isn't much I can do about it. Rich was always catting around with this woman or that woman, but after his wife died, he seemed to get worse, out with a different one every time he came here."

"Do you know any of these women's names?" she asked.

"A few. I'll give you a list of those I can remember."

It probably was too much to ask that any of these names would produce the killer, but this was the sort of tedious police work they all had to go though in order to produce a lead, any lead. That and a bit of luck, of course.

"Hey, Amber, get over here," Simmons shouted. "These detectives want to ask you a few questions. Looks like Rich Murdoch got himself killed last night. Now you tell them anything they wanna know, and you tell them the truth, you hear?"

The young woman's eyes widened. She was a beautiful girl in her early twenties whose heavy honey-blonde hair contrasted with enormous chocolate brown doe eyes, so dark they appeared black. The short waitress outfit with the low neckline she wore emphasized her voluptuous figure and long, shapely legs.

"Oh, my God? Killed? But I don't know anything," she whispered.

"It's okay, Miss Norton," Alix assured her. "Don't be frightened. We just have a few questions. Were you with Rich Murdoch last night?"

"Sorta," the young waitress replied, blushing. "At least when he first came in. I was working my regular shift and I didn't have time to sit down and visit. It was Saturday night, and the place was jumping. We were just kinda fooling around, nothing serious. He wanted to take me out after my shift ended."

"Did the two of you go out often?"

Amber shot a furtive look at her boss. "Once or twice. He was a nice-looking guy, and knew how to show a girl a good time."

"What happened after you talked about a date?"

"A woman came in. I never saw her here before. Rich hooked up with her and never gave me the time of day after that."

"Did you see them leave together?" Alix asked.

"No. I wasn't feeling good, so I went home a bit early. They were still here when I left."

"Would you recognize the woman if you saw her again?"

"Oh, sure. She was pretty good looking, in a cheap sort of way. She and Rich seemed to be getting along real good."

"How long have you known Mr. Murdoch?"

"About two years. He'd come in for a beer or two when he was in town and we'd talk. Said he didn't get along with his wife, that she didn't understand him. You know, like they all say, and …"

She broke off, suddenly indignant. "Oh, no, you don't!" she exclaimed. "You're not going to hang that on me! You think I killed him because he dropped me for that other woman, but I swear I didn't. Rich meant nothing to me. He was just somebody to have a good time with. Besides, I went straight home. You can check with my parents."

"You live at home?"

"Yeah. I can't afford my own apartment. The folks were up when I came in at around twelve thirty, and I stayed up with them to watch an old movie until about two in the morning. I'm usually too wound up when I get home from work to go straight to bed. They had one of those old westerns on TV. Something with Henry Fonda in it."

"And you never went out again after that?"

"No. I was beat and had a headache. And my feet were killing me, so I took a bath and went to bed. The folks will tell you. You can check with them."

"We will, thanks. Here's my card, Amber," Alix said. "Please call me if you remember anything else about the woman."

"Okay, sure. Is it all right for me to go back to work now?"

"Sure," Alix said, "and thanks."

Alix was silent during their drive back to the precinct.

"You're awfully quiet. What are you thinking about?" Dave asked as they drove back to the precinct.

"That woman in the red dress. She was probably the last person to see Murdoch alive, but if she went home with him, why kill him? Makes no sense, Dave. From what Simmons says, she'd just met the guy. If she wanted to rob him, she could've taken his wallet when he slept and then slipped away, but his wallet wasn't missing. It just doesn't add up."

"What if he woke up and caught her at it, then roughed her up, and she shot him in self-defense?" Dave suggested. "Some women do carry guns to protect themselves in case their johns get rough. All I know is that we've got to find her and bring her in for questioning, and the composite will help, but where do we start looking? She may have only been passing through."

"Yes, but what about the execution method, Dave?" Two bullets in the back of the head? A hooker trying to protect herself probably wouldn't have done it that way. Maybe this woman was carrying for protection, I'll go along with that, but the rest doesn't fit," Alex replied.

"Then we'd better find her and bring her in," Dave repeated.

"Well, we know one thing for sure," Alix said grimly. "The killer wanted to make certain that Rich Murdoch didn't get up and walk away."

* * *

Alix arrived in her office just in time to receive a call from Harry Simmons. He told her that he had just remembered overhearing the woman who had been with Murdoch the night before say that she was a waitress looking for work.

Now at last they had a starting point. If the woman was an out-of-work waitress, it meant showing the composite at all the restaurants, bars, taverns, every place food and drink were served. It would take a lot of time and patience, but Alix knew that the success of an investigation was seldom brought about by divine intervention. Breaking a case was the result of tedious, back-breaking, time-consuming work, sifting through unending details, reading reports over and over again, beating the pavement, and interviewing people. Lots and lots of people. And of course, a bit of luck helped, too.

Dr. Gardner called around noon to tell her that the gunshots to Murdoch's head had definitely been fired through the pillow, undoubtedly to muffle the sound.

"I found fragments of foam in the wounds," he told her. "Looks like the victim had quite a few beers before he died. There wasn't much else in his stomach except a few pretzels. And about intercourse, that's negative."

Alix was stunned. "Negative?"

This was not at all what she had expected, given the crime scene.

"That's right." He paused. "An interesting thing, though. The angle of the shot indicates the shooter was standing. Murdoch was either kneeling or sitting on the floor, facing away from the killer. It was definitely a downward shot."

"Can you estimate the height of the shooter?"

"That's all it is, Alix, an estimate. Maybe five six, five seven."

That meant that the killer could have been either a man or a woman. Alix digested this information, wondering whether it weakened the theory of a woman as the killer, and decided it did not, particularly in view of the statement the tavern owner had made about the woman's height.

As for the victim, his rap sheet revealed a long history of misdemeanors—fighting, drinking, disturbing the peace, but nothing that shed any light on the reason for his death. A check with the company Rich had worked for indicated there had been incidents where he had been caught speeding and using drugs and also driving more hours than the company allowed. The lab reports also disclosed traces of sawdust in the Murdoch bedroom, which matched samples from the King's Tavern, probably tracked in by Murdoch or by the woman who had accompanied him.

Who *was* the mysterious Jen? Was she the killer?

Alix could only hope that the composite of the woman in red would elicit some results. But aside from several long, brown hairs, a couple of cigarette butts, the .25 caliber casings, and the two bullets, the evidence vacuum had picked up nothing of real value, particularly since Eileen had had long, brown hair. Whoever had killed Murdoch had been careful or clever enough to leave no trace of his or her presence. The only adult fingerprints found at the scene were those of Eileen, Pruitt, and Rich Murdoch.

Alix sequestered herself in her office until mid-afternoon and finally called Dave in.

"Don't you find it odd that there was no sign of intercourse?" she asked him. "Rich Murdoch picks up this woman at a bar and presumably brings her home, but they don't have sex. So what did they do? Play Monopoly? Exchange quiche recipes? Discuss the Jewish-Iranian situation?"

"Yeah, I see what you mean," Dave replied, frowning. "So you're thinking she lured him home for no other reason than to kill him?"

"That's what I think, but the big question is why, and more importantly, who? And then there's that business about the angle of the shot. According to Doc, the victim was either kneeling or sitting on the floor when he was murdered. That and the two shots behind the ear reek of execution."

Two killings in one month. One robbery-murder with no clues, no suspects other than the victim's wife, and no apparent motive. And another murder, one that might have been committed by a woman, also with no apparent motive, and absolutely nothing to indicate a connection between the two cases.

Had Red Pine suddenly become the nation's new murder capital?

Alix knew that the answer would, in large part, depend on her.

CHAPTER 10

Meagan's doorbell rang and she went to answer it, heart pounding. But instead of the police, she found one of her colleagues, Dan DeVoe, standing at the door and holding a bouquet of exquisite ruffled daffodils. Like her, Dan taught criminology at the university. Meagan was well aware that he had been hopelessly smitten with her for years, even though he tried valiantly to hide it. Now that she was a widow, she thought he might become even more of a nuisance when all she wanted was to be left alone.

"Meagan, I'm sorry to barge in on you like this," he said haltingly, "but I called, and there was no answer. I thought your machine was off and I was afraid that you might … I was concerned that … I thought you might need something," he finally said.

Meagan struggled to find an appropriate response and forced a weak smile. "That's very nice of you, Dan, thank you."

Why was he here? Had someone from the university sent him to spy on her? She was in no mood to visit and had a lot on her mind, but basic courtesy dictated that she be polite to him. Had Alix made a connection between his murder and Steven's and did she suspect something?

"Would you mind if I came in for a few minutes? And these flowers are for you," he said, oblivious to her feelings.

Why couldn't he just go home and leave her alone? "I have to leave in a few minutes," she said, trying to hide her annoyance.

"I won't stay long, I promise," he said as he stepped inside the door.

She had entertained him in what now seemed like so long ago because Steven, sadistic as usual, had enjoyed watching the little man grapple with his feelings toward his wife. And now, ironically, she still had to be pleasant to him in order not to raise his suspicions.

People would be watching her closely in weeks to come, perhaps not consciously, but one never knew what ideas might come into people's heads and she knew that she had to watch her every step.

"They're beautiful, thank you," she forced herself to say as she accepted the flowers. "I'll put them in a vase." She buried her face in the yellow bouquet that smelled of sunshine, eager to avoid eye contact with him.

Meagan knew how Dan felt about her, but she also knew he would never mention it. Gentle, shy, almost colorless, he was the antithesis of Steven's flamboyant good looks and extroverted personality. Dan's best trait was that he was an excellent listener. Many people sensed they could trust this reserved, intense man who seemed to care and who exuded such a quiet aura of understanding. Which was all well and good, but she had nothing to tell him. Nothing to tell anyone. Nothing at all.

What did he want? Who had sent him? "Was there a reason for you to drop by today other than to bring me flowers, Dan?" she finally asked as she fetched a vase and filled it with water.

Dan nervously brushed back sandy hair that was beginning to recede. "Well, I wanted to make sure you were all right. You're all alone here now, Meagan, and I thought you might need some help around the place. You know, yard work or something. Or maybe I could run to the store for you and … Well, you know what I mean."

He looked sincere enough, but maybe, just maybe, the police were involved in his visit. Maybe he was here to report to Alix. Maybe …

"Thanks, Dan," she said, "I appreciate that. I can't think of a thing, but I'm glad you came. You're my first visitor other than the police and my family since the … you know."

It was easier to cry than she would have thought. Burying her face in her hands, she began to sob.

"It's okay, Meagan, I understand," Dan said. She imagined that he was finding it difficult not to put his arms around her to offer comfort. "But if you need anything, anything at all, all you have to do is ask."

As if she were likely to ask him or anyone else for anything, let alone comfort. But now was not the time to let him know that. Perhaps later when she could do anything she wanted, say anything she wanted.

"Meagan, what about dinner sometime?" he said as he was leaving. "I know how you felt about Steven, and there's no way I could … I mean, he was such a great guy, and the two of you seemed so happy. But if you ever need a friend … That is, if you don't think it's too soon …"

Wiping her eyes, she glanced at him sharply. Was he mocking her? Had he somehow uncovered her secret about the true state of her marriage?

"I can't promise anything right now, Dan," she said, forcing a smile. "I need to sort out a lot of things in my life and don't know where to start. To be honest with you, I'm not ready to socialize, but when I do, I'd like it to be with you."

She didn't mean a word of it but she knew he wouldn't leave unless she offered him some hope.

"This means a lot to me," he told her, beaming. "Look, I won't bother you, but I'd like to check on you once in a while, if you don't mind, just to make sure you're okay."

"I'd like that, Dan," she said trying to hide her impatience.

Meagan was irritated at this invasion of her privacy, yet what else could she say? She didn't relish the idea of Dan dropping in to check on her unannounced, even with the best of intentions.

She would do anything, say anything to send him on his way. She didn't need him or anyone like him in her life.

* * *

Earlier that day, Meagan had talked to her protegée, Paige Chatfield. Now, as she thought about their conversation, unease filled her again. Paige was a beautiful, smart, compassionate girl who planned to attend graduate school in the fall and work with teens at risk. Meagan had, in fact, become something of a sister to her. But Paige seemed so distracted lately. When questioned, she had told Meagan about her new love interest, sounding quite smitten.

"He's great, Dr. Rathburn, and so handsome! He has dark hair and blue eyes, and he looks a little like Mel Gibson. He sent me a gorilla-gram last week for my birthday and gave me the biggest box of candy I've ever seen! He's a little older than me and he's got a good job, a very responsible position. Last night he told me he loved me and asked me to move in with him."

"How long have you known him, Paige?" Meagan had asked the girl.

"A couple of months, but I feel like we've known each other forever."

It wasn't until after she had gone to bed that Meagan focused on what had bothered her about the conversation. She remembered Daphne's description of the man she had lived with when she had addressed the support group and her blood froze—dark and handsome, blue eyed, in a responsible position.

A counselor? A minister? A politician? A policeman?

The guy had hurt Daphne so badly that she was still afraid to say his name out loud, and refused to warn any new girlfriends about her own experiences. Could he be the new man in Paige's life?

She had to talk to Daphne, find out who he was once and for all, and then warn Paige. She must not let anything happen to her.

CHAPTER 11

Meagan leaned back in her black leather chair and tried to relax. It had been a frenetic morning: three classes, a departmental meeting during which she had been more than a little distracted, and a lecture by a guest criminologist to whom she had been introduced and whose name she could not remember. It was only one o'clock, and she still had an evening class to teach and papers to correct.

Normally, she breezed through her Wednesday schedule with energy to spare, but nowadays, any effort seemed to require all of her concentration. Right now, she felt as exhausted as if she had competed in a three-day marathon with five-pound weights strapped to her ankles. And she couldn't shake the cold symptoms that refused to go away.

The stress, brought on by the murders and compounded by her weariness, was taking a heavy toll on her emotional and physical well-being. Trying to keep up the appearance of a normal life while living with her secrets was a huge burden, choking her, wearing her down. She felt no remorse for her crimes, since she fervently believed that both Steven and Murdoch had deserved to die. Yet no matter how she tried, she could no longer pretend that her life would be the same.

She looked at the papers and reports lying on her desk without really seeing them. Her lengthy leave of absence had cost her dearly, and she realized now that she would have to take work home if she expected to catch up. She had assignments to correct, a mid-term exam to prepare, a session tomorrow with the support group, and a paper that was a long way from being finished and that she was due to present at a conference in Atlanta in two weeks. Suddenly, it all seemed too much to deal with. She felt so alone, but that was the way it had always been. Certainly no one had tried to help her, protect her, not even her mother. She had been her own defender. Always. And she had learned to be alone.

She had gone over every detail of the Murdoch execution and felt sure she had left no clues. Alix and her detectives would be hard pressed to find the woman in red. After seeing the composite in the newspapers, she thought it would be a miracle if anyone made the connection between the woman depicted in the police rendering and the chic, elegant professional now sitting behind her desk.

As for the weapons she had used to commit both murders, she had disposed of them by dropping them into the river, wrapped in plastic and weighed down with rocks, in one of the deep pools of the river that serpentined in a slow, lazy pattern, about a mile from where she stood.

Today she wore a pale yellow Givenchy suit with a Hermès silk scarf the color of her eyes, and a golden scarab pin with matching earrings. Shoes of buttery soft Italian leather in the same cream shade completed her ensemble. She looked composed, cool, and beautiful despite the dark circles under her eyes that defied make up. Still, no one had remarked on her changed appearance. And if they did, she could always blame the insomnia that had turned her nights into torment because of her "grief." After all, she *was* a widow, and the fools who surrounded her would believe anything she told them.

She looked out the window, her rêverie interrupted by the sound of students' horseplay below her office.

Pussy willows, cattails, and Queen Anne's lace grew with wild abandon on the river's banks, home to raccoons, wood ducks, deer, and pheasants. It was not unusual to catch sight of a doe suddenly bolting from the protection of the shrubs, startled by another animal or by joggers running along the bike path that followed the river.

The day was cool and crisp, so clear that she could see the mountains in the distance still covered with snow and shrouded by mist, looking like the trailing veils of timorous vestal virgins. She watched the gardener's monotonous up-and-down stroll as he rode his mower under her windows and could almost smell the promise of warmer summer days to come in the clean smell of the newly mowed lawn.

A flock of raucous Canadian geese, returning from their southbound winter foray, flew overhead in perfect V formation, their necks elegantly stretched, their webbed feet tucked under them. They were flying so low she could almost hear the rhythmic, steady *whoomp-whoomp* of their powerful wings.

The sight of the river and the birds swooping overhead suddenly brought back some poignant memories of a day long gone when she and her father had gone fishing. She remembered the care he had taken to bait her hook with its brightly-colored feather lure, his patience at her first bungling attempts to throw the line, his excitement when she had felt the first tug, and the thrill with which she had brought in her first fish all by herself. The fish, a lovely rainbow trout with reddish bands down its sides, olive back, and black spots, was too small to keep, so they had tossed it back in. But that had not mattered. Nothing had mattered that day except the joy of being cared for, as a child should be. For a few hours, she had been able to forget the horror of the nights, the sound of his feet on the stairs.

Afterward, they had eaten lunch on a grassy knoll near the river—egg salad sandwiches, soda pops, even the misshapen chocolate chip cookies she had baked for him with such care. It had been a wonderful day, and she had felt loved and very special.

"I love you very much, Meagan," her father had said, "and what happens between us is our secret, so if you tell someone, things won't be the same. We must share our secret with no one."

The ringing of a phone in the office next to hers jolted her back to the present and a chilling loneliness flooded over her. She had never had playmates or girlfriends with whom she could share her innermost secrets, giggle, talk on the phone, or discuss the latest heartthrob. Her life had always been tightly coiled, filled with shadowy secrets she could share with no one. For most of her life, she had felt like a playgoer, seeing happiness unfold in other people's lives while she remained captive of her fears and taboos. Society might not see that justice was done, but she would. And there would be no nonsense about proof and legalities. She would go straight to the source of what she hated most and eliminate it.

And she would never look back.

* * *

"Anything on the woman in red?" Alix asked Dave who was sitting across the desk from her, sipping one of his newest coffee creations—Amaretto, vanilla, and a touch of cayenne pepper.

"Just some false leads," he replied. "We tried all the restaurants, eateries, taverns, and bars, but it's like the woman vanished from the face of the earth."

"We've got to find her, Dave. You know she's crucial to this case. How're we doing with the women Murdoch dated?"

"Slow going," he told her. Murdoch wasn't exactly shy with his favors. Most of the women have alibis, some still need to be located, and there's got to be more we don't know about. Pruitt was right, though. Murdoch wasn't particular about their marital status. At least half of those we've already talked to are married."

Alix looked at her mustard-colored walls and sighed—they reminded her of something normally found in a baby's diapers, but on the bright side, the cigarette smell seemed to have dissipated somehow. Maybe her talk with Shawn Connors had produced some results after all.

But hearing that no leads as to the woman's identity were forthcoming was not the news she had hoped for. "I think I'm going to pay Jon a visit," she told Dave.

Getting to her feet, she left the precinct and drove to the university. Her lack of progress and Lloyd's increasing discontent with her schedule were causing her to feel edgy and despondent, and she knew that Jon sensed her state of mind as they faced each other across his desk and he waited patiently for her to speak.

"Coffee?" he offered. "I even have some condensed milk to go with it, just the way you like it."

She looked at him suspiciously. "Is it the stuff that tastes like it was made with toilet water?"

"Certainly not!" he replied indignantly. "It's some of that great coffee your Aunt Sarita sends you from Nicaragua each year. You shared some with me, remember?"

"In that case, I'll have a cup."

You know, you never told me why you take your coffee that way," he said. "Why the condensed milk?"

"I don't know," she replied, shrugging. "*Mamá* and *papá* always drank it that way, and once I was old enough to be allowed coffee, I started to drink it that way, too."

She sat back in one of his deep leather chairs, closed her eyes, and listened to the music coming from his CD player. "Wonderful stuff," she told him. "Is that one of your Jelly Roll Morton CDs?"

"You've got a good ear," he replied. "It's *Shreveport Stomp*, one of my favorites. I find that it stimulates the little gray cells. I do love your American boogie woogie, especially the stuff from the twenties and thirties."

She nodded. Music *did* stimulate the thinking process, although her taste leaned more toward salsas, Chopin, and Edith Piaf. But the ambiance Jon had created was delightful. She was silent for a long time as she looked around his office. Long ago, it had been a plain-looking room whose only redeeming features were its ample proportions and corner location. Jon had moved into it after the death of one of his colleagues, and it now featured two comfortable leather chairs flanking an eighteenth-century Frank Partridge desk that had belonged to his father.

Books on psychology and Meso-American art lined some of the bookshelves. An unlit meerschaum pipe sat in a heavy crystal ashtray, and Mayan figurines from the Mexican provinces of Nayarit and Colima looked down on visitors with somber expressions. Trophies earned at various karate tournaments revealed yet another aspect of Jon's multifaceted personality.

Hearing the squeaking of his chair, she looked up at him with an expression that matched that of the figurines. "I feel like I'm shadowboxing with a ghost, Jon. How can someone suddenly appear out of nowhere and then disappear in a town this size? Where is the damned woman? If she really is an out-of-work waitress, we'd have caught up with her by now."

"How about nearby towns?"

"We've covered everything within a hundred-mile radius and have turned up nothing, zilch, *nada*. The elusive Jen is undoubtedly long gone by now."

"She's probably moved on," Jon said. "Jobs aren't plentiful in Red Pine this time of year."

"Perhaps, but in the meantime, the chief's about to replace me with a computer, the press is on my butt, and the DA's been camping on my doorstep pressing for an arrest."

He laughed. "Alix, Chief Harrison knows you're giving these cases everything you've got. A computer wouldn't have your hours. And Pat Conwell is always pressing for an arrest. It's his job, remember?"

"I need some answers, Jon," she said dejectedly. "Red Pine's a peaceful community. We aren't used to this type of violence here. I took this job because I loved this town and thought I could make a difference. I walk the streets and the merchants know me. I call them by their first names and ask about their kids. When I stopped by the bakery the other day, I forgot to bring money, and Angelo Salvatore said I could pay next time I came in. Small things, but they're the reasons I call Red Pine home. I won't see it become a haven for murderers."

"Have you discarded the ridiculous notion that Meagan killed Steven?" he asked her.

"No, I won't lie to you," she said grimly. "I'm sure she did it. Maybe somebody saw her leave campus. Maybe I'll discover her motive. Either way, I'm going to keep at it until I can prove it, but if something's going to break, it had better be soon!"

"It will. It's just a matter of time, old bean. Yes, I know," he said as she started to interrupt, "I sound like a broken record, and I'm sorry I can't be of more help."

"Thanks anyway," she said, getting to her feet. "And now I'm off to enforce law and order. Cheerio!"

Now he's got me doing it, she thought with amusement.

As she drove back to her office, she thought that it was a shame that Jon found it so difficult to believe her. In the end, his loyalty to Meagan might hamper her progress, but he was no fool. If and when she could make the case, he would believe her, but right now, at this very moment, she was tempted to doubt herself—something she had always sworn never to do.

CHAPTER 12

Meagan heard a knock and saw Dan DeVoe peering around her door.

"I hope I'm not interrupting," he said as he walked into her office, looking dapper in a three-piece navy-blue suit, "but I wondered if you were presenting at the Atlanta conference next month."

"If I ever get my paper done," she told him wearily, looking up from her computer. "Now if you'll excuse me, I have to go to the Women's Center."

He looked dejected. "I'm sorry to disturb you. I'll get out of your way and let you finish your paper," he said quietly and left, closing the door behind him.

The interest he was showing in her did nothing but send up warning signals. She hoped he would go away and leave her alone. She had too much on her mind and she didn't need him adding to her worries.

On her way to the Center, she stopped to see Daphne at the tiny apartment she shared with another woman.

"I can't, Dr. Rathburn," Daphne had wailed when Meagan asked about her former boyfriend's identity. "What if you tell his new girlfriend and he finds out I told? He'll hurt me real bad, just like before. Please don't ask me to do this! I've tried so hard to put it all behind me!"

"Daphne, I know you're afraid, but how are you going to feel if he's the same guy who's dating my student? What if he does to her what he did to you? Can you live with yourself, knowing you could have prevented it? Whether or not it's the same man, I promise you I won't mention your name, okay?"

Reluctantly, Daphne had told her, and it had confirmed Meagan's worst fears. Shawn Connors was a policeman with the Red Pine PD, and Meagan was almost certain he was Paige's new love interest. She was sick about it, but she had to tell Paige about his proclivities before it was too late. The girl was in Idaho visiting family, and Meagan wondered what her reaction would be since she seemed obsessed with the guy. Would she listen to reason?

As she reached the Center, she noticed that the building was sorely in need of repairs: the paint peeling away from the wood siding, the torn window screens, the gutters and downspouts barely hanging on.

She and Kelly had tried hard to raise money for the Center, but somehow a home for abused women did not seem to rate as high with affluent donors as a new arts pavilion, a sports arena, or even a city zoo. Yet somehow, the money had to be found. She would talk to Kelly to see if she might consider going on with the fundraising on her own without telling her why. Hopefully, Kelly would understand and maybe even forgive her some day.

She was so weary. So tired. So very, very tired!

She parked in front of the Center and got out, barely aware of the warm spring sun and the lilacs around the building that filled the air with their incomparable scent. Pink and white dogwoods dotted the Center's grounds, and the patch of lawn and blooming azaleas softened the building's dilapidated exterior. The flowers were beautiful, and yet she seemed to have lost that affinity for nature that had once had had the power to maker her so happy. Would she ever really feel it again?

As she walked up to the front door, she saw Vivian O'Neil get out of her car and run up to her, disheveled, and looking very frightened. "Meagan!" she cried. "I'm so glad you're here. Can we talk in my car?"

Jasmin, her toddler, was strapped in her car seat, tears staining her chubby cheeks. Her big brown eyes, so much like her mother's, were beginning to close with fatigue.

"What's the matter?" Meagan demanded, narrowing her eyes.

But she knew. Before Vivian opened her mouth, she already knew. And Meagan felt herself filled with excitement, her exhaustion forgotten.

"It's Paul," Vivian told her. "He found out we're staying at the shelter. I think he followed me there a couple of days ago, and today he was waiting for me. He forced me into his car and started slapping me around."

She paused to wipe away the tears that were running down her face. "When I told him I was leaving him for good, he threatened to hire a lawyer and take Jasmin away from me. Said he'd make sure I never saw her again and called me all sorts of awful names. A couple of people saw us, and must have called the police, because the cops came while we were still arguing. They let me go when I told them I didn't want to press charges."

"Why didn't you?" Meagan demanded.

She knew that, were it not for her, abused women would never take action on their own. It rankled to see them so helpless, and gone was the realization that she had been there herself not so long ago.

"I didn't think they'd believe me," Vivian wailed. "The way the officers looked at me, I knew they thought the whole thing was my fault. And I didn't want to cause Paul any trouble. I just want to take my baby and go somewhere where we can be safe, so I came straight over to wait for you."

"You've been here since this morning?" Meagan asked her. "Why didn't you call my office?"

"I knew you were teaching so I decided to just come here and wait."

She looked at Meagan as hope filled her tear-washed eyes. "Can you help us?"

Help? If she only knew, Meagan thought with grim satisfaction. Yes, she would help Vivian be rid of Paul forever. But first, there were practical considerations, and she must pretend an interest in what Vivian was saying if she hoped to get her out of harm's way.

"Do you have any money? Any place to go?" Meagan asked her.

"About fifty dollars from the house money but not enough to get us to my family in Maine. Paul knows I have a sister, but she moved recently, and he doesn't know where. Boy, am I glad I never told him! And we have to leave the shelter. They've been very patient letting us stay as long as they did, but now they have to make room for others."

"Vivian, what do you want to do?" she asked, pretending a calm she didn't feel. "I can't make that decision for you, you know that."

"I want to be with my sister Ruth in Maine, but how are we going to get there?"

"What about a checking account? Can you use some of that money?"

"My name isn't on it, only Paul's."

How typical of him to keep her dependent by not letting her have any money of her own, Meagan thought angrily.

"Do you know where he is right now?"

"He probably went back to his office," Vivian replied. "He was still talking with the officers when I left. He must be furious, wondering if his partner will find out. His firm is pretty stuffy, and it might mean the end of his career."

Why would she worry about the worthless man's career when her life and that of her child were on the line? Despite her growing anger, Meagan forced herself to calm down. She would take care of everything, and then Vivian would be glad that Meagan had handled the problem for her.

"Okay, now listen to me. If you're absolutely sure that's what you want, I'll help you," she told Vivian. "Go back to the shelter, pack a bag, and wait for me. I have to go to the bank to get some cash. Then I'll call the airlines and make reservations. I'll pick you up in an hour and take you to the airport. The tickets will be waiting for you. Don't go back to your house. Just call your sister and tell her what's going on. You can also call your mother, but don't tell anyone else. You said your husband doesn't know where your sister lives, right?"

"That's right. Thanks so much, Meagan!" Vivian hugged her, crying with relief. "There's a special place in heaven for people like you. Today was the last straw. I know Jasmin sensed something was wrong when I picked her up this morning. She's been clinging to me ever since. Look at her! She's scared out of her wits! We just can't live like this anymore."

She gave Meagan a wry smile. "Just the other day at the meeting, we all said that each of us would make our decision in our own time, in our own way. I guess I made mine today. And to think that just a couple of days ago, I was thinking of going back! You've been so good to me! I swear I'll pay back every cent I owe you."

When they reached the small airport on the outskirts of town, it bustled with activity—travelers arriving and departing, redcaps loading luggage on hand carts, cars disgorging passengers, tinny, disembodied voices blaring over the intercom to announce flight numbers and page passengers.

"Here's a hundred dollars," Meagan said, handing Vivian an envelope. "Call my home in a couple of weeks and let me know how everything's going. I promise no one will find out your whereabouts. At least not from me. You two are going to be just fine, Vivian, trust me"

"Thanks so much, Meagan. I'll call you as soon as I can."

"Leave a message on the answering machine with a phone number where I can reach you. Here's my home number. It's unlisted, so hang on to it."

She gave them both a final hug and stayed until their plane took off, watching it diminish in size and then disappear.

She realized that Vivian and Jasmin's safety now rested in her hands. Helping them would ease the pain with which she lived daily.

She did not give a single thought to the fact that she was about to kill for the third time. Somehow, it was no longer important. She was unable to stop. Her need for her special brand of

CHAPTER 13

Alix had met Darrin Kirkwood the year before at one of the night classes on criminology that she often taught at the university. The young man had impressed her so much with his eagerness and intelligence that she had recommended him for an internship. But she had forgotten that he worked days as a trucker until he reminded her when he came to the office, his young wife, Sandy, in tow, to talk to her about Rich Murdoch.

She liked this young couple. They seemed so happy together, making them a nice change from the bitter, hostile people she often met when she was on a case. Yet today they looked unusually sober.

"Okay, you two," she said. "What's going on? You look like you've lost your last friend."

"There's something you should know, Detective Mendez," Darrin said, looking decidedly ill at ease. Maybe it's got something to do with Rich Murdoch's death and maybe not."

Interested now, Alix leaned forward and encouraged him with a smile. "Let me be the judge of that," she said. "And don't worry. If you suspect something, you should tell me, and if you are wrong, then no one will be the worse for it. You can't get an innocent man in trouble. Not with me, at least."

Darrin nodded. "Well, it's like this. Sandy and I were coming back from camping out at Bear Creek Lake the weekend before Rich Murdoch was killed. We didn't get back until much later than we had planned, and we were tired and hungry, so we stopped at Hiram's Truck Stop for a bite to eat. It was dark and getting pretty cold when we left the diner, and we were hurrying to our car, when we saw Rich standing by his rig arguing with Vince Hagstrom, a trucker friend of mine. Vince had a hold of Rich's jacket, and he was shaking him and yelling at him."

"Could you hear what they were saying?"

"Sure, we couldn't help it," Sandy piped in. "We were the only ones in the parking lot, but the guys couldn't see us because of the way the truck was parked. Vince was shouting at Rich to leave his wife, Midge, alone. Sounded like he'd just found out about Rich and Midge, and Vince said he'd kill him if he ever went near his wife again."

"Vince pushed him against the truck so hard Rich's head bounced," Darrin added. "Rich was a big guy, but Vince out-weighs him by about thirty pound and he's built like a tank. Personally, I wouldn't want to tangle with him. We weren't close enough to see the expression on Vince's face, but there was no doubt about his body language. I think he meant every word he said."

Alix felt a flash of hope and remembered the hesitation in Pruitt's voice when questioned about the possibility of a jealous husband. Had he been thinking of Vince and Midge Hagstrom? If so, why had he been reluctant to mention her name? Unless of course, he had not wanted to risk tangling with Vince.

"Mmm, I see," she said. "I understand Murdoch dated quite a few women."

Darrin nodded. "That he did."

"Thanks for telling me, Darrin. Did you know about the affair?"

"I'd heard rumors. Look, I don't want to cause Vince any trouble. He's a good man, and I honestly don't believe he killed Rich. But if the guy was messing around with his old lady … Anyway, Sandy and I thought you ought to know, even if it means losing Vince's friendship."

"You did the right thing, Darrin, and I owe you. And maybe your friend's innocent, although I must say he's got a hell of a motive."

Alix was elated. This was her first solid lead, and she felt like jumping up and down. She and Dave had interviewed most of the women who had shared Murdoch's favors, but no jealous husband or boyfriend had surfaced. One thing for sure, though, Rich had been a busy man.

When she called the trucking company where Hagstrom worked, Alix was told he was in Seattle and would return to Red Pine in a few days. In the interim, she planned to speak with his wife, Midge. Maybe this was the break she had waited for.

She couldn't wait to get home to give Lloyd the good news. In the interim, she called Jon to bring him up to date.

"I was wondering whether you'd left the country," he grumbled. "I haven't heard from you in days."

"I had nothing to report until today. I think we're on to something, Jon, and it's a pretty good lead. A young man I'm sponsoring for an internship told me about a fight between Murdoch and another trucker by the name of Hagstrom. Seems like Rich and the guy's wife were sharing pillow talk. Hagstrom's out of town right now, but I plan to talk to him as soon as he gets back. In the meantime, I'm going to interview his wife."

"Well, you sure sound better than when we talked last time," he said. "Let me know what you find out."

"To be honest with you, Jon, I'm almost afraid to hope. Say, have you seen Meagan Rathburn lately?"

"I stopped by her office this morning but she seemed busy and I didn't want to bother her. She looked like she didn't want to talk to me, so ..."

"But you guys are friends! What's going on?"

"I think she's got a lot on her mind. She's going to Atlanta to present a paper in a few weeks, which is a lot of work, but we all have to do it if we hope to advance professionally. And she has her support group and a home to care for all by herself now. I don't think it was personal. I probably just caught her at the wrong time, that's all."

It was more than that, Alix thought, although she decided not to say so. Jon already believed that her obsession with Meagan's guilt bordered on paranoia. As he kept pointing out, there was still the itsy bitsy matter of an alibi she hadn't been able to shatter and a motive she had yet to uncover.

* * *

Meagan was sitting in her living room, wondering if Jon had noticed her curtness when he had stopped by her office. He had walked in just as she was planning a crucial aspect of her next mission, and his concern had seemed more like an intrusion. She had been trying to remember a lecture she had attended last year, one given by a visiting toxicologist whose topic was poisonous animals indigenous to the area, and the details had been eluding her. He had said something about a rough-skinned newt and a fatal toxin from its skin whose symptoms mimicked respiratory failure. Hopefully, she would find the notes she had taken that day. If not, she would do some research at the library or on the Internet because she needed the information now. Immediately.

Although she had often felt a bit apprehensive about the home's isolation before Steven's death, now she loved the privacy it afforded, although she no longer took the pleasure she once did in the scent of the daphne, honeysuckle, and lilacs Steven had planted around the deck. The majestic live oaks studding the property sported leaves again after a harsh winter and hosted flocks of redheaded woodpeckers, black and white flickers, and tiny, canary-colored finches. And soon, the hummingbirds would be back.

The pasture, where the deer came daily, blazed with purple lupines and yellow mustard plants, and the little pond shimmered in the distance. As she looked toward the pasture, she saw a doe and her still-spotted fawn coming out into the clearing, watching her without fear. Distracted as she was lately, she had found it difficult to enjoy the beauty of the house and grounds. If only she wasn't so tired all the time! She wished her headaches and exhaustion would go away and longed to recapture her usual energy.

Having forgotten to make a doctor's appointment again, she decided to do so right away. Perhaps a few iron pills would do the trick. The vitamins tablets she had recently purchased sure did not seem to help much, and she found herself forgetting things more and more lately.

The window seat had always been one of her favorite spots. Built under the large bay window facing the pasture, it had been the perfect place to watch the birds and the squirrels at play or to lose herself in a favorite book.

And now it was a place where she could plan another murder. Despite the insomnia and huge weariness that were part of her daily life, she felt energized, renewed somehow.

She spied two gray squirrels chasing each other, tails aloft, as they ran up and down the trees, chirping madly and carrying leaves and bits of vegetation. She thought that it would be nice to have a cat or a dog to keep her company, now that Steven was no longer around to object. Now she could do whatever she pleased, be whatever she wanted to, with no one to tell her what to do or how to act. She herself was the master of her own destiny. She would take care of Vivian's problem just as she had taken care of her own and Eileen's, as she would continue to help those others whose husbands or boyfriends abused them. She was in control now.

A cat. That was it. Cats were smart and independent and affectionate and made good companions. She would look for a Siamese or a Persian and check the newspaper ads this week, but first …

Her expression clouded as she looked up and noticed the mistletoe beginning to choke some of the older oaks and made a mental note to call Joe's Tree Toppers. Mistletoe could kill an adult oak if allowed to propagate, slowly choking the life out of it, and she decided to make the call while she thought of it.

Ironic, she thought. Hadn't she, too, been slowly sinking into the morass of a destructive relationship? Like the tree, she might have died, the life choked out of her. Or shot.

She shivered, and, uncurling from her sitting position, she

went to her study where she called about the oaks and made an appointment with her doctor. Then, reaching for the telephone book, she looked up the number of Paul O'Neil's accounting firm and punched the number in.

A pleasant voice answered. "Edmonds and O'Neil, may I help you?"

"My name is Joan Campbell. I'd like to make an appointment with Mr. O'Neil."

"Certainly. Mr. O'Neil makes his own appointments, so let me put you through."

Within seconds, a male voice, deep and confident, said, "This is Paul O'Neil. What can I do for you, Ms. Campbell?"

"I am in the midst of divorce proceedings. Our assets are fairly substantial, and I was recommended to you by an acquaintance. I'd like to discuss possible tax consequences with you."

"Of course. Let me check my calendar." After a short pause, he said, "Would Wednesday afternoon at three work for you?"

She looked at her own calendar. "That's just fine. Thank you, Mr. O'Neil."

No need to write it down. She would not forget this particular appointment and did not want to leave unnecessary tracks.

"My pleasure. I'll look forward to seeing you then," he said, and she could tell from the sound of his voice that he found hers intriguing.

Meagan's own interest was piqued. She found it difficult to reconcile the pleasant, confident voice with the image of a wife beater. Yet why should she, having lived with such a man for years? She had planned her strategy with great care, using the information gleaned from Vivian about Paul during their counseling sessions, as she had done with Eileen Murdoch. Again, there could be no mistakes, no slip-ups.

She thought briefly about Dan DeVoe and felt a twinge of guilt as she remembered his obvious disappointment when she had refused yet another dinner date, but her plans had changed. Now that she was tracking a prey again she couldn't afford any distractions, no matter how innocuous. It was far too dangerous.

Once again, she was on a mission to prevent the harm she

knew would come to Vivian and Jasmin unless she intervened. It was up to her to protect them.

She would not fail them.

CHAPTER 14

The tantalizing aromas of freshly brewed coffee and frying bacon drifted through the O'Rourkes' kitchen, but not even the lively snap-crackle-and-pop noises emanating from the Franklin stove could bolster Alix's foul mood.

It was a perfect spring morning, bursting at the seams with the rowdy colors and heady perfumes of a partygoer dressed for Mardi Gras. The sun, slanting through the Levelor blinds, created a zebra-like pattern on the kitchen floor, while the mourning doves' plaintive call, the raucous cries of bluejays, and the barking of the two dogs playing in the back yard filtered through the partially opened windows. The honeysuckle near the kitchen's door was in full bloom, its cloying fragrance reminiscent of long-gone days when living was slow paced and murder only an occasional occurrence.

"Have you seen my glasses, Alix?" Lloyd asked, looking around helplessly.

"You're holding them, dear."

"Sorry! Somehow I never seem to … Are you all right?" he asked, peering myopically at his wife's haggard face.

"Yeah, but I tossed and turned all night, and you know what that does to me. I'm as cheerful as a starving pit bull in the morning. Those damned cases are really getting me down, Lloyd."

She still hadn't brought up his failure to relay Dave's message, which wasn't helping her state of mind, and again she wondered why. It wasn't like her to procrastinate. Did she, subconsciously, fear what she might learn?

"Did I keep you awake?" she asked.

"Not really," he told her. "You were talking in your sleep but I couldn't understand a word and had to draw my own conclusions," Lloyd replied.

"Did another man's name pop up?" she asked with mock alarm.

"Well, I heard you say something about Rich. Any cause for concern?"

"Not really. As you know, he's dead. I must've been dreaming about the Murdoch case again, and it's enough to give anybody nightmares. I need a break, Lloyd. The chief is uptight because the DA's office and the press are hounding him, and they all look at me like it's my fault there aren't any leads."

She picked up the morning paper but tossed it back on the table. Reaching for a bagel, she slathered it with cream cheese and marmalade, then put it down and pushed her plate away, dispiritedly pouring some condensed milk in her coffee.

"Not hungry?" Lloyd asked.

"No, and I guess I better start watching my diet again. I've put on a few pounds."

At almost five foot ten, well proportioned and big boned, she carried her height with considerable poise, but, like her mother, Alix had a tendency to gain weight easily.

"One of my suspects— actually, my only suspect—is due back in town any day now," she said, "and Pat Conwell's already salivating at the prospect of an honest-to-goodness arrest, so maybe ..." An eloquent motion of her hand finished the sentence.

Lloyd chuckled. Alix knew he admired her tenacity, her ability to adjust, her energy and boundless optimism, and her superb tact. Newly arrived in Red Pine as the department's first female police officer and the only Hispanic, she had faced sundry forms of harassment ranging from insensitive remarks to blatant slurs, which she had handled with firmness tempered with dignity, patience, and grace. Her detective unit now was a cohesive, hard-working unit that was second to none. Slowly, gradually, she had earned the respect and affection of her detectives, except for a few older, disgruntled men who had since retired or left for greener pastures.

"You're due for a break, my dear," he said in an attempt to cheer her up. "And it's bound to boost your morale. I know how hard you are on yourself when things don't go as well as you think they should."

"Goddamit it, Lloyd, don't patronize me. I know all that!" Alix exclaimed, slapping the kitchen table with the palm of her hand. "I'm not a child. Why do you always feel you have to cater to my feelings?"

She saw immediately that Lloyd was stunned by the suddenness and virulence of her attack. During their three-year marriage, they often disagreed, but fights between them were rare. It was unusual for Alix to raise her voice and lose her cool, and, in retrospect, she fervently hoped he knew that her outburst was an indicator of the frustration she was experiencing.

"I'm sorry, honey," she said, repentant and overcome with remorse when she saw the startled expression in his eyes. "I don't know what got into me. You don't deserve this and I apologize. What can I do to make amends?"

She watched his face closely and saw him suppress a grin. This was Alix at her best. Her thermonuclear temper could flare as suddenly as spring squalls and vanish as fast as Christmas cash. She knew she had been forgiven when he rose and took her in his arms, stroking her fall of cinnamon hair.

"Come home early tonight and I'll show you," he said with a salacious twinkle in his eyes. "Look, kiddo, I know you're stumped and have to let off steam, and I promise not to take it personally. You took me by surprise, that's all. Seeing your Latin temper in action is truly an unforgettable experience and one I am still getting used to," he added with a chuckle.

"Am I really hard to live with when the going gets tough, Lloyd?" she said with a weak smile.

"Of course you are, but I love you anyway. And besides, I,

too, have my moments."

She raised her eyes to heaven. "*Gracias, Señor*. A perfect husband would be a total bore. You know," she added somewhat dejectedly, "I was wondering just the other day whether I was drunk, mad, or both when I chose law enforcement. Police work is like nothing else. Most people think that all we do is follow clues and apprehend criminals. What do they know about the long hours, the boring work, the forms we fill out, the myriad of reports we sift through for that one clue that might break a case? One look at the stack of DD5s on my desk would make most people puke."

She stopped long enough to take a bite of her bagel.

"And what about the obnoxious members of the press we must be nice to, like that repulsive Joel Nehring?" she continued. "The Great Detective sure knew what he was talking about when he said, 'It is a singular business, Watson, and on the surface, most unlikely'."

Alix had been weaned on Sir Arthur Conan Doyle and Sherlock Holmes, and often joked about their influence on her choice of career.

"I've often wondered whether my parents were right," she went on. "Maybe they knew what they were talking about when they told me I should stay in Santa Barbara, pour tea at fundraising events, and manage the Mendez Foundation with *papá*. My life sure as hell would be a lot simpler."

"I know you can pour tea with the best of them, Alix," Lloyd said, trying to suppress a smile, "but somehow, I don't see you making it a lifelong occupation. In fact, that scenario has got about as much of a chance as my being asked to sing *The Barber of Seville* at the Met."

She laughed despite herself. What a wonderful guy he was, and how lucky they both were to have each other! She really loved his sense of humor, which kept her sane at times like these.

"You're going to solve those cases," he said firmly. He took her hand and kissed her palm. "And the reason I know is because I saw first hand what you did when you solved Dorothy's murder. It was your courage, your conviction, your bulldog tenacity that brought my wife's killer to justice. In my book, you're the best. You're so good at what you do, Alix! That sixth sense of yours borders on clairvoyance, and your career speaks for itself. So why do you doubt yourself so?"

She eyed him thoughtfully. He was a man. Would he understand?

"Lloyd, I'm competing in a field dominated by Anglo males," she said quietly. "It's been only a short time since policewomen were accepted into the ranks, and then only grudgingly. It's harder for us to be tolerated, to be promoted, to be recognized as equals. The camaraderie male officers find so natural is lacking with us. Women officers don't seem to have that kind of rapport. There aren't enough of us, and the men have been at it a whole lot longer. No matter how hard we try, we're never 'one of the guys'."

She watched him as he thought for a while about what she had said. "Yes, I see," he said finally. "I think I understand."

"It's like I'm always on trial, always being tested, Lloyd," she went on. "I can never let my guard down. If I screw up, it's because I'm probably suffering from PMS. I have to work twice as hard and be twice as good to prove myself, not just because I am a woman but because I'm a *Hispanic* woman."

"Just think of the awful consequences if you had, though," Lloyd said pensively.

"Had what?" she said, startled by his nonsequitur.

"Chosen to stay home and pour tea. You wouldn't have become a cop. And you wouldn't have been in charge of Dorothy's murder investigation. And I wouldn't have met you."

She got to her feet, put her arms around him, and kissed him soundly. "That's a lovely thing to say. You're a one-of-a-kind husband and sometimes I don't think I deserve you."

"It's all right. Sometimes I don't think you deserve me either," he said cheerfully.

She kissed him again. "Seriously, Lloyd, this Murdoch case is really strange. His murder was like an execution carried out with cold-blooded precision—totally out of character for a hooker. There were strong feelings at play, and I wish to hell I knew what they were. I keep going back to the jealous husband-boyfriend-girlfriend theory. Hot, raw jealousy would make sense, which is why I bet he was killed by a woman."

"Then go with your instincts, my dear," he said quietly. "They haven't failed you yet."

She gave him an affectionate smile. He was a good man despite his self-admitted flaws, and the two of them were a good match. She remembered her doubts following Lloyd's proposal yet it was difficult to remember what her life had been like before they had met. Upon her return to Red Pine after the psychology department murders, Lloyd had relentlessly pursued her. She was thirty-four years old, he fifty. Married only three years now, they had a loving, stable marriage, enjoying their time together but not guarding it so jealously to prevent pursuing their individual interests.

Suddenly, and for no apparent reason, she remembered the undelivered message from Dave.

"Lloyd, Dave says he called the morning of the Murdoch murder and left a message for me," she said. "Did you forget to tell me?"

"I wondered when you were going to bring it up," Lloyd said sheepishly. "I wasn't sure how you'd react."

The look she gave him was one of sheer confusion. "Well, whatever your reason was, it must have been a damn good one, but I can't begin to guess what."

He let out a sigh and looked at her. "It's just this, dear," he said slowly. "Have you ever thought about resigning from the force? Maybe do some private consulting so that we can spend more time together? We don't really need the money, and it would be great to have the time to take some trips, read lots of good books, play tennis, or sun ourselves on the beach together. It's a big world out there, and I'd love to see it with you. I guess that's what I was trying to tell you."

Stunned, Alix remained silent, not wanting to interrupt him as she saw a shadow cross his face. Being a cop was her whole world. She had worked very hard to achieve success in her career, and giving it up would be like tearing her heart out. But what about her marriage?

"Dorothy was about to retire when she was murdered," Lloyd went on. "We had planned to do all those things together, and then she was gone in a heartbeat. Then I married you, knowing full well how you felt about your work and how much younger you were. But it was wrong of me to try to manipulate you. Now that I think of it, the whole thing seems pretty childish and ridiculous. Forget it, honey, I'm sorry."

"Lloyd, quitting my job isn't something I can do on a whim," Alix said, choosing her words carefully. "Couldn't we have discussed this like mature adults? Not telling me about Dave's call didn't solve anything, and yes, it *was* childish. Do you suppose it's because you feel at loose ends now that the book is finished and you don't have something else in the works?" she asked.

"Yes, that may be part of it," he said slowly. "Look, like I said, it was a dumb thing to do. I don't know what I was thinking."

Alix was simultaneously warmed by his love, moved by the sight of his contrite face, and upset at his omission.

"Honey, why don't we talk about it again in a couple of days?" she said. "Let me think about it, okay?"

"Sure. Forgive me?"

"Of course I do, but this is quite a bombshell to drop first thing in the morning on a woman who hasn't even combed her hair!"

Lloyd was right, she thought. They didn't need the money. Her income from the Mendez family trust and his retirement and prudent investments afforded them a comfortable living. She did love Lloyd, deeply so. But give up her career?

The thought gave her chills.

Still, she told him she loved him before she left. And she did love him, perhaps more than he would ever know. But she was who she was, the woman he had fallen in love with, and if she were to change just to fit some preconceived notion about wives and their role ...

But she wouldn't think of that now, she told herself as she drove to the station. As long as she had a job to do, she would do it. But as she chewed on her dilemma while driving to the station, she realized she had forgotten to tell him about her latest activities regarding Meagan Rathburn.

* * *

Several days ago, Alix had tenaciously, painstakingly retraced her steps one more time. She had re-interviewed the people who had attended the lecture and the reception on the day of Steven Rathburn's murder, even taking them back to the auditorium where they had pointed out the approximate spot where Meagan had sat in the back of the room and nowhere near the two sets of double doors leading to the exit. Meagan could not have left her seat, gone down the aisle to either door, and exited without being seen by those sitting nearby. And no one with whom Alix had spoken remembered seeing Meagan leave.

The auditorium was a stately structure built in the early thirties. Alix took in the floor-to-ceiling red velvet curtains that covered the graceful curving walls, the white opaline and ruby chandelier, the giltwood wall mirrors and Victorian curlicues. She had already tested both doors leading from the auditorium into the foyer and discovered that, just as she has assumed, both opened with a whooshing sound that made it impossible for someone to leave without drawing attention to oneself.

So how had Meagan managed to go through one of those doors, drive home, murder her husband, and return without someone seeing her? She could not have left during the reception. Too many people had seen her there. Several of her colleagues had walked with her from the auditorium to the reception room while another had escorted her to her car afterwards.

Once again, the interviews had been hopeless.

"Yes, I saw her," one of Meagan's criminology colleagues had told Alix. "She was seated a few rows behind me."

"No, I never saw Dr. Rathburn leave the auditorium," a student said. "She was there when I left to go back to my class."

"I saw her head for the reception right after the lecture," another professor had told Alix.

"Yes, I definitely saw Professor Rathburn come into the auditorium and again at the reception where she and I chatted for quite a while," a Spanish professor had stated.

In addition, the university president had claimed to have seen Meagan in the auditorium and at the reception where they had discussed the proposed addition to the campus museum.

"I sat next to Meagan during the lecture," a woman from the psychology department had said. "But I had to leave early because my youngest son was ill at home."

No one had seen anything. No one knew anything that would help her prove her case. Discouraged, yet still convinced she was on the right track, Alix kept hoping that by shaking the tree, something would fall from it. She was a cop, trained to see facts logically and clearly and fit them into a rational pattern. Nothing made sense, yet there was no doubt in her mind that Meagan, no one else, had killed Steven. All she had to do was figure out how and why, and then prove it.

How had the damn woman managed to leave her office, the auditorium, and the reception and return unseen? She was not a ghost. She could not have gone through walls, for God's sake!

There had to be an explanation. Obviously, she was missing something. Something she had not thought about. Something she did not know about.

Okay, then. Her next job was to shoot down Meagan's alibi. And then she could go after her motive.

And then I'll nail her for murder.

* * *

The following Monday, Alix received the promised call from the owner of the trucking firm Vince Hagstrom worked for, and she and Dave went down to the large complex where the trucking firm's offices and garage were located to find the yard buzzing with activity. A few trucks were being serviced in the far corner of the yard. Others were just pulling in, their drivers staggering with fatigue, faces drawn from wrestling with the elements and a tight timetable.

Hagstrom was washing his big rig. The rolled-up sleeves of the checkered red flannel shirt he wore revealed biceps that rolled and rippled. As Darrin had told Alix, he was a huge man with a massive torso. When he saw them as they approached, Alix noted that he looked first perplexed, and then resigned. His faded jeans looked as if he had spent long hours in the driver's seat, and his old leather work boots and black Stetson had seen better days. Curly blond hair framed a strong face with a square jaw. He looked bone-tired, his eyes were bloodshot, and he needed a shave badly, but despite his shabby appearance, there was a calm, dependable look about him.

"Mr. Hagstrom, I'm Detective Mendez," she said flashing her badge. "And this is Detective Barnes. We need to talk to you about an argument you had with Rich Murdoch a week or so before his death."

Vince's eyes darkened and he scowled. "That scum! He wouldn't leave my wife alone and I told him in no uncertain terms to stay away from her. Can't say I'm sorry he's dead."

"Did you threaten to kill him?"

He looked at her steadily. "Sure did. I was real upset. Midge was talking about leaving me. I thought we had a pretty good marriage until he came along and swept her off her feet, and now she's ashamed and won't even speak to me. But I didn't kill him. If I had, I would have done a real favor to a lot of other guys, though."

Alix's instincts told her to trust this gentle giant. Obviously, he had the brawn to take care of anything that might threaten his family and his marriage, but somehow she believed him.

"I tried to call your wife while you were gone and found out that she was visiting family in Kansas," Alix said. "What about you? Where were you the night of March 28th when Murdoch was killed?"

"On the road. I'd have to look at the log to make sure where. You know," he added whimsically, "I knew you'd show up sooner or later. The way I felt about Rich was no secret. The other guys here knew, and they might have heard me say I'd kill him if he didn't leave Midge alone, but I didn't do it. I couldn't kill anybody, even slime like Murdoch. Besides, I was hoping to patch things up with Midge and it'd be kinda hard to do that from prison."

He paused to wipe his dirty hands on the old towel he had pulled from under the driver's seat.

"Rich was a coward," he went on, "and I think I scared him good. And then Midge found out he was seeing other women at the same time he was giving her the rush, so the affair was pretty much over. But she has her pride, I guess, so now I gotta convince her that I still love her and that I want her back."

Alix smiled at the big trucker's honesty. Her instinct told her that Vince hadn't killed Murdoch.

Opening the diesel truck's door, Vince grabbed a clip binder holding some sheets of paper. Pulling one out, he handed it to her. "The night Rich was killed, March 28th, I was on my way back from Seattle. I got in at two in the morning."

"Trouble is, the medical examiner says he could have been killed later," Alix told him. "Did you go see Murdoch after you returned from Seattle, Mr. Hagstrom?"

It was a shot in the dark.

Hagstrom was silent for a while. "I almost did," he admitted. "Drove to his house right after I got back. But I swear on my mother's grave I didn't go in. When I saw his pickup parked out front, I sat in my car and wondered what I was going to say to him that I hadn't already said. Midge was gone, so what was the point in talking to him again? I wasn't there more than a coupla minutes, and that's God's honest truth."

Alix and Dave again exchanged glances.

"Mr. Hagstrom, this is very important," she said. "Did you see anyone while you sat in your car near the Murdoch home?"

She watched him closely and saw his straw-colored eyebrows meet above his eyes.

He nodded and said finally, "A young couple. They got into a light-colored car and drove away. They looked slightly drunk, you know, horsing around, joking, laughing, that sorta thing. But it was just them. Them and the woman."

Alix felt her pulse quicken. "What woman?"

"A woman wearing a scarf. But I don't know what house she came out of or where she was headed. I'd already started my car and gone down about a block. She had her back to me and was walking in the other direction. I just caught a glimpse of her in my rearview mirror. It was just a flash, maybe two seconds."

His brown eyes focused on Alix, his look intent as he toyed with the rag in his hands. "I didn't kill Rich, Detective, much as I would've liked to," he said earnestly.

And then, suddenly, the implication of her question seemed to dawn on him. "You think a woman might have killed him?"

"I don't know," Alix confessed. "Can you remember anything else about her? Her height? What she was wearing?"

"No. She was just a figure walking away from me with a scarf over her hair. She wore some sort of light-colored coat, I think. Like I said, she appeared out of nowhere."

"Could she have been coming from the Murdoch home?"

"Maybe, but I just couldn't swear to it."

"Did she look around when she walked, like she was afraid of being seen? Anything like that?"

"No, she never turned around."

"Did you see her get in her car?"

"No. As I said, I only caught a glimpse of her back for a few seconds just as I turned the corner going the other way."

Alix decided to change the thrust of her questioning. Clearly he had told her as much about the woman he had seen as he could. "When did you say your wife left for Kansas?"

"Couple of days before I got back from Seattle. I called her from up there to ask her to wait until I got home so we could talk, but she said she needed some time to think things out. Hell, I want her back right now. Sorry, ma'am," he said sheepishly. "Sometimes my language gets away from me."

Dave had verified Midge Hagstrom's whereabouts through telephone records when Vince's wife had called her neighbors about her cat, and he knew she couldn't have been the woman in red. So Vince was still their only bet. And now the woman he claimed to have seen. Could she have been the mysterious Jen or just an innocent bystander? Was she the same woman seen at the

King's Arms? And had Hagstrom seen the murderer leaving the Murdoch home?

"Would you be willing to take a lie detector test?" Alix asked Vince.

"Yes, ma'am. Sure thing," he said, nodding vigorously. "In fact, I insist!"

* * *

Meagan sat in her study, eyes glazed, forehead beaded with cold perspiration. Her brain was numb, making her doctor's diagnosis difficult to absorb. He might have spoken in Aramaic for all the sense his words had made. She had fled his office, blind to his startled but compassionate look, deaf to his plea to make another appointment, wanting only to get out of there and be alone. She felt as if a bomb had exploded under her, leaving fragments of herself scattered everywhere.

Keeping her weight down had never been a problem. She was not a big eater, stuck to a sensible diet, and followed a fairly regular exercise program, working in her yard and biking whenever she could. Given that regimen, she had effortlessly remained at the same weight for the past several years. But she could no longer ignore her present weight loss. Her oval face was now angular, her once-curvaceous body emaciated. And she had found no answers to her persistent, cold-like symptoms that had been present for months now.

Until now.

Meagan had been stunned by the diagnosis and its implications. Although she knew such a possibility had existed, it had remained buried deep in her subconscious. Now, however, she could no longer evade the truth, even though she wanted to hang onto the notion that this had nothing to do with her, that perhaps her records had gotten mixed up with someone else's at the lab.

But down deep, she knew there was no mistake.

AIDS!

Who would have guessed this short word could carry such terrible connotation, such finality.

AIDS.

Steven's final legacy and her death sentence. She had known that Steven's sordid affairs had put her at risk, that she might have carried this killer in her body for sometime, and now she knew she didn't have long to live.

She also knew she must deal with this terrible blow, but having neither the strength nor the mental capability to cope with it right now she sat, eyes vacant, frozen in her chair like a statue.

She considered the vagaries of life that had controlled her destiny and never felt more alone.

There must be someone she could talk to, but who?

Kelly? She and Larry were on vacation in Hawaii.

Her mother? She smiled sardonically at the very idea. The notion of being comforted by her mother was an oxymoron. Wouldn't it be ironic for her mother to have to explain to her society friends that her daughter was dying of AIDS?

Jon and Margot? Although she knew they would be supportive and would try to help her, she still could not bring herself to bare her soul to them.

What about Dan DeVoe? Despite the way she felt about him, the temptation to tell him was almost overwhelming. He exuded the type of stalwart strength she needed right now. But she rejected the idea as quickly as it had come into her head. He would probably react with … what? Disgust? Pity? Horror? No, not possible. Not him either.

Once again, she was alone, totally alone. There was no one else, and she was only kidding herself to think that she could share this with someone. It was just one more burden that she must bear alone.

Her illness was yet another secret she must keep buried in the recesses of her mind, a true chamber of horrors that only she could unlock. Her subconscious, no longer driven by society's conventions, corrupted by her overwhelming need for revenge, would not let her. She was hamstrung by her need to protect her private life, no matter what the cost, yet knowing with blinding clarity that her only salvation lay in reaching for help and stopping the killings.

Mind still reeling as she felt tears rolling down her cheeks, she put her head down on her folded arms and finally gave way to uncontrollable sobbing until there was nothing left but a huge emptiness. Was it so much to ask to want someone's arms around her, have her hair stroked, be told everything was going to be all right by someone who cared?

She had been through hell. First, incest, then nine years of abuse. Now, with the ultimate loss of her life, she realized there would be, finally, an end to the pain and despair that now filled her existence.

First she felt fear, and gradually, inexplicably, relief.

There was nothing more to lose now.

* * *

Red Pine's downtown area, all six blocks of it, bustled with activity, an undeniable sign that summer was just around the corner, bringing with it its yearly influx of visitors bearing much-needed cash. Yet tourism was a double-edged sword. The locals resented the increased traffic that clogged up their streets and parking lots, although visitors also filled shops, theaters, and restaurants. And, ironically enough, the merchants had come to realize that their winter survival depended on those very people they professed to loathe. Red Pine's popularity was both its curse and its blessing.

Many of the shops had been renovated in anticipation of the visitors' arrival. Bed-and-breakfast inns, hotels, and motels all stood at the ready to host those who descended upon the town between early spring and late fall in a seemingly endless flood. Small stands scattered along Main Street sold everything from hotdogs to fresh flowers, and the streets were already filled with people eager to sample the town's fine restaurants, theaters, and the tiny shops that seem to proliferate from year to year. Depending on the economy, some made it, others didn't. Where a vegetarian restaurant flourished one year, it might be replaced by a fashionable boutique or a shop featuring Portuguese imports the next.

The plaza was a picture-postcard scene, the air brimming with smells guaranteed to stimulate the most reticent appetite and loosen the most jealously guarded wallet. Actors in authentic Elizabethan costumes caroused through the park to the tune of period instruments. University students mingled with visitors to feed the ducks and swans in the two ponds, fed by a pristine creek that ran the entire length of the park. Even the sun was doing its thing, shining brightly on the festivities.

Near the park's center stood a small bandstand where the city band performed every Sunday. Families brought picnics, spread makeshift tablecloths, and ate on the grass, picnic style. Menus ranged from soda pop, sandwiches, and potato chips eaten on paper plates to elaborate feasts featuring Waterford crystal, Rosenthal china, *paté de foie gras,* and chocolate truffles.

Margot and Jon strolled hand in hand, enjoying the familiar sights, sounds, and smells. Drawn by the aroma of the hot dog stand, they each had a foot-long dog with all the trimmings, which they ate standing up, hot mustard dribbling down their chins as they attempted to minimize the damage to their clothing with the help of huge paper napkins.

"How's it going, Herb, and how's the baby?" Margot asked the young man tending the stand.

"Just great, Ms. Cavanaugh. He's seven months old now and looks like a miniature football player."

"He'll have a good teacher. Your days as a quarterback aren't that far behind you."

Herb beamed with pride. "I can't wait 'til he can toss a ball."

He had been the university's star quarterback a few years ago and was now working on a degree in chemistry. The hot dog stand, which was fairly lucrative during the busy summer months, helped defray the tuition.

Jon and Margot had brought popcorn and bread, and as they made their way to the first pond, they were soon surrounded by a raucous flock of birds that knew a feast when they saw one. Used to humans, they had lost their natural fear and come to equate people with food. And they never went hungry.

As they walked up the path toward the second pond enjoying

the beautiful day and the dogwoods in full bloom, Margot suddenly stopped and put her hand on Jon's arm.

"What is it?" he asked.

"Over there," she replied, pointing with her chin toward a bench where a lone figure sat. "It's Meagan. Let's go say hello."

A huge dogwood whose canopy spread over most of the lawn—a magnificent, sixty-year-old specimen that was the park's *tour de force*—shaded the bench. Meagan's head was down, her whole demeanor reflecting utter dejection and surrender. She was so engrossed in her thoughts that she didn't hear them approach and jumped as Margot spoke to her.

"Sorry, Meagan, I didn't mean to startle you," Margot said as she saw the haunted, almost terrified look in the other woman's eyes. "Jon and I were just wandering through the park and we saw you sitting here and wanted to say hi. It's been so long since we've seen you, and we've missed you. Are you okay?"

"I'm fine," Meagan said. "I needed to get out of the house for a while, but I've got to run now," she added, looking at her watch and getting to her feet. "I've got a conference coming up in a couple of weeks, and I need to work on my paper or it'll never get done."

Without giving them a chance to reply, she gave them what was more like a grimace than a smile and hurried toward the graveled area where her car was parked.

"What was that all about?" Margot exclaimed. "She acted like she didn't want to talk to us. And she's so thin! She always looks like a model, but I've never seen her look so haggard and disheveled! What's wrong with her?"

Jon shook his head. "I'm not sure, Margot. I think she was devastated by Steven's death, and I guess it's going to take time for her to get over it. I've noticed how distracted she is at work. She used to eat lunch with me and other people in the cafeteria. Now I never see her, and whenever I call or drop by her office, she's always busy. Looks like the adjustment is proving more difficult than I thought."

Margot shook her head. "I think there's more to it than that, Jon. She looked almost frightened when she saw us. I hope she isn't turning into a recluse. Isn't there anything we can do?"

"I'll visit with her and offer my help, Margot," he told her. "I feel a certain responsibility. Maybe she's hoping for my help but is reluctant to ask," he added.

That must be it, he decided, reassured. I'll go see her tomorrow.

* * *

Meagan was furious with herself. She had let her guard down and allowed her friends to see her as she grappled with her situation. Who would have thought they would also be at the park at the same time? But she had felt an almost compulsive need to leave the house for a while and go somewhere, anywhere, to think among the trees, the cool rippling sound of the creek, and the impersonal noises of the crowds. She could not allow them to suspect, yet time was not on her side. Soon, they'd know. Soon, everybody would know. More than ever, she had to stay calm and keep her wits about her.

Tomorrow was her appointment with Paul O'Neil.

* * *

Hoping to project the image of an attractive, well-heeled but unimaginative young matron leaning on a man for financial advice, Meagan had dressed with great care in a dark-green crepe suit, gold and pearl jewelry, and black leather pumps with modest heels. Her blonde wig and blue contact lenses completed the ensemble. As a last flash of inspiration, she added some nonprescription eyeglasses with square frames that made her now-blue eyes appear even bigger.

The suit was loose on her now, but her weight loss was a small matter compared to the task ahead. She dismissed the thought. She could not let herself dwell on her illness right now.

Arriving at Paul O'Neil's plush suite of offices at the appointed time, she was immediately shown into a very masculine room with deep leather chairs, forest green carpeting, and English hunting scenes on the dark paneled walls. He rose to greet her, a tall, darkly attractive man with hooded black eyes, olive skin, and perfectly barbered hair. She noticed his hands, a musician's hands with long fingers and manicured nails.

She thought that he reminded her of a gigolo and smiled inwardly at the unexpected thought.

He wore a conservative dove-gray suit that complimented his height and professional mien. Precisely one inch of snowy-white shirt protruded from the sleeves of his jacket. She identified his aftershave lotion as the same one Steven had used, and for a few seconds, she was overcome by irrational panic. There was an underlying hardness, a total lack of warmth in the dark eyes that surveyed her, first with definite approval and then overt admiration.

She felt faint and caught herself on the chair he offered.

"Are you all right?" he asked, clearly concerned. "Can I get you a glass of water?"

She shook her head and attempted a smile. "Thanks. I'm fine, just a bit warm, that's all."

She could tell that he was impressed by the well-cut suit, the Italian shoes and matching bag, the pearls at her ears and throat, and the large, flawless diamond sparkling on her right hand. And she was well aware that he found the subtle aura of helplessness that surrounded her most appealing. She was also pleased that she had decided to wear a delicate, flowery perfume reminiscent of Monet paintings, fields of daisies, and girls on swings, which, she knew, suited her.

He came around his desk to pull the chair out for her and seated her with all the gallantry the Duchess of Windsor would have expected at the *Tour D'Argent,* then sat next to her in the companion chair rather than across the desk in his partner's chair. None of this went unnoticed by Meagan. Everything was going swimmingly, just as she had planned.

She declined the water he offered her with a slight shake of her head and a smile.

"Now, Mrs. Campbell, what I can do for you?" he said.

"You've been highly recommended by a friend of a friend,"

she told him. "As I told you on the phone, I'm in the middle of a divorce and need someone to represent my financial interests. I am fairly ignorant in such matters, Mr. O'Neil. I need someone who can work with my attorney and go to bat for me. I hope you'll be that person."

"I'd be delighted," he told her. "What can you tell me about your finances?"

Meagan delivered the story she had rehearsed with her usual care. She had not brought any documents since she had none, of course, but made a point of stating that she was here only for a preliminary consultation, continuing to belabor the point that he had been recommended as the best in his field.

Scornfully, she watched him preen and listened to him rattle on about his qualifications and experience. But she pretended to find him utterly fascinating, and at the end of her conference, she rose and extended her hand, looking up at him, her head charmingly tilted sideways in her trademark mannerism as she gave him her most beguiling smile.

She was doing everything but fluttering her eyelashes, she thought, but felt unashamed of her southern-belle act.

"Thank you," she told him, rising. "I really appreciate your help and you've given me a lot to think about. I'll get my documents together, and I can't tell you how relieved I feel, knowing that I'm in such competent hands."

"Mrs. Campbell …"

She interrupted him. "Won't you please call me Joan?"

"Joan," he said, smiling at her, "I'd like to meet with you again as soon as possible so that we can discuss other options that I think will work to your advantage."

"Of course. Should I schedule another appointment with your secretary on my way out?"

He looked at his watch. "I have another client coming in shortly, but …" He paused. "I wonder if perhaps we could meet later for coffee at the Yellow Pelican? Or have a drink somewhere, say, around six? And won't you please call me Paul?"

So it had been as easy as that. Men were such fools, so easy to manipulate! Call him Paul indeed. She would do far more than that! He was under her control now. Too bad he didn't realize it yet.

"I'd like that very much, Paul, but I can't today," she told him, giving her another heart-melting smile.

She'd meet him again later, all right, but definitely not under the circumstances she could see he was anticipating.

"I also worry that someone might see us," she added, frowning. "My attorney stressed discretion while the divorce is pending. This is a small town, although I know this wouldn't be a date or anything," she hastened to add. "But if we were seen out together, it might give the wrong impression and make a settlement more difficult. I know you understand."

Meagan could see that he felt his prey slipping away as she watched his hard black eyes darken.

He swiftly changed tactics. "Well, then, how about coming to my home? I know my wife, Vivian, would love to meet you."

I've got him, she thought, elated. It had been so easy!

She hesitated. "Well ... that might work, I guess. I'd really like to talk to you again and meet your family," she added, motioning toward the smiling pictures of Vivian and Jasmin in elaborate silver frames behind his desk.

"Why don't you call me and let me know what evening would work for you?" he said nonchalantly, but Meagan knew it was a pose. "I'll give you directions when you call and let my wife know you'll be coming. Maybe later this week?"

"I'll check my calendar when I get home and get back to you as soon as possible," she told him. "Thank you, Paul. I hope this won't be inconvenient. Meeting at your house, I mean."

"Not at all! I look forward to it," he said, looking deeply into her eyes as he took her hand. For a sickening second, she thought he was going to kiss it.

"Is there some special drink you like? I make excellent martinis," he told her.

She tried to hide her overwhelming revulsion at his touch. His anger at the mention his wife and daughter had not escaped her. The flash of rage that had crossed his face was a reflection of the one she had seen many times on Steven's face. Nor had she overlooked his failure to mention his family's absence. She wondered what excuse he would come up with to justify it. She didn't have to ask herself what he wanted of her, having met many men like him, some of them not so transparent.

Under his suave exterior, she knew a killer lurked. For that was what he was under the forced smile and the polished manner. He would destroy Vivian's life, given the opportunity. And were it not for Meagan, who was wise to him, he would ultimately kill her. Stupid man! He was a fool, just like all the others. Who did he think she was, thinking that she could be lured to his home with the promise of a few drinks and not know what he expected of her?

"I love margaritas," she simpered, "the kind made with tiny ice cubes instead of the usual way with crushed ice. My husband and I had them that way in Old Town Sacramento once and they were wonderful!"

"Then margaritas on the rocks it is. They're also my favorite drink."

Sure, she thought. She could see right through this self-important idiot. Had she mentioned Purple Tornados with a twist of lemon, he would probably have claimed that they were also his favorites, even though she had just made them up.

She left his office, energized, her mind churning with anticipation, her weariness temporarily forgotten as she thought about their meeting and allowed her thoughts to digress. Paul O'Neil was an attractive man in a cold, dark way. Under other circumstances, she might have been tempted by his obvious interest and let herself be seduced. After all, she was still a woman and it felt good to be desired.

But she also saw him for what he was and was repelled by the abuser hiding beneath the man-of-the-world façade. Besides, she enjoyed the control she now held, knowing that he was playing right into her hands. Oh, how it amused her to see him fawn and, at the same time, play the innocent. Yes, she knew what he was after, all right. And she alone knew precisely what he would receive. And Vivian and Jasmin would be safe. Flirting with him was one thing, but being seduced by him was quite another. He

CHAPTER 15

The Browns were quarreling. This in itself was rather extraordinary since Eula and George Brown had been married fifty-one years, seldom argued, and definitely never quarreled. In fact, they never seemed to disagree about anything. They even looked like mirror images of each other—two small, gray sparrows with alert faded blue eyes, silver hair, and barrel-shaped bodies. And in the way of couples married for many years, they were prone to finishing each other's sentences and reading each other's minds. One day followed the next in their pleasantly dull routine as each year, they grew a bit grayer and a bit shorter together.

Today was definitely not that kind of a day. Eula Brown, with atypical obstinacy, stood her ground as she looked at her husband, one hand on her hip, the other holding the broom she had been using to sweep the back steps, cold blue eyes fixed on him with a mixture of frustration and scorn. Her look could have pierced a boil at twenty paces and, had it been an arrow, George Brown would be a very dead man indeed.

Not to be outdone, George glared back at her, hair standing straight up, giving him the look of an elderly elf plugged into an electric socket. His face was screwed up in a manner he hoped was menacing but was only comical.

"Dang it, woman, if I say I saw something that night, then I saw something that night. I know I've got problems sleeping, but I don't usually spy on the neighbors when I'm up, you know, and I'm telling you that there was a strange car parked near the Murdoch home."

"So what? Now I suppose you think the FBI's going to come knocking on our door looking for one of the Ten Most Wanted and wanting to interview you, right?"

"Go ahead. Poke fun all you want. I know what I saw. And what I saw was a car I'd never seen before pulling away from the Murdoch's house, and I think I should tell the police."

"And tell them what? Who was in the car? What kind of car was it? Did you take down the license number?"

"How could I tell? I didn't have my glasses on. It was just a car—small, dark, but it must have been there 'bout the time Murdoch was killed."

"How do you know that whoever drove the car came out of the Murdoch house?"

"I don't know that for sure. It was parked behind Murdoch's pickup truck, so I just assumed …"

"You assumed. You assumed! Maybe it was someone visiting one of our other neighbors."

"At two-thirty in the morning?"

"Why not? Come on, George! Think! The whole thing makes no sense. So you saw a car as it pulled away from the curb. You don't know what the make was or even the color. And you don't know the license number. And you don't even know if a man or a woman was driving. How's that going to help the police?"

He looked at her and nodded. "Yeah, I guess you've got a point, Eula. I'm sorry I lost my temper."

Her face softened. "George, you're a good man, but you know how you love spy novels. We aren't talking about a Robert Ludlum thriller here. This is real life."

"For God's sake, woman, don't you think I know the difference between a novel and real life?" he shouted, fired up again. "I'm telling you I saw a car out there leaving just about the time they say Murdoch was shot and maybe there's a connection."

"So like I said, what are you gonna tell the police? It could have been somebody coming out of the Pekarek home, or the Callaway home, or the Garvin home. And it's none of our business who our neighbors entertain or how late unless they have drunken orgies and keep us up 'til all hours with one of them danged boomboxes. Now if you had a description of the car or the driver, I'd be the first to tell you to call the police, but under the circumstances ... C'mon, George, this is dumb! What makes you think that car had anything to do with the Murdoch murder anyway?"

George scowled. "Okay," he reluctantly agreed. "I'll think about it a while. Then I'll decide what to do."

"You do that," she said, throwing up her hands in frustration. "Look, George, we told the detectives everything we knew when they came after Murdoch was killed—that we heard nothing and saw nothing. It's going to look awful funny if we bring this up now. They're going to wanna know why you didn't say something before. They may even think you're some geriatric old coot wanting attention who will say anything to get it. What are you going to tell 'em then?"

"But Eula, I just forgot about the car! And it didn't seem important at the time. I guess you're right, but even if I look like a fool, I still think I ought to mention it."

"Fine. Do whatever you want. I give up."

She turned around and went into the kitchen where she demonstrated her displeasure by taking pots, pans, and dishes out of the dishwasher with an ear-busting cacophony of banging and clanking. She wondered what the police would think of George's story regarding a car he could not describe, whose license plates he could not read, whose driver he had not seen and could not identify, and who could have come out of any number of houses in the neighborhood.

Sometimes she really wondered about George.

CHAPTER 16

Meagan picked up the phone after the third ring and heard Vivian's excited voice.

"Everything's going great, Meagan!" Vivian exclaimed, her happiness oozing over the phone. "Jasmin loves the beach, and you should see Ruth's house! It's so beautiful, up on a knoll overlooking the ocean. I was raised in Canada's flatlands, so living near the beach is like a miracle. And everybody's been so nice to us! We love it here! And guess what? I'm giving piano lessons to the children of Ruth's friends and working part-time for a computer firm. I can't believe my luck! I feel needed and appreciated, and the whole thing is like a dream come true. And we owe it all to you!"

"I'm so happy for you," Meagan told her once Vivian had stopped to catch her breath. And she was, although it was difficult to give the appropriate responses when her nerves were as taut as violin strings. Meagan thought that Vivian sounded like a new person, light-years away from the frightened woman who had fled in fear for her life only a few weeks ago.

Not long ago, she would have rejoiced at Vivian's enthusiasm, but now she felt only impatience, wanting to get off the phone as soon as possible so she could go on planning Paul's forthcoming demise.

"I'm glad you're with family, Vivian," she said wearily, "but even with all the good things going on in your life, you still face some rough times ahead, and having loved ones nearby is really helpful," she added, forcing herself to sound helpful and upbeat when all she wanted to do was hang up.

"But Meagan, I wonder if I did the right thing. I mean, I love my new life and all, but I wonder if I shouldn't go back to Red Pine and see if I can fix things between Paul and me. I'd be willing to try again if I wasn't so afraid of losing Jasmin. After all, he did provide a roof over our heads and put food on the table. What if he promises to change?"

Meagan's throat constricted with a mixture of fear and dismay. "I can't tell you what to do, Vivian, but I really think you ought to find a support group there. You still have lots of unresolved feelings and will suffer lots of ups and downs. I know you feel guilty for leaving Paul, but what about you and Jasmin? Do you really want to go back to that same situation?"

Meagan tried hard to suppress her annoyance. Here she had provided Vivian with the opportunity to free herself and get a new life, and all Vivian could do was to go on about how she might want to stay married to a man who would provide for her when all he had really given her was a living hell, the kind of hell Meagan knew only too well!

Vivian sighed. "Not really, but people can change, right? And what about Jasmin? She keeps asking about her daddy. Do I have the right to keep her away from him?"

"Everything you're going through is normal," Meagan said more sharply than she had intended. "Many women in your situation have gone through the same thing. You've taken a major step by leaving Paul, and you've got to keep working through the process. I won't lie to you, it's not going to be easy, but you'll get through it."

But Vivian's next sentence raised her level of apprehension another notch.

"I think Paul has hired a private detective, Meagan. He called my mother and was furious when she wouldn't tell him where we were."

"What makes you think that?" Meagan asked as she felt her blood run cold.

A private detective? How dare Paul interfere with her plans by trying to find his family, undoubtedly with the thought of doing them further harm! Vivian was indeed fortunate that Meagan was looking after her safety. It was just a shame that she did not know it.

"Because Mother says that after she refused to talk to Paul, a man came around asking questions," Vivian told her. "Maybe it's just nerves, but I'm terrified I'll lose my baby, Meagan. Maybe I should go back and try to work things out for her sake. If I apologize and promise to change, maybe Paul will take us back."

Trying hard to contain her agitation, Meagan realized that she was out of time. If Vivian was thinking of returning to Red Pine, she needed to make her move, and she needed to make it now.

The timetable had to be moved up.

She tried to think of an appropriate response, but her mind was already working on the problem, having carefully thought out her strategy after her meeting with Paul O'Neil and knowing that her planning was about to pay off when he had taken the bait. If he was closing in on his family, there was no time to waste. Things would not change in Vivian's life if she came back. She would merely be caught up again in the same cycle of an abusive relationship, and she needed Meagan to take care of things for her, once and for all.

"Vivian, don't do anything before we talk again," Meagan told her, trying to suppress the quiver in her voice. "Give me your phone number, and I'll call you in a few days."

She took the information down and slipped it into the top drawer of her desk. After she hung up, she stared at the phone. Her mind was racing and her brow was damp with nervous perspiration. Why would Vivian even think about returning to Red Pine after what she'd been through? But, at least for now, she and Jasmin were safely tucked away in Maine. The police would not suspect Vivian even if Alix turned up something to raise doubts during the investigation.

But there would be no investigation.

She had paid for her office conference in cash, and had given Paul's secretary a false address for the fictitious Joan Campbell. The woman, busy with the telephone and other clients, had barely glanced at her after showing her into Paul's office, and Meagan did not think that anyone in the waiting room had taken a good look at her. Besides, she had been wearing her wig, contact lenses, and glasses.

As she had rounded the corner just outside Paul's office, she had almost collided with one of her colleagues. It had given her quite a fright, but the woman had excused herself and given her a mechanical nod and a smile without showing the slightest hint of recognition. Having put her second disguise to the test, albeit involuntarily, she now felt confident that no one would recognize her at a distance.

She found Tudor Lane on her map and saw that it was located in a quiet, upper-income neighborhood. Finding the best place to park during the brief time she intended to spend at Paul's house would be vital. Parking too close might be chancy, but she would run a greater risk of being seen and remembered if she left her car several blocks away and walked. She would refine her plan after scouting out the territory.

The blonde wig and blue contact lenses would work well for this foray, and her three-inch-heel leather boots would increase her height. The weather had turned blustery again, bringing some unseasonably cold rain and snow showers. A scarf over her wig and a raincoat would help her further conceal her appearance. The critical times would be when she went in and out of the house—scarf, boots, and raincoat would definitely look out of place if the weather suddenly turned balmy, which she knew could sometimes happen this time of year.

She closed her eyes and leaned back, overcome by the now-familiar exhaustion. The episodes were becoming more frequent and intense. Only her determination and the fire burning deep within her kept her going. Giving in to her illness now was out of the question. There was too much at stake, too much to do.

And nothing more to lose, she reminded herself.

She thought about the trip to Atlanta coming up in less than ten days that loomed over her like a dark cloud. She sure wished she could bow out, but she was already on the agenda, and canceling might attract unwanted attention—she had to keep going about her normal duties if she hoped to carry out of her plans.

The results of her protracted research on the toxin had paid off. She had ample details about the poison now, the method of extraction, its symptoms, and its final aftermath.

Meagan walked down to the small swampy pond at the end of her property. Her research had told her how to readily identify the small, rough-skinned newts that bred in the spring and abounded in the pond's stagnant water and the reeds that surrounded it. After several clumsy attempts, she finally succeeded in catching about a dozen of the small creatures, which she stored in the refrigerator to make them sluggish and simulate hibernation. She hoped that chilling them would numb them to the pain she would have to inflict upon them.

The next day, having gathered all the materials needed to extract the poison—most of them available in her own home—she donned the rubber gloves. Then, as swiftly and humanely as possible, she decapitated the small creatures with a razor-sharp knife, feeling guilty and sick at heart.

She worked awkwardly at first but gained more confidence as many of the fragments of the toxicologist's lecture and the information obtained from her research came back in a series of flashes and bursts. First, she grasped each newt and made a shallow cut around the animal in front of its hind legs. Taking hold of tail and hind legs in her left hand and gripping the edge of the cut skin with a pair of needle-nose pliers in her right hand, she pulled it forward, turning it inside out as it peeled off the body and over the front legs.

She turned the animal around, grasping the skinned body with her left hand. Clamping onto the cut edge of the skin with her pliers, she pulled the skin off the hind legs and tail. Finally, she slit open the belly of gravid females and removed the egg sacks and ovaries, reflecting upon the symbolism of using the toxin-laden eggs of female newts to kill abusive men. She then flushed the residue down the garbage disposal.

She had to separate herself from her grisly task by visualizing the ultimate results of her efforts. But somehow, as she toiled on with enforced detachment, she could not help but think of herself as a modern version of one of Shakespeare's witches in Macbeth as they chanted around the boiling pot:

> *"Double, double toil and trouble/fire burn and cauldron bubble/fillet of a fenny snake/in the cauldron boil and bake/eye of newt, and toe of frog ..."*

Wasn't she, like the witches, after the same result?

Snipping the skins into small pieces, she soaked them and the eggs overnight in ethyl alcohol to dissolve the toxin before pouring off the liquid, a procedure she would repeat the next day, using fresh alcohol. Next, she filtered the residual alcohol extract through a coffee filter into a porcelain bowl, allowing the thick liquid to slowly dry and using an electric fan to speed up the evaporation process. Finally, she cut up the coffee filter into tiny pieces, grinding it and the remaining skin fragments in the garbage disposal, flushing everything away, including the vestiges of her own revulsion.

Left with a gummy residue at the bottom of the bowl and the problem of how to encapsulate it, she wondered how she would get some of the poisonous extract into Paul's drink without detection and without poisoning herself. Despite her mental and physical exhaustion, she forced herself to study several possibilities, the gruesome task of extracting the toxin now forgotten.

Going to her medicine chest, she pulled apart a cold-medication capsule, dumping out its powdery contents, washing them down the drain, and replacing them with a bit of the poison she had scraped with a toothpick. But how would she find a subject to try the capsule on? Getting a dog or cat from the animal shelter for her experiment, even if the creature's fate to be put to sleep had already been decided, was out of the question—she just couldn't bring herself to do it. Animals were innocent and did not deserve a violent death while their human counterparts ... Well, that was another matter, and she was here to remedy the many wrongs men inflicted on women. And she would continue to do so as God directed her toward each mission, as He had so far

Then she remembered the rats she had seen running along the barn's aged timbers and the harmless Havahart trap Steven had bought several years ago. It allowed the animal to go in after the bait, and the small gate-type door would close behind it and capture it inside, unharmed. In a rare show of rebellion, she had refused to allow him to use a more cruel way of snaring the raccoons that came to the kitchen's back door in search of refuse and had become a real nuisance. Catching them in the cage and releasing them elsewhere had solved the problem, albeit temporarily, since they always seemed to return in ever-increasing numbers.

Going to the garage, and after much foraging through items she had forgotten she owned, she located the trap. Wrapping up the doctored capsule in a piece of soft jack cheese, she placed it inside the trap with gloved hands to eliminate the human smell, took it to the barn, and propped its door open.

Whimsically, she visualized Paul as the rat and herself as the bait as she placed the trap on the barn's floor.

* * *

Police work was partly luck, but luck often had to be nudged, so Alix decided to review the interviews gleaned from the Murdoch neighbors one more time, knowing it wasn't unusual for someone to remember something they had thought insignificant at the time or had merely forgotten. Besides, she was desperate for leads and maybe she would get lucky.

She settled down to read, focusing on anything that had to do with the case. After about an hour, her attention began to flag. But just as she had about decided to take a break and go out for a sandwich, something caught her eye. She sat up in her chair.

George and Eula Brown. Retired. Living a couple of houses down from the Murdochs. George was an insomniac.

Was he up the night of the murder? Had he seen something? The report merely stated that neither he nor his wife had seen or heard anything unusual, but it sounded like something worth pursuing. Feeling a spark of hope, she quickly made a note to call them.

Gritting her teeth, she sat down at the computer, determined to make it work for her, but when Dave Barnes arrived a few minutes later, she looked up at him with relief.

"What are you doing?" he asked.

"Trying to figure this damned thing out. According to the chief, it's supposed to make things easier for us and do everything but wash dishes. I'm sure that in time, it probably will, but right now I'd be thrilled to just get the thing to do something. Anything."

Dave leaned over her shoulder, hit a few keys, and the screen came alive.

"Wow!" Alix exclaimed, spreading her arms and knocking over a cup filled with pencils. "You're a miracle worker! I had no idea you were a computer nerd."

"Does this mean I get a raise?" he asked, picking rolling pencils off the floor.

She grinned up at him. "Don't push your luck, buster. What can I do for you?"

"Two things. First, we've got the results of Hagstrom's lie detector test."

"And?"

"Inconclusive," he said, sighing. "Roger, the technician, won't commit himself one way or the other, but he's leaning toward Vince telling the truth."

"I suppose I already knew that," she sighed, "but it was worth a shot. Send Hagstrom in before he leaves, would you, *amigo*?"

He nodded and started to leave, then hesitated.

"Something on your mind?" she asked.

"Pat and I just heard from the adoption agency," he told her, a huge smile lighting up his cadaverous face. "We'll soon be the proud parents of not one, but two Korean orphans, two-year-old twin girls. We couldn't bear to separate them, so we took them both. They'll be here next week."

Alix rose from her chair and hugged him. "That's great, Dave. That's just great! Congratulations to you both. Got any pictures?"

"I'll bring them tomorrow, now that we know the adoption is a done deal. Wait 'til you see them, Alix, they're adorable. They look like little matching bookends. I hope you'll stop by to see them. Pat and I can't wait to show them off."

Still smiling, he went out and ushered the big truck driver into her office.

"Mr. Hagstrom, you're free to go," Alix said quietly. "Thanks for coming in and taking the test."

"You're not sure I'm not guilty, are you?" he said, looking at her steadily. "But I swear to you I'm not. I spoke with my wife last night, and she's flying home tomorrow so we can give our marriage another try. She'll come in and talk to you if you think it'll help."

He paused, twisting his worn Stetson in his big hands. "I know I had a damn good reason to kill Murdoch, but I'm not stupid. Murdoch wasn't worth messing up our lives."

"I believe you. And yes, I'd like to speak with your wife."

He left, leaving her to wonder what to do next as she looked with dismay at her messy office, the computer screen which had once again mysteriously darkened, and the stacks of reports on her desk.

Was anything positive ever going to happen with these damned cases? Between the lack of leads and the bombshell Lloyd had thrown at her, life had somehow not been the proverbial bowl of cherries lately. She was sitting back in her chair, rubbing her eyes, when Dave knocked at her door again.

"You're okay, boss? You look beat."

"Yeah, fine Dave," she said wearily.

"You're not fine. I've seen that look before."

"It's these murders, Dave. We've got suspicions we can't confirm, a woman we can't locate, theories that don't jell, and suspects that turn out not to be suspects. What I am doing in this job, my friend? I feel like packing it all in and retiring as Lloyd suggested."

His eyebrows rose, but all he said was, "Go on."

"Lloyd wants me to quit."

"And?"

"And nothing. I told him I'd think about it."

"You're not serious, are you?" he said.

"What's not to be serious about? Can't say that I feel particularly effective as a cop these days."

He sat down in the chair across her desk. "Boss, you remember what happened with the psych department murders a few years back? We had no clues, no leads, nothing. The chief replaced you with Alan Cooper, your career looked like it was in the john, and your pride was as full of holes as a colander. But then you regrouped and showed them all: the chief, the mayor, the university president, everybody. And brilliantly, I might add."

She smiled up at him. "And you saved my life when I tried to corner the murderer and thought I was a goner."

"You can't quit, Alix. The loss to the department would be too great. Besides, you love your work and, unorthodox as your methods are, there's nobody better at it than you. I'm sure you and Lloyd can work things out without putting your career or your marriage on the line."

"Easier said than done, *paisán*." She sighed, looking away. "Would Pat ever ask you to find another job, now that you have kids?"

He grinned. "No, we've been married too long, but I think I understand where Lloyd's coming from. He's older and has already lost one wife to violent death. And now he worries about losing another. You can't blame him, you know. He's crazy about you, and maybe the retirement thing is his way of saying it. Our work isn't exactly hazard free. Cheer up," he added with a smile. "We're going to solve these murders. You'll see."

"We'd better. If I could only prove my suspicion ..."

"What suspicion?"

"That Professor Rathburn killed her husband," she said frowning. "But I can't, and it's driving me nuts."

Dave started to say something.

"No, don't try to talk me out of it!" she said, shaking her finger at him. "Jon's already told me that I'm fighting windmills, but I've just got to keep digging."

She knew that Dave wanted to warn her that this was becoming an obsession with her. But at least he knew better, and proving Meagan's guilt gnawed at her like a beaver at a log. As Dave was leaving, her intercom buzzed.

"What!" Alix barked.

"Sorry," Louise, her secretary, said apologetically. "Sounds like things aren't copasetic in there. I did warn the chief that computer would turn out to be nothing but a pain in the ass for you."

"And you were right. What's up, Louise?"

"There's a Mr. Brown on the phone. He wants to talk to you about a car."

"A car?" Alix repeated. "What car?"

"I don't know. He just said he wanted to talk to one of the detectives in charge of the Murdoch case."

"Okay, put him on," Alix said wearily. "And I'm sorry I snapped at you, Louise. I've been a little tense lately."

Alix closed her eyes and took a deep breath. She worked hard to curb her temper, not always successfully. It was bad enough when she lost it with Lloyd, but she could not take out her frustrations on her co-workers who did not deserve it any more than he did.

Her eyes returned to the flashing red light on her phone. A man about a car? Probably someone whose neighbor's kid had put a dent in his renovated Model A. She really did not need this today, but she was, after all, a public servant …

The caller, who had introduced himself as George Brown, sounded like an older man.

"Me and the wife talked to one of them detectives when they came around asking about the Murdoch killing," he said in a voice that tended to tremble. "And I've been thinking about something and decided you should know."

"Know what?" Alix asked, curious now.

About the car I saw the night Mr. Murdoch was killed."

Shooting to her feet, Alix knocked her chair over and white-knuckled the phone. Was it possible that the stroke of luck she had been praying for had just knocked on her door?

And then it clicked. George Brown. Rich Murdoch's

neighbor. The insomniac she had planned to interview again after perusing the reports.

"This is quite a coincidence, Mr. Brown," she told him. "I was about to call you myself. In going over the reports, I noticed that you suffer from insomnia, and I wanted to talk to you in the event you might have seen or heard something that night that might have slipped your mind. What time was it when you saw the car?"

"Two-thirty," he told her. "I know because I looked at the clock on the nightstand."

"May I come over so we can talk about this in person?"

"Sure, come on ahead," he said. "Me and the wife aren't going anywhere."

Shouting for Dave to come along, Alix snatched her jacket from the coat rack and charged out the door. Dave tried to keep up with her as she brought him up to date. Twenty minutes later, they both joined the Browns in their tiny living room, cluttered with twice as much furniture as seemed needed. It was obvious from the couple's demeanor that the detectives had interrupted a family disagreement. Eula, while attempting to be hospitable, looked stern, but George, giving his wife a warning look, came right to the point.

"Eula says I'm going to look like a fool because I didn't say anything when you folks were here before," he began, sitting up very straight in a rocking chair beside the fireplace. "There really isn't much to tell, but I think you should know, for whatever it's worth."

"Why don't you start from the beginning?" Alix said gently. "You know, sometimes things that may seem insignificant to you can be valuable leads for us. And many witnesses often forget details when they're first interviewed, so this isn't unusual, believe me."

"You think so?" he said hopefully.

"Yes, I do. So why don't you go ahead, tell us what you remember?"

George, white hair askew and emphasizing his words with considerable hand and arm gestures, repeated his conversation with Eula of a few days ago.

"So you say you couldn't sleep, had a headache, looked at the clock on the nightstand, got an aspirin without turning on the lights, and saw a small dark car from the window, pulling away from the curb near the Murdoch home," Alix said, paraphrasing him.

"That's it exactly," the old man told her.

"But you couldn't tell what color it was and couldn't see the license plate or the driver."

"No," he said dejectedly. "I didn't have my glasses on. And even if I had, I probably wouldn't have seen much. It was pretty dark and starting to rain. Maybe it's nothing," he added, "but I thought I should tell you."

"You were right to do so, Mr. Brown," she assured him. "And I appreciate it. Tell me, can you remember anything else about the car?"

"Yes! I remember now!" he said after a moment's thought. "First, I'm almost sure it was an import. Me and Eula, we buy American and I'm kind of a car buff. I don't think this car was U.S. made, but I could be wrong. There's so many gall danged models on the road now it makes your head swim. Was easier to recognize cars in the old days. Studebakers, Buicks, an occasional Edsel ... Sorry," he hastened to add as he saw Alix's eyes beginning to glaze over. "It was too dark to be sure. And the car's lights were off when it pulled away from the curb. I didn't need my glasses to see that. And then, when it got to the middle of the block, I saw the red tail lights glowing and thought that the driver must have forgotten about the lights and then remembered."

Or wanted to get away without being seen, Alix thought as she and Dave exchanged a glance.

Alix was euphoric. There was no doubt in her mind that the murderer had driven the car. But a small, dark car! It was like looking for one specific grain of sand on a ten-mile beach, but she knew from experience that such details often solved a case. Right now, she was grateful for any clues, no matter how slim.

Vince Hagstrom had seen a woman near the Murdoch home around the time of Rich's death, and now George Brown had observed a car pulling away, also within the right time frame. Was there a connection? Had a woman been driving that car? The woman they had been looking for?

The two detectives thanked the Browns. Once they were back in their unmarked car, Alix turned to Dave and said, "I want the neighborhood checked again. I want to know who was entertaining that night, who the guests were, what kind of cars they drove, what time they left, anything you can find out. Somebody else may have seen something, and we might just get lucky."

A clue! Slim, but a clue nonetheless.

* * *

Midge Hagstrom, a delicate young woman with pale blonde hair pulled back in a girlish ponytail, came to see Alix upon her return to Red Pine, but could add little by way of information.

"The whole thing was a huge mistake," she admitted sheepishly. "And when I found out Rich was also seeing other women, I made up my mind to call the affair off. I was flattered by his attentions, I guess, and Vince was on the road so much. But he loves me enough to give me another chance, and he's twice the man Rich Murdoch was. I'm glad I finally realized that."

There was no doubt that she had been in Kansas at the time of the murder and therefore could not have been the woman in red. When asked if she knew the other women Rich had dated, Midge shook her head. "No, but I know now there were quite a few. What a fool I've been!"

Murdoch had done plenty of damage in his lifetime, and Alix was glad that the marriage of two basically decent people wasn't one of the casualties he had left in his wake.

* * *

Meagan and Paige Chatfield, who had just returned from Idaho, sat on a bench behind the criminology building. The girl attacked her tuna sandwich with the appetite of youth while Meagan, after taking only one bite of hers, threw the rest away in a nearby trashcan. She was silent for a while, hoping to find the right words to ask Paige about her new boyfriend. In the meantime, she had to keep up her role of friend and adviser, although it was becoming increasingly difficult for her to make the effort.

"So how're things going with your new heartthrob?" she hedged.

"Just great, Dr. Rathburn. He was so happy to see me back. I know how upset he was when I went home to see my folks."

"Why would he be upset? Doesn't he like you to visit family?"

"He hates it when we're apart," Paige explained, "and he wants me to move in with him so we can be together all the time. Isn't that sweet?"

Sweet? This was almost more than she could bear. Was she the only one who could see what was as obvious as if it had been written on a sign and waved in front of the girl that this man was dangerous?

"Paige," she said as she rose, "before you make such an important decision, I've got to talk to you. It's really important. I think that ..."

"Dr. Rathburn!" The voice of the department secretary, who was coming up the pathway on the run, interrupted her. "I've been looking everywhere for you," the secretary told her. "Dr. Stanfield has called an urgent department meeting in fifteen minutes. Seems Dr. Harper just had emergency surgery, and Dr. Stanfield wants to meet with the whole department about class coverage."

"Be right there," Meagan replied. "Paige, I've got to run but remember, we need to talk, so let's meet after class tomorrow. It's really important, although you probably aren't going to like it," she added as she got to her feet. "But you know I care about you and about your future. You'll be there, won't you?" she added, attempting a smile.

Was she saying this the right way, Meagan wondered. It seemed as though the girl was looking at her strangely but perhaps she was imagining things. So much stress! It was a wonder she could even pretend to some sort of mindless normality. But she had to warn Paige. It was literally a matter of life and death.

CHAPTER 17

Meagan found a rat, deader than the proverbial doornail, in the trap she had set. It had worked, she thought excitedly. How clever she had been to research the poison and try it out on the rat. The next question was, would the gelatin capsule dissolve in a margarita without leaving a residue?

There was only one way to find out. She mixed a small batch of margaritas and placed the capsule in a glass. Much to her disappointment, it would not dissolve. Because of the poison's gummy consistency, putting the substance by itself in a pitcher of margaritas or in Paul's glass would not work.

So what will she wondered. Agitated now, but unwilling to give up, she tried to think of other alternatives, systematically rejecting each one as unsuitable. And then, as she was about to throw in the towel, she suddenly hit on a solution, one so simple she chided herself for not thinking about it before.

Going into the garage, she found a stepladder and searched the top of her pantry shelf where she found a tiny, old-fashioned ice-cube tray she had not used since the advent of icemakers. She partially filled six of the diminutive cavities with water and waited until the tray was almost frozen before placing pea-sized lumps of the toxin in each ice cube, adding more water and returning the tray to the freezer.

Her plan was to take some of the ice cubes in a small ice bag with a screw-on cap that would fit in her shoulder bag without a problem. They would need to remain frozen for only an hour or so, long enough to get to Paul's house and be offered a drink.

Up to now, she had found a gun a useful weapon, but this was so much more intriguing! And there was an extra fillip to death if it could be accomplished in disguise. This way, she could outwit everyone. Even the police would have no reason to think that Paul had died of anything but a normal death. How clever of her to think of this!

During the course of her research, she had found that tetradotoxin was one of the most toxic non-protein poisons known to man, and that even a small amount would cause muscular paralysis, resulting in hypotension and respiratory arrest. There was no antidote. If not put on life-support systems immediately until the poison could metabolize into less toxic materials, the patient would certainly die in as little as thirty minutes as the poison blocked the nerve impulses, paralleling the symptoms of cardio-pulmonary arrest.

There was only one thing left to do: check out Tudor Lane. Filled with nervous excitement at the prospect of seeing the results of all her planning now, she could not wait to conduct her scouting expedition. She made it a point to go at about the same time she planned to arrive at the O'Neil home for her date with Paul later that week. This way, she could get the feel of the area and decide where to park her car.

But despite her eagerness to move on toward the ultimate and inevitable denouement of Paul's death, the more she thought about it, the more her plan's dangers became apparent. More people would be home in the early evening and children might be playing in the street, increasing her chances of being seen and remembered. She forced herself to rein in her impatience, although she found it almost impossible to do so.

Barely able to contain herself, she decided to check out Paul's street in the daytime instead. With people at work and kids in school, she would minimize that danger.

* * *

Meagan thought she would scream when Jon rapped on the door of her office and peered in. Why couldn't everyone just leave her alone? She had so much to think about, especially now that she was about to meet with Paul O'Neil.

"Got a minute, Meagan?" he asked. "I just came over to borrow a book from Dan DeVoe and stopped in to say hello."

Meagan felt sure that he suspected nothing. She had been too careful, too focused, too smart. And she knew that there was no way Jon or anyone else would think that she was anything but a grieving widow trying to get over her husband's death, rather than the powerful woman she had become who dealt well-deserved death as God's instrument of justice.

She motioned him to one of the chairs that faced her desk and saw the concern in his eyes. Meagan knew that her clothes now hung on her as a result of her weight loss and that her face was colorless and wan, but these were small matters when compared to what she had gained. Anything else paled by comparison.

"How're you doing, my friend?" Jon said, noting the smear of mascara under Meagan's eyes. "I wanted to apologize for startling you the other day in the park. You looked so sad that I thought maybe you might want to talk," he hedged.

"Thank you, Jon. I guess I'm not over Steven's death yet," she said as she tried to curb her impatience.

It was taking such a great deal of effort to lie of late. Down deep, she knew that Jon did not deserve the deception, but the old barriers held. What was there to talk about? The incest? The abuse? Her illness? The killings? She no longer needed or wanted to indulge in such weakness. She did not need anyone's attention or sympathy, now that she was strong, in control, filled with the power her destiny demanded. She neither wanted nor relished pity or understanding from friends or colleagues.

But she sensed that Jon was not satisfied with her answer as he asked, "Meagan, have you seen a doctor? I worry about you. You look so thin. Are you eating properly?"

She could only nod, barely hiding her annoyance now as he

reached for her hand, almost skeletal in its thinness. "Are you sure?" he probed.

"Yes, I'm sure. Thank you," she said, pulling her hand away and finding it impossible now to suppress the annoyance in her voice.

"Meagan, the mind plays a powerful part in the body's healing," Jon persisted. "Have you thought about seeking professional help?"

"I'm fine and I don't need any help, Jon, but thanks for caring. Now if you don't mind, I've got a lot of work to do," she said, rising. She hoped he would take the hint and leave.

He sighed and, getting to his feet, he said, "Look, if you decide you want to talk, please remember that I'm available, day or night."

As if she would need him or anyone else, she thought as she watched him go, her mind already working on the next step of her plan.

She could not wait for the end of the week to arrive and for her meeting with Paul O'Neil.

CHAPTER 18

As Meagan approached Paul's street, she looked to her right before turning onto Tudor Lane, an upscale neighborhood of somewhat pretentious homes set on half-acre lots and shaded by stately old maples and oaks. Some homeowners had opted for large lawns edged by multicolored flowerbeds while others had combined evergreens and shrubs with redwood bark and decorative stone to minimize upkeep. All the homes reflected solidity and affluence.

The O'Neil house was a light-gray Victorian of imposing proportions with lots of intricate wood curlicues and a steep pitched roof, located in the middle of the block. The lawn was edged by purple, lavender, and yellow primroses, and the wide brick walkway led to a darker-gray front door sporting beveled glass inserts.

Meagan watched the front door open and spotted Paul walking toward the garage where his black Mercedes was parked. She saw him glance briefly in her direction and, taken by surprise, she caught her breath as she felt her heart pound wildly against her ribs.

How confident he looked. How self-assured. He didn't know she was watching him or the danger he was in. No, more than danger since what would happen to him was a certainty. She made no mistakes when it came to extracting vengeance. The king of the world in his fancy Mercedes would soon be a dead man.

Attempting to get over her shock, she remembered that, since this was merely an exploratory trip, she wasn't wearing her blonde wig, so she quickly covered her flamboyant copper mane with her silk scarf and donned her sunglasses. She then proceeded straight ahead on Stratford Avenue rather than turning right as she had first intended. Turning around, she parked another half block down the street, glanced down Paul's street as she passed it, and saw him open the garage door, get into the Mercedes, and drive off.

Why was he leaving the house now when he should already be at his office? The hammering of her heart abated as she saw him go in the opposite direction from where she was parked. It had been a close call, although she was certain he had not seen her. Yet, even if he had, he would not have recognized the woman he knew as Joan Campbell. Just to be safe, she waited a few more minutes before continuing her reconnaissance. Confident that he had left for good, she went down the Tudor Lane cul-de-sac and looked for a propitious spot to park her car when she would return as a guest.

She had delayed a few days before calling Paul to set a date for their next meeting, deciding to let him stew a bit, but Vivian's call had precipitated the event. Her strategy had paid off. "Joan!" he had exclaimed, sounding relieved. "I'm glad to hear from you. I was beginning to think you had forgotten our meeting."

"Of course not," she reassured him. "I'm looking forward to it. It's just that I've been very busy, and it's only now that I've had a chance to catch my breath. Would Wednesday evening around six be okay?"

He had told her it would, and they had made a date.

As she slowly drove, she suddenly spotted the perfect parking place just a few houses down from Paul's home, yet not so far that she would have to walk a long way to and from her Toyota. A huge weeping willow, fully clothed in its narrow, pale green leaves, would shroud her car, and she hoped that the space would be available the night of her visit. The tree was obviously very old. Its roots, looking like gnarled limbs, had started to buckle the concrete sidewalk, and its graceful branches curved downward like a waterfall.

She made a mental note to watch out for the protruding roots and concrete outcrops when she returned to her car in the dark wearing her high-heeled boots. Going down to the end of the block, she slowly reached the end of the cul-de-sac, turned around, and went back down the street, exiting once more on Stratford Avenue.

She did not see the freckled-faced woman observing the Toyota from an upstairs bedroom window across the street from Paul O'Neil's house.

* * *

"Damn!" Laura Wingate exclaimed as she ran downstairs to catch the license number and make of the small sedan that had slowly driven past her home a few seconds ago. From her son Timmy's bedroom where she had been dusting, her vision hampered by the angle of the roof, she had been unable to see anything but the top of the car. Panting heavily from running down two flights of stairs, she reached the kitchen window where, had she been there in the first place, she could have easily seen both car and driver.

Laura Wingate was a big woman, but despite her bulk, she moved quickly. But not quickly enough, she thought with considerable annoyance. By the time she reached the kitchen, the car was turning left and she caught only a brief glimpse of its muddied plates and the back of the driver's head as it rounded the corner.

Well, no matter. She'd keep an eye out for it in case it came back. Maybe it was a delivery person or someone looking for an address. One thing was certain. She wasn't going to summon the police and embarrass a complete stranger and herself without something more alarming to report. It was one thing to be cautious and quite another to panic because a strange car had gone by a couple of times. It certainly did not prove that a child molester was on the loose in her front yard.

In retrospect, the more she thought more about it, the sillier she felt. She was glad now that she had not called the police immediately.

Because of the flyer Timmy had brought home the day before alerting parents about the possibility of a pedophile on the loose in their neighborhood, she and her husband had sat down with the child and set some rules.

"We don't mean to frighten you, Timmy," his father had told him, "but you know what your teachers and the policeman who came to your school said. There're some bad people out there, and we don't want you to get hurt."

"I know, Dad. The policeman said we shouldn't get into strange cars and to yell if someone tried to make us."

"That's exactly right. Here's a whistle your mom and I bought you. Wear it around your neck, and if someone tries to make you do things you don't want to do, just blow it as hard as you can and run for help. And remember that it's not a toy, son. It's only to be used in case of emergency. You understand?"

"Like the boy who cried wolf and no one paid any attention to him when he really needed help?"

"Exactly like that."

Alan and Laura felt the drill had made an impression on Timmy without frightening him, and felt better knowing that they were doing their best to protect their son while teaching him how to protect himself. With that in mind, the urgency of tracking down and identifying the car faded from Laura's mind. Later, distracted by a long-distance call from her mother, she promptly forgot about it.

* * *

Meagan had planned the evening with the utmost care. In addition to the blonde wig and blue contact lenses, she wore a black silk angora sweater, a matching skirt, and her high-heeled boots. She softened the almost-funereal effect by draping a multicolored Hermes silk scarf across her shoulders, fastened on the pearl earrings she had worn to Paul O'Neil's office, and donned the big square glasses. In her purse, tucked in the small insulated bag, she carried a few ice cubes containing their deadly cargo. She added a handkerchief and the thin surgical rubber gloves to the purse's contents. On her way out the door, she grabbed a black cashmere coat, making sure another other silk scarf was in its pocket.

Earlier today, she had been overcome by yet another wave of the ever-growing exhaustion that had become part of her daily life. The insomnia and cold sweats were a nightly occurrence now, and to prepare for the evening, she had taken a nap after her last class and felt somewhat refreshed. She had felt quite calm at first, but as she dressed the anticipation of what was about to happen returned and excitement replaced the weariness she had felt earlier. How wonderful it was to know that Paul would soon be dead, victim of his own deeds through her cleverness and detailed planning!

* * *

Earlier that day, fear had gripped her when she learned that Alix had been poking around the auditorium and was again talking to colleagues and students.

"By the way, Meagan, Detective Mendez came around again a couple of days ago asking more questions about the day Steven was killed," one of the younger sociology professors had told her. "And she also wanted to know if I'd seen you leave campus between two and five that afternoon. They can't possibly suspect you, can they?"

"Of course not, but Detective Mendez is very competent and thorough. She's committed to catching Steven's killer," Meagan had replied, trying not to bite off the words. "She's just doing her job. What did you tell her, Thea?"

"That I was sitting next to you at the lecture but had to leave early because Jake, my son, was sick and that I never saw you leave the campus. I'm sorry they haven't caught the killer yet

Meagan. It must be really hard for you, knowing he's still at large."

What was Alix up to? Meagan had been so sure that Alix was satisfied about her alibi. There was only one explanation; Alix knew, and it was just a matter of time now before she arrived at her doorstep.

Meagan also felt sure that Alix had not been able to crack her alibi or discover her motive. All she had were suspicions, but she was a very smart woman, and it might not take her long to make the connection between Steven's and Rich Murdoch's murders.

And, ultimately, to her.

But she was much smarter, much more clever than any policewoman, and she would outsmart them all. She was sure of that. Nothing, no one, would interfere with her missions.

* * *

It was six o'clock and already dark when she arrived at Paul's home and, after parking her car, she was pleased to confirm that it was almost invisible under the tree's green shroud. It was a relief to be on the move, to put her plan into action.

Thunder, which had crept progressively closer, suddenly exploded over her head as she started down the sidewalk, making her jump, followed by a spectacular zigzag of lightning that stitched sky to earth. The musty, rain-soaked smell of wet ground rose up to meet her, bringing with it memories of childhood. Oh, God! She could not think of that now!

She felt the soles of her boots getting wet but, as she neared the door, she was overcome with the anticipation of what would soon take place. As she ran up the steps and rang the doorbell, she saw that the street was still deserted. Behind the closed door, she would again feel the adrenaline and watch an abuser grovel at her feet.

She was concerned about the porch light shining on her, but Paul came to the door almost at once, dressed as nattily as before in gray slacks, a navy-blue sports jacket, and a white silk turtleneck. His hard black eyes brightened when he saw her, and he opened the door to let her in.

"Come in before you get soaked!" he said cheerfully. "Quite a storm, isn't it? Looks like you found the house without a problem. Were my directions helpful?"

"They were perfect, and thank you so much," Meagan simpered, "because I'm hopeless with directions."

"I hope you will forgive my family's absence," he said, taking her coat. "They were looking forward to meeting you, but they had to go visit Vivian's mother who was hospitalized a few days ago. They'll be back in a few days, but I saw no reason to postpone our meeting. I hope you don't mind."

Of course she didn't mind. It was just what she had planned, but he was too stupid and filled with his own self-importance to read her face and see the contempt she felt for him.

"Sorry to hear about your mother-in-law," she said soberly. She walked over to the beautiful baby grand piano and picked up a picture of a toddler in an elaborate silver frame.

"That's Jasmin, my little girl, she's almost three," Paul said. "She's a real sweetheart."

But you didn't mind scaring her half to death and hitting her mother, you bastard!

Suddenly, her father's face interposed itself between them. There was no difference between him, or Paul, or Steven. But now she could get her revenge with impunity! And, in a strange way, to exact it on her father as well! She smiled at Paul. How lucky he was to be the representative of all the men who had wronged her in her life, and how lucky she was to be able to rid him of all of their sins and to allow him to pay the penance that he absolutely had to pay.

The furnishings were Victorian in keeping with the house's exterior and looked authentic. But aside from the family photographs, the room lacked the imprint of the owners' tastes and personalities. She picked up another photograph, this one of Paul, Vivian, and Jasmin taken at what looked like a vacation resort, all clad in bathing suits and looking happy and tanned. She returned the picture to the top of the piano and ran her hand over its surface, feeling the rich, velvety softness of its wood under her fingers.

Meagan knew Paul resented Vivian's playing. Vivian had often told her during the counseling sessions how he used to fly into rages, resenting the time her music took away from her household chores—meaning him—and criticizing what he called "all that banging" to demean her talent.

And now, thanks to her, Vivian was free to enjoy her music and teach in Maine, safe at last, and after tonight, she would be safe forever.

Meagan had to fight the overwhelming impulse to tell him everything. To tell him how she had sent his wife and child away. To tell him how she was about to free them forever from further fear and abuse.

She knew, of course, that he was oblivious to her thoughts as he regaled her with anecdotes about his hobbies and his work. He was an amusing raconteur, and under different circumstances, she might have actually enjoyed herself.

But you aren't clever enough, she thought as she watched his performance, her mind's eyes already anticipating his death throes.

After a few minutes, he went into the kitchen and soon returned with a tray of hors d'oeuvres, which he placed on the coffee table, and two margarita glasses, their frosted edges gleaming with perfect circles of salt.

"You said you liked margaritas," he boasted, "and I happen to make the best in town."

Meagan could not help but notice that he had remembered the comment she had made in his office about the margaritas made with ice cubes rather than crushed ice and she was grateful for his attention to details since it suited her plan perfectly.

She accepted the proffered glass but deliberately caught her right elbow on the chair's arm, spilling her drink and drenching her skirt.

"Don't worry," he told her, hearing her exclamation of dismay. "I'll be right back with another drink."

Meagan watched as he returned to the kitchen with her empty glass. She heard the phone ring and saw Paul vanish into his study.

Opening her purse, she quickly unscrewed the top of the insulated ice bag and poured three small ice cubes into his glass, which sat on the coffee table across from her, noting with relief that they closely matched the size of the cubes already in the glass.

Meagan was once again seated in her chair when he returned with a fresh margarita and two damp dishtowels.

"Sorry," he told her. "That was my partner on the phone and he does have a tendency to ramble on. May I propose a toast? To a fruitful professional association and a budding friendship."

He toasted her with his glass, his eyes holding hers, and took a healthy sip.

"Very nice," Meagan murmured, sipping from her own glass.

"Glad you like them. They're my favorite drink, too. Really, I wasn't just saying that to please you. And the small ice cubes do add a certain interesting dimension to the drink," he said.

They sure do, she thought, thinking of the toxin.

The margaritas were excellent and revealed an expert hand. She kept watching him under her long lashes to see if she could detect any change, although he had taken only two sips, but so far, nothing. Killing a rat with a doctored capsule was one thing, but would it really work with a man? Would the dose be strong enough? There were so many unknowns! But she knew it would work. It had to because she had planned everything so carefully, tested the toxin, and was convinced she had overlooked nothing.

A gray cat lazily entered the room and came over to her, startling her and almost upsetting her drink for the second time. As she bent to pet it, the cat purred and jumped on her lap but soon, tiring of the attention, it jumped off and wandered into the kitchen. Meagan reached for one of the hors d'oeuvres to cover her nervousness. Why was he still sitting here like nothing was happening? She was trembling with impatience when she suddenly heard his voice as if in a fog, her mind focused only on why the poison was not yet taking effect.

"Tell me about your husband," Paul was saying, leaning toward her and putting his hand on her knee. "What caused the divorce? Do you mind talking about it? I can't imagine any man letting someone like you go."

She resisted the urge to slap his hand away as she waited for some change, any change, to take place.

She was beginning to wonder if it was *ever* going to work. Fifteen minutes had already passed since he had taken his first sip, yet it felt like three hours. They were both on their second drink, and he still showed no signs of ...

He spoke to her in a low, intimate voice, and her thoughts started to drift until she suddenly noticed a thickening in his speech and saw a puzzled look come into his eyes. She saw him rise unsteadily and hurry away, in a lopsided gait. She knew that some of the toxin's symptoms were vomiting, numbness, tingling of lips and tongue, and that it often had emetic properties, but these symptoms could vary, and she had no idea what to expect with Paul.

Meagan watched him closely as he came back into the living room. She noticed beads of perspiration on his forehead and, with growing satisfaction, she saw that he walked with ever-increasing unsteadiness and stumbled as he resumed his seat next to her chair.

She was transfixed by the scene, wanting to run away, afraid to watch, yet mesmerized by it all, like a child watching a horror movie through spread fingers. She could tell that he was wondering what was wrong with him, and she saw incomprehension followed by terror coalesce as he saw her staring at him, silent and aloof, watching with cold detachment and increasing elation. She smiled as she watched his mouth open and close, but no words came out.

Now Meagan got to her feet and took off her wig, tossing it on the chair. Shining red-gold hair now framed her face as he gave her a look she recognized as incomprehension.

"You have no idea who I am, do you? I'm your wife's avenging angel, and you will never hurt her or that precious little girl again, you slimy bastard. I am your judge and jury. You've been found guilty, and this is your punishment."

Her impatience growing now, she watched him feebly trying

to reach for the telephone, and she moved it just out of his grasp as she saw his eyes clouding over. She stood rooted to the floor for a few seconds, staring at him as the familiar rage flowed through her. Where was his bravado now, and his belief that no woman could resist him? That he could do with them as he pleased? She had ground them into the carpet on which he lay.

But her subconscious kicked in, forcing her to act. The longer she stayed, the more vulnerable she became. She put on the surgical gloves she had brought, snatched the two glasses and the pitcher of margaritas, and dumped them, as well as the rest of the hors d'oeuvres, into the garbage disposal. Washing the glasses twice with hot soapy water to obliterate any traces of the toxin in his glass or lipstick marks on hers, she put them and the pitcher back in what she hoped was the right spot and washed the tray on which the hors d'oeuvres had been so beautifully displayed such a short while ago, also returning it to the cupboard.

Moving with the speed of a well-trained athlete, her illness and exhaustion temporarily forgotten, she grabbed her handkerchief and wiped everything she had touched. She looked up at the antique clock on the wall. Seven fifteen. She had been in the house just under an hour.

No sign remained of her visit except for Paul's body lying on the floor, eyes set in a frozen stare, hand extended toward the telephone which she picked up and replaced in its original place on the table next to the sofa. A quick look around reassured her she had left nothing incriminating behind. Grabbing the wig from the armchair where she had tossed it, she patted it into place, covering it with the silk scarf, then put on her coat and grabbed her purse. She remembered to turn off the porch light as she opened the front door and cautiously peered outside.

Nothing.

Still wearing the rubber gloves, she locked the front door from the inside and closed it after her, moving briskly toward her car. She thanked the foul weather that was keeping everyone inside. Except for the yowling of fighting cats and the distant whine of a truck's engine laboring on Interstate 5, the neighborhood was peaceful, the rain mixed with wet snow softly pat-patting down on the sidewalk.

Her boots, with their rubber soles, made no sound as she hurried to her car. She opened the door, simultaneously turning off the overhead light, and got in. As she had done after the Murdoch murder, she did not turn on her headlights until she was halfway down the block.

When she got home, she went to her medicine cabinet and grabbed a couple of aspirins for the headache that clutched her head, probably a delayed reaction from the stress she had been under for the last couple of hours. She swallowed the tablets with a big glass of mineral water and waited for her nerves to settle.

Shedding the sweat-drenched angora sweater and skirt, she dropped them on the floor and looked at them with revulsion. She hurried into the kitchen to look for a paper bag and stuffed the offending garments into it. After starting a fire in her living room fireplace, she waited until it burned bright and hot and threw the bag in.

Then, running a bath as hot as she could stand it, she poured some of her favorite oil in the steaming water and sat in the tub, hugging herself and shaking violently. The lavender-scented soap dropped from her grasp to the bottom of the tub.

She would thank God again once she heard confirmation that Paul was dead and only then would she allow herself to rejoice. She felt herself trembling, then shook her head. No, she would not think of that. The aftermath of his murder was something she did not want to consider. Would not consider. He was slime, and she had dealt him exactly the kind of death he deserved, the kind all abusers deserved. She had shown him who was in charge, who the powerful one was.

But she felt so tired! Her head pounded and her entire body ached, and despite her glee at having eliminated yet one more abuser, she thought that it would be so easy, so very easy to end it all if she just had the nerve. It was so tempting to …

Tears pooled but did not spill. As she had sworn after Steven's murder, there would be no more tears, only a steely resolve to guide her own destiny. She sensed her death close at hand, feeling it inching closer every day as her health deteriorated. She would pay, but in her own way, with dignity, and in control of her own life.

And now in control of her own death.

She would never be a victim again.

CHAPTER 19

Alix looked up and saw Louise peering around the door. This morning, her secretary wore a dark wig styled in a pageboy hairdo topped by a pink velvet pillbox. She wore a matching pink wool suit, a pearl choker, and conservative dark-blue pumps with sensible heels.

"Jacqueline Kennedy?" Alix inquired.

"Excellent!"

Alix suppressed a smile. "Well, it's not as flamboyant as some of your other stuff, but it's very nice. You could pass for her twin, Louise. What's up?"

"Well, first my sinuses thank you for whatever you said to Shawn Connors about not smoking inside. And second, we got a formal complaint from a field worker who says Connors threatened to turn him over to the Immigration Service, even though his green card is in order."

"*Madre de Dios!* Not again! This guy's like a cactus permanently affixed to my butt. Give me the paperwork, Louise. I'll take care of it before he involves us in an affirmative action suit. Anything else?"

"Yes. Dave says a man was found dead in his home on Tudor Lane this morning. Looks like a heart attack. The man's partner, Lee Edmonds, told Dave he and the deceased were supposed to be in court today about a tax case. When he didn't show up, Mr. Edmonds went to the house to see what was going on. The door was locked, but he could see a body on the floor through an opening in the living room drapes and all the lights were on."

"What's the guy's name?"

"Paul O'Neil," Louise told her. "Mr. Edmonds says that he talked to him last night and he seemed fine. Dr. Gardner's going to do an autopsy this morning."

"Why would he do that if it's a heart attack?" Alix asked, surprised.

"Isn't an autopsy always done in the case of an unattended death?"

"Yes, of course. So no one else was home? I wonder if he has a family and if so, where they were?"

Dave came in as Louise was about to leave. "You heard about the guy who was found dead at his home this morning?" he asked, throwing himself down in a chair and propping his feet on the corner of Alix's desk.

"Yeah, Louise just told me. I was wondering about his family."

"I spoke with his partner and went to the scene myself," Dave replied. "Doc Gardner is taking the body to the morgue. Looks like a heart attack, although Edmonds says O'Neil was a fitness freak, ran every day, that sort of thing. Edmonds also said that he has a wife and a little girl, but they weren't at home."

Alix frowned. "Any idea where they are?"

"Edmonds doesn't know," Dave said, spreading his hands, "but he thought maybe the wife took the kid to visit relatives or something. He's trying to get a hold of them."

"Tough break," she told him. "Had someone been there, he might still be alive. Say, not to change the subject, but have you got any news about the car Mr. Brown saw the night Murdoch was killed?"

"A young couple, the Garvins, live two doors down from Murdoch," Dave replied. "They had some friends over for dinner and a game of cards. One couple left after dinner, but the other couple left much later because they decided to stay and watch a video. They apparently own a large, light colored vehicle, so it doesn't sound like our mystery car. No one else in the neighborhood had company that night or saw the dark car."

"I'd like you to talk to that couple again and see if they saw anything when they left."

"Consider it done," he said as he rose to leave.

Who did the little dark car belong to? And who was driving it the night of the murder? The more Alix thought about it, the more convinced she became she was on to something.

Alix was surprised to get a call from Lee Edmonds, Paul O'Neil's partner.

"I called Paul's mother-in-law," he told her. "Her name is Susan Henderson and she lives in Canada; Calgary, to be exact. I told her that Paul was dead, that I had found him when I went to his house after he didn't show up in court this morning on a tax case we were working on. I also told one of your detectives that I'd let Vivian, his widow, know. But the thing is, Vivian isn't staying with her mother, which is where Paul had told me she was going for a visit."

Alix listened to him without interrupting. This was getting stranger by the minute.

" But Mrs. Henderson said she had not heard from Vivian lately," Edmonds continued, "and she gave me that information only after she'd called me back at my office. She said she wanted to be certain that I was who I said I was. The reason I'm calling is because of what Mrs. Henderson said next. I could hardly believe it when she told me that she thought Paul might be up to one of his tricks in an effort to locate Vivian. Apparently, she had left him once before and this time, he's hired a private detective."

"Mr. Edmonds, did Mrs. Henderson tell you why Mrs. O'Neil had left the first time?"

After a brief pause, he said, "Yes. She said that Paul had abused his wife on several occasions. I couldn't believe that my partner could be an abuser."

Alix barely thanked him before hanging up the phone, stunned into silence perhaps for the first time in her life.

CHAPTER 20

Meagan and Paige Chatfield were sitting on a bench in front of the library when Shawn Connors strutted up on his shiny black motorcycle. She noted that he cut a handsome figure in the Red Pine City Police uniform that fit his six-foot-three movie star physique like a second skin.

Paige waved when she saw him. "Oh, here's Shawn now. I gotta talk to him for a minute, Dr. Rathburn. Be right back."

"Go ahead," Meagan replied. "But let's catch up later." She was glad to see that the couple had moved to a bench nearby where she could overhear their conversation.

"Who's that?" Shawn exclaimed, staring at Meagan.

"That's my professor, Dr. Meagan Rathburn. She's terrific," Paige said proudly.

"Wow! What a looker! She could pass for a student."

"She is beautiful, but she's lost a lot of weight since her husband died. He was shot and killed during a robbery at their house a few months ago."

"Oh, yeah, I remember. Our snooty chief of detectives is in charge of the investigation. So that's Dr. Rathburn. I gotta tell you that I never had professors that looked like that!"

"You keep that up, and you'll make me jealous," Paige told him teasingly as she leaned over to kiss him.

Meagan could not believe her ears. Was Paige so blind that she could not see the guy for what he was, making comments and staring at other women right in front of her? She had to admit that they did make a handsome couple. Paige was a striking girl, tall and slim but curvy in all the right places, her hair so light it shimmered like liquid platinum and it hung down almost to her waist, creating a startling contrast with her huge black eyes.

"Well, just because you and me go out doesn't mean I'm blind," Shawn snapped.

"Take it easy, Shawn, I was just kidding," Paige replied, stroking his cheek.

Meagan seethed as she continued to watch the couple. She saw a group of students emerging from the library, laughing and chatting. Among them was a short, dark-skinned young man wearing a turban. With his black hair and almond-shaped eyes, he looked like a figure out of the Arabian nights. He smiled and waved at Paige. "Do we still have a date to study at the library at two?" he asked her.

"Sure, Ali. See you then."

Shawn's eyes darkened with anger and he roughly shoved her hand away. "Who's the darkie? And why are you meeting him this afternoon? You're cheating on me, aren't you?"

What a jerk, Meagan thought. Feeling threatened by something as innocuous as a study date. What an insecure idiot he must be.

"Ali is not a 'darkie,' Shawn," Paige replied uneasily. "He's from Kuwait and happens to be one of the smartest students in our class. He's doing me a real favor by studying with me for our mid-term."

"I don't want you seeing anybody else. Doesn't this idiot know you and I go out?"

"Ali and I aren't 'seeing' each other. We're just studying together, and there's no need for you to feel threatened," she said, looking exasperated now.

Meagan, who was listening to every word, had to summon all her calm to remain on her bench in order to hear more. She could barely contain her anger and frustration. Who did this guy think he was, talking to Paige like this? And why was the girl taking it? She did not know how lucky she was that Meagan was able to judge what kind of man this Shawn was. She would definitely tell her protégée what she thought and order her to stop seeing him!

She strained to hear more while pretending to read the book that sat on her lap.

"You've got some nerve suggesting that I can be threatened by a darkie!" Shawn yelled.

He reached for Paige and dug his thumbs into her forearms, so hard that she winced in pain. Stinging tears of hurt and embarrassment filled her dark eyes, and her involuntary cry made the heads of the students nearby turn in their direction.

"Shawn, you're hurting me. Let go of me!" she exclaimed.

"I'll let go when I'm good and ready. And I want a decision this week about your moving in. I'm not gonna wait forever, you know," he told her angrily, giving her a final shake as he released her.

It took all of Meagan's self-control not to get up and tell this guy what she thought of him. If this did not cause Paige to break off the relationship, nothing would. Why could she not see that this guy was violent and dangerous?

Meagan needed to step in since Paige obviously was not clear headed enough to realize that she was dating an abuser and that her life might be at stake. She was indeed fortunate that her professor had been right here to overhear and witness the whole episode, and who better than Meagan to put this wrong to right one more time?

Meagan locked eyes with Shawn, hoping he felt the icy contempt and hatred emanating from her. The challenge in her eyes seemed to sober him up until finally he averted his glance.

This man has all the marks of a man who enjoys roughing up women, Meagan thought angrily. Was Paige either too blind or too much in love already to see it?

As she struggled to keep her emotions under control, Meagan heard him tell Paige, "I'm sorry, babe. It's just that I love you so much I can't stand the thought of you seeing other guys. You understand that, don't you?"

Meagan watched as Paige rubbed her arms and tried hard to suppress her tears.

It's like déjà vu, she thought as she remembered the many instances when Steven had shaken her until her teeth rattled, thrown her across the room, beaten her, and she had reacted the same way as Paige, had not done anything to stop it. She hoped Paige would come to her senses and carry through with her plan to leave Shawn. She knew that the girl did not see him as a batterer, but Meagan did and she would have to step in if he continued to see Paige. Ultimately, the girl would be grateful for Meagan's efforts, she was sure of it.

"I'm trying, Shawn, but the way you reacted was uncalled for," Meagan heard Paige say.

"Look, honey, you're a beautiful girl and I worry about guys taking advantage of you, especially foreigners like him," he said, looking in Ali's direction. "You can't blame me for being jealous, right? Say, how about going to a party Saturday night? It's nothing special, just a few friends. Cops, mostly. We'll have a good time and we can talk about you moving in with me."

"I don't know, Shawn. Let me think about it. I've got a lot of studying to do for next week's midterms. And moving in with you is a big step. I'm not sure I'm ready for it," she said wearily.

Meagan sensed that Shawn was smart enough to let the issue drop for the moment. "I'll call you later, all right?" he told Paige as he rose and bent to kiss her.

After he left, Meagan went over to Paige. "Are you all right?" she asked. "I couldn't help but notice that ..."

"I can't figure this guy out," Paige interrupted, giving her a weak smile. "He can be real sweet, and then he acts like he did just now. It's like dating Dr. Jekyll and Mr. Hyde. How about you? Are you okay? You look so pale," she said, peering into her professor's face with concern.

"I'm fine, Paige, not sleeping well, that's all."

"I never know where Shawn's coming from," Paige went on. "I have this huge, easy-going family, and we're big on talking things out. Maybe if I try to communicate better with him, things will get better."

Sure they will! Meagan thought. She knew that "talking things out" with someone like Shawn would be as productive as trying to catch a bird with her bare hands. She was disappointed in Paige. She had always thought her to be smart, yet she appeared to be unable to see through this guy's phony charm.

Fortunately, she was here to care of things. She would deal with Shawn.

"Has he ever hit you, Paige?" she asked.

"No," the girl said, looking startled. "But to be honest with you, I realize now that I don't want to see him anymore. There's something strange about him. I don't like his moods, I don't like the way he treats people or the way he acts. Sometimes he scares me."

"I think you're making the right decision, Paige," Meagan said, breathing an internal sigh of relief. "It's wiser to back off from a relationship than make a mistake. Look, if there's anything I can do to help, or if you ever want to talk, just call me, okay? Here's my card. It has both my office and my home numbers on it. Call me day or night if you ever need me."

"Thanks, Dr. Rathburn, I really appreciate that. You're the best!"

Squeezing the girl's hand, Meagan left. She had to go home and pack for the Atlanta conference, and she was running late. As she got into her car and threw her briefcase on the passenger seat, she spied Dan DeVoe in her rearview mirror but pretended not to see him. She was deeply disturbed by what she had just witnessed but hugely relieved to hear that Paige had decided to end the relationship.

When she reached home, she called Alix before leaving for the airport under the pretext of checking on the progress of the investigation, knowing that it was expected of her. Although Alix was always pleasant when Meagan called, she sensed an underlying current, something she could not put her finger on.

Meagan was neither stupid nor blind.

Alix knew about Steven's death.

She was sure of it.

* * *

Alix stopped briefly to visit Pat and Dave Barnes and meet the twins who had just arrived. She played with the children for a few minutes and wondered what kind of mother she would have made. She smiled at the thought. She could just see Lloyd's face if she were to ask him how he'd like to hear the patter of little feet around the house!

Afterwards, she drove to her office, enjoying the scenery until the roar of a motorcycle's engine broke her rêverie as she saw Shawn Connors speed by her unmarked car without seeing her, his face tight and angry.

She scowled. She had loathed him on sight when he had first joined the Red Pine PD, and the entire precinct not only shared her dislike but also resented the bad name he was giving the department. Alix knew that beneath the matinee-idol looks lurked a vicious temper and the personality of a sociopath. She suspected that Connors thrived on the misfortune of others, and hid behind his badge and uniform in order to bully the weak, the poor, and all those his twisted mind considered inferior.

She had shared her concerns with Barnes. "He's every decent policeman's nightmare, Dave," she had told him. "We're proud of our department and have worked very hard to earn the public's cooperation and trust. Cops like Connors give the entire profession a black eye. He represents everything I hate in law enforcement, and I'm sure he knows how I feel. He wants to make detective in the worst way so he walks on eggshells around me, but I know what he says about me behind my back. His chances of making detective are about as likely as the Bard riding into my office on a skateboard to chat about a TV version of *Othello II*."

"We're all watching him, Alix," Dave had assured her. "That business about calling the INS on the Hispanic farm worker was his first major slip up, especially when the worker was here legally. If the man doesn't retain a sharp lawyer and sue, it'll be a miracle."

* * *

The plane was full. Meagan, returning from the conference, was exhausted from the three-day presentation. Dark smudges ringed her eyes as she leaned back and tried to rest. Time was running out, valuable time she desperately needed to plan what to do next. She did not for a moment underestimate Alix, sensing that every day she was inching closer to the truth, a formidable adversary as dedicated and focused as herself. And she saw the questions in Jon's eyes every time they met. Her missions were over. Now it was just a matter of time before Alix confirmed her suspicions.

One thing was certain. She would not face a trial, and only she would choose the payment society demanded. She did not yet know how or when, but she felt sure that a sign would come to point her in the right direction. After all, she was in control of her destiny now, and everything she had done had been for the right reason: to protect and avenge the women God had placed under her protection. And she knew that no one could have done it better. Only she would decide on the next step. Nothing, no one could stop her now, no matter what she decided to do.

But at night, she could not help seeing the faces of Steven, Rich Murdoch, and Paul O'Neil forever etched in her brain. The nightmares, which were becoming more and more frequent, would wake her and she would sit up in bed, drenched in cold perspiration, heart hammering in her chest, unable to remember who or where she was. Her headaches were growing more frequent now, her vision steadily getting worse, forcing her to squint in order to be able to see.

Last night, her sleep has been filled with such nightmares, and for the hundredth time she had relieved Steven's murder. She no longer wondered why she had not told the police that he had threatened her life, that they had struggled for the gun and it had gone off. It would not have worked, she knew, because it was her fault for keeping the abuse secret. They would not have believed her.

Down deep, and despite her growing madness, she knew that she had no one but herself to blame. But she could not explain the nightmares. She was doing God's work, wasn't she? He was guiding her steps all the way. She was certain of it.

But she wanted the nightmares to stop. She wanted to be at peace. She wanted …

The young woman seated next to her rose and excused herself, interrupting her thoughts, as she squeezed past Meagan on her way to the lavatory.

When she returned, she said, "It's nice to be able to get up and move around, isn't it? These seats aren't exactly built for comfort, especially on a long trip. I've been visiting my dad in Atlanta," the woman added. "How about you?"

"I went to a conference," Meagan said curtly. She closed her eyes to preclude further conversation. Exhausted, she settled down for a nap before the dinner service, but when it arrived, she took only one bite before pushing her tray away.

Irrationally, in a brief moment of clarity, she thought that it would be nice to tell this young woman what she had done. Deep down, and even though she was unable to acknowledge it, this was the worse part of her secret life: the isolation, the lack of human contact, the inability to talk to someone about what she felt and the horror of the murders.

But the moment of weakness soon passed. She did not need anyone to hear her story. It was hers and hers alone. People were too ignorant, too blind to understand what she had done and why. They would not acknowledge how clever she was, how well she had handled the problems of the women entrusted to her care. Well, she'd shown them all.

Lulled by the droning of the plane's engines, she closed her eyes again and finally fell into an exhausted sleep.

CHAPTER 21

After receiving Jon's summons, Alix went to his office and was surprised to see his grim, unsmiling face as she sat across from him.

"What's up?" she asked.

He was silent for a while. "Alix, Dan DeVoe, one of Meagan's colleagues, just left me," he finally said. "He told me he sensed that something was horribly wrong with her, but he had no idea what it might be or what to do about it, and knowing that Meagan and I were friends, he wanted to share his concerns with me. Apparently, he's been infatuated with her for years."

Alix leaned forward and motioned him to go on. She could tell this was difficult for him, and her heart went out to him.

"He asked if I had noticed how sick she looked," Jon said, "and how she was avoiding everyone, even though she had always been so gregarious and friendly. When he finally gets her to say a few words, her answers make no sense, and I have experienced the same thing myself. It's like she's in another world. Neither of us has a clue what to do about the situation."

"So what did you tell him?" She had a pretty good idea, but she did not want to put the words in Jon's mouth. Was he finally coming around and seeing that guilt was causing Meagan's apparent state of mind?

"I told him that I felt sure it had to do with Steven's death, but that I also sensed there was more to it than that."

Alix thought for a moment, trying to absorb his words. "Did she date Professor DeVoe?" she asked.

"Apparently Dan has asked her out repeatedly and she refused each time, but he sensed something behind her refusals that had nothing to do with Steven's death."

"Jon, have you tried to talk to her yourself to see if she'll confide in you? You guys are good friends, so ..."

"I tried," Jon interruped, sighing, "I really did, but she put me off and refused to discuss it. I'm convinced there's more to it than losing her husband, but I told Dan that if she didn't want to talk about the issue, neither he nor I could force her. She's a free agent."

Alix nodded pensively. Indeed, something was going on there. She had seen Meagan, who was always so immaculately groomed and put together, and wondered about the smeared lipstick, the disheveled clothes, the uncombed hair, and the haggard look in her face.

"Anything else?" she finally asked.

"Well, Dan senses that something bad is about to happen, an opinion I share, by the way, but since Meagan won't talk to us ..." A wave of his hand finished the sentence.

"Any idea what that might be?"

She saw Jon hesitate. "No, not really. I just have this feeling, that's all."

After she left his office, she, too, was filled with the same presentiment that something terrible was about to happen.

CHAPTER 22

Alix was at her desk surrounded by the usual array of files, phone wedged between shoulder and head as she made notes on a lined yellow pad while listening to Dr. Gardner.

"Paul O'Neil died of respiratory failure, Alix," the medical examiner said. "He seemed to be in perfect health, but this wouldn't be the first time hypoxemia has killed someone who was in great shape. I hate to admit it, but we doctors aren't God. It happens. You can release the body to the widow now."

Death! She was sick of it, whether it was natural, accidental, or murder. Why not let someone else worry about the violence, the family quarrels, the disappointments, the lack of appreciation? Maybe this was time to hang it all up and do what Lloyd had suggested.

Yet the thought of leaving the job she loved filled her with sadness, and worse, resentment. Still, she had promised Lloyd she would think about it, and think about it she would.

Soon.

Next week.

Eventually.

She lifted the phone from its cradle, intending to call Jon, only to discover he was holding for her on the other line. "Jon ..."

"What?"

She hesitated. "Nothing, never mind," she said finally, deciding that there was no point in telling him about her renewed efforts to track down the one elusive witness who might have seen Meagan leave campus. They had already discussed it to death, and his obstinacy bordered on blindness when it came to Meagan's guilt.

"I just wanted to let you know that Dr. Rathburn called me to check on the investigation before she left for her conference," she said.

She paused, reflecting on their previous conversation. "Odd, don't you think, that she won't talk to you about what's troubling her? You're a friend, a colleague, and a psychologist to boot. You'd know what to say and how to help."

It was Jon's turn to hesitate. "Maybe, but as I told you and Dan DeVoe earlier, there's nothing I can do unless Meagan asks. God knows I've tried, but she refuses to admit anything's amiss."

"She's probably trying to work things out in her own way."

Neither she nor Jon knew how right she was.

* * *

Paige called Meagan upon her return from Atlanta. "I've decided to break up with Shawn," Paige told her. "We're going to a party on Saturday, and I'm going to tell him then that I won't be seeing him anymore."

She went on to tell Meagan that, after much soul searching, she had finally admitted to herself that they were wrong for each other; that she liked Shawn, maybe even loved him a little, and she'd miss him, but not enough to put up with his temper tantrums and his moods.

Meagan felt that Paige had been sensitized by their earlier conversation and that she now realized that she had to call the relationship off. It sounded like Saturday would be the perfect opportunity to do so. She was relieved that she would no longer have to worry about Paige's safety, especially since she had no way of knowing how long she would be available to watch over her.

* * *

Vivian called Meagan after returning to Red Pine for Paul's funeral, and they agreed to meet at the Yellow Pelican for coffee.

The diner was an anachronism, a relic from the fifties that had been renovated without compromising its charm. It was a cozy meeting place, a favorite of college students, residents, and visitors attracted by its quaint and authentic ambience and by the colorful personality of its aria-singing owner. Its booths were dark, intimate, and conducive to private conversations. It was in one of those booths where the two women sat.

"I can't believe Paul's dead," Vivian said tearfully. "He was always so healthy. He never even caught a cold. And respiratory failure! Who would ever guess? And I still loved him despite everything, and I feel sad and guilty that he died alone. Maybe if I had come back and tried to work things out, I could have gotten him some help and he'd be alive today. I can't help thinking that it's all my fault."

"It might have happened whether you were home or not," Meagan said as she tried to hide her frustration. Sometimes she wondered why she had risked so much for women like Vivian who didn't seem to appreciate it and clung to the pathetic life they had known.

"And don't forget all those years of abuse and the two babies you lost because of him," Meagan added.

"How could I forget?" Vivian replied, her eyes filling up with tears. "But it was the only life I knew, Meagan. At least I had a home and someone to look after Jasmin and me."

Meagan struggled to hold in her temper. "What do you plan to do after the funeral?" she asked.

What am I doing here anyway, she thought with dismay. She was exhausted, light headed, and her head was pounding. This meeting with Vivian was the last thing she needed right now. Too bad Vivian didn't know that Meagan had done her a huge favor instead of shedding tears for a man who would have almost certainly continued to abuse her, maybe even killed her.

"We're going back to Maine," Vivian answered. "It's home now. I have a job I enjoy, and my sister and her family are nearby. Jasmin seems happy and she's too young to understand about her father's death. I hope she'll grow up with only good memories of him. I've joined a support group as you suggested, and they've been terrific."

She looked away, biting her lip. It was clear to Meagan that she was trying hard not to cry. *What's wrong with you?* Meagan almost screamed. *Why are you crying for your abuser and missing him instead of applauding his justly deserved death?*

"I'll sell our house here," Vivian continued. "It holds too many sad memories. Everyone knows by now that Paul abused me, and I feel that Jasmin and I need to put the past behind us."

This is too much, Meagan thought as Vivian droned on. She wondered now whether the women she had tried so hard to protect deserved what she was doing for them, the danger she was putting herself in. It had to stop now. She was just too weary, too disillusioned. But she knew how to put an end to it, and she would do it. Nothing, no one could stop her now.

With a supreme effort, Meagan nodded and got to her feet in an attempt to end the meeting, but Vivian kept on talking.

"You're doing the right thing by moving to Maine, Vivian, and please keep in touch," Meagan finally said, heading for the door. The diner's pleasant atmosphere now suffocated her, and the sight of her car parked at the curb had never seemed more appealing.

"I promise. Thanks again for all you've done, Meagan. I'll never forget you," Vivian said, following her across the room.

But Meagan knew they would never see each other again.

CHAPTER 23

As Alix was getting a cup of coffee in the precinct's lounge, Steve Belford came up to her. "Got a minute, boss?"

She motioned him toward her office and grimaced after taking a sip. Dave had been at it again. "I swear I'm going to issue an APB on Dave, Steve," she told him. "This coffee is nothing short of attempted murder. What's up? You look pleased about something."

"I just thought you'd be glad to know that our crime prevention program and the flyers we've been passing around the schools are producing some results. The program is really going great guns. We made one arrest this morning, and the folks out there are really a lot more aware, and it's making our job of keeping the creeps off the streets a lot easier. We've also had a couple of reports of unfamiliar cars driving around neighborhoods and of sightings by concerned parents, most of which turned out to be nothing. Yet one led to the arrest I just mentioned."

Well, she could sure use some good news today. She believed that there was nothing worse than men who preyed on small children and, were it up to her, she would gladly see them locked up for the rest of their miserable lives!

"That's great, Steve," she told him, smiling. "If we catch just one of those guys it's worth the effort."

"In fact," Steve said as he leaned over her desk, "I got a call a while back from a woman who saw a compact, a dark-colored car drive up her street a couple of weeks ago, but she could not give us a good description and she hasn't seen it since, so we didn't pursue it. But it shows you what I'm talking about. She was alert enough to call us, even if she never saw the car again and even felt a bit foolish about reporting it."

Warning needles pricked Alix's subconscious. Steve's words suddenly flashed in her brain like a huge Broadway neon sign.

A compact. A dark-colored car.

"What street was that on? And when did it happen?" she asked, eyes bright.

"Why the interest? I just told you nothing came of it."

"It rings a bell. Can you get me the information right away, Steve?"

"Be back in a sec," he replied. True to his word, he returned in less than five minutes and placed a sheet of paper on her desk. "Here's a copy of the report with the date and name of the woman who reported it. A Mrs. Laura Wingate. She lives on Tudor Lane."

Alix felt a pulse of excitement as something clicked. It just could not be a coincidence, could it? A dead man, an absent wife. Was her luck finally turning?

"Tudor Lane, Steve, isn't that where our loner death occurred?" she asked eagerly.

No need to connect the lines for him. Not yet. This was her baby and if she was wrong, she wanted to be the only one who knew it.

Steve seemed only mildly interested. "Yes, same street. Why do you ask?"

Alix knew that like so many of her colleagues, Steve took his cases step by step, distrusting creative leaps of imagination—the sort of leap she had just made. Besides, there was no reason why an executive, a man who lived under a great deal of pressure from his work, might not have died of respiratory failure, no matter how young he was.

What was it that Freud had said? Sometimes a cigar is just a cigar.

"Where's Dave?" she asked him.

"Out there talking to Jaime Ordoñez," he said pointing toward the hallway.

"Send him in right away, would you, *amigo*? And thanks, Steve, thanks a lot!"

Steve scowled, and after thinking about it, she realized why. He wanted in on her thought processes and he hated the fact that Dave was her first choice when it came to strategizing. But he was a good guy and he knew his limitations.

When Dave Barnes came in he took one look at her face and said, "Uh-oh, what's up, Alix?"

"Dave, Steve just told me that a dark-colored compact that didn't belong in the neighborhood was seen on Tudor Lane before O'Neil was found dead. Didn't he live on that street?"

"Yes, he did. So what?" he said, looking puzzled.

"But don't you see, Dave? It may be the same car George Brown saw the night Murdoch was killed."

"But so what?" he said again. "O'Neil wasn't murdered, Alix! Gardner said he died of respiratory failure, remember? What are you getting at?" Used as he was to her leaps of thought, he seemed at a loss to see where all this was going.

"Dave, please indulge me for while, okay? George Brown saw the car after Murdoch's murder, right? And then someone else sees a car that could be its twin around the time O'Neil died, right? I don't like it, Dave, I don't like it at all, and I want to talk to this Mrs.... " she looked at the report Steve had brought in, "Wingate, and I want you to come with me."

"But there must be hundreds of such cars in Red Pine alone!" he protested. "What do you expect to find?"

"I haven't got a clue, if you'll pardon the pun," she told him. "It's just one of my super-duper, world-class hunches."

Laura Wingate was home and agreed to see the detectives at once. When they arrived, she offered them tea and freshly baked cookies. Alix looked at them with longing, her sweet tooth battling with her common sense. Giving in meant an extra swim session at the Y and a five-mile run with Zeus. Common sense lost—the cookies were melt-in-your-mouth delicious.

"Mrs. Wingate," Alix said, "Thanks for seeing us on such short notice. You told Officer Belford that you saw a strange car on your street a few weeks ago," she added, coming right to the point in her usual no-nonsense manner, "and I wonder what made you decide to call with that information?"

"Well, a couple of weeks ago, my son brought this flyer home from school, and …" Laura went on to relate what had transpired since the flyer's arrival and how she had caught sight of Meagan's rented car during her daytime excursion up and down Tudor Lane.

Smart woman, Alix thought. She looks like the kind of person who doesn't let grass grow under her feet. Wish there were more alert citizens like her out there. People like her make our job a whole lot easier.

"But then my mother called, and I forgot all about the car," Laura continued, "and since it didn't come back, it no longer seemed important. I figured it was a delivery person or someone looking for an address. But when Timmy, my son, told me that some man approached one of his friends just a couple of blocks from here, I started to worry all over again.

"I thought to myself, what if there's another molester out there?" Laura added, reaching for a cookie. "Maybe there was something to that car after all, so I decided to report it, although a couple of weeks had gone by."

"But you never saw it again?" Alix asked.

"No," Laura said, shaking her head. "But I did keep looking for it, just in case."

"When was that, Ms. Wingate?" Alix asked her.

"Oh, roughly two weeks ago."

Before Paul O'Neil's death! No, this was really too much of a coincidence. And Alix did not believe in coincidences. The little, dark car seemed to be the key that connected the two murders.

"Were you home the evening of the eighteenth when your neighbor, Paul O'Neil, died? And if so, did you see anything un-usual?" she asked Laura.

Well, one could hope, right? And Laura seemed the type of person that would not miss anything that went on in the neighbor-hood, particularly if it might affect her family's well-being. Alix was becoming convinced that Laura Wingate was the kind of witness every investigator hopes for.

"Why do you ask?" Laura said sharply. "Was there something suspicious about Paul's death, detective?"

Yes, indeed, she is as smart as I think she is, Alix thought with admiration. She's definitely wondering where I'm headed with this.

"No, I just wondered if perhaps you might have seen the car again that day, or anything else out of the ordinary," Alix answered cautiously.

She saw that Laura wasn't satisfied with her response, but she rose to consult the wall calendar in her kitchen.

"There was a recital at Timmy's school that night," Laura told her. "We left the house a little before six o'clock and didn't get back until around nine. I saw nothing suspicious, and if that car had been anywhere near, I know I would have noticed because I know most of the cars our neighbors drive."

Now for the important questions. She wondered if Laura's answers would confirm her suspicions.

"Any idea what kind of car it was?" Alix asked.

"It was just an impression, but it looked like a small Honda or Toyota. Maybe a Datsun, about that size, you know? My mother has one like it."

"What about color?"

"Dark blue or black, I think."

She was on the right track, she knew it since George Brown had also mentioned a dark import.

"Can you tell me anything else about it?" Alix asked hopefully. "Was it a two-door or a four-door? Perhaps a recent model?"

"I'm sorry, I don't know," Laura said dejectedly. "It was only a glimpse."

Time for yet another important question. "Was a man or a woman driving?" Alix asked.

"Couldn't tell. Here, let me take you upstairs to show you where I was at the time so you can see for yourself," Laura said, getting to her feet.

She took both detectives up to Timmy's bedroom and pointed to the window from which she had observed the car. Alix saw that the pitch of the third-story roof and the angle of the house made it difficult to see little more than the top of passing cars.

Another expectation dashed. Another dead end. Another disappointment. Alix never got used to it. Damn, she thought, why couldn't she ever get a break in these murders? It was as if she was suddenly cursed with endless bad luck, and the feeling was foreign to her.

As Alix was about to thank Mrs. Wingate and rise to leave, Laura suddenly said, "You know, I couldn't swear to this under oath, but when I got to the kitchen and saw the car going around the corner, I got the impression that the driver might have been a woman wearing a scarf, but it could just as easily have been a man with a cap. I'm just not sure."

A woman wearing a scarf! The same woman Vince Hagstrom had seen at the scene of the Murdoch murder? Halleluiah! Was she finally getting the break she had been praying so hard for?

"Mrs. Wingate, did you know the O'Neils well?" she asked.

She saw Laura's demeanor cloud. "No, Vivian O'Neil didn't go out much. A few times, we heard Paul's raised voice and someone crying. My husband and I were sure Paul had a nasty temper and often wondered if he hit her. Our suspicions were confirmed when I saw Vivian sporting a shiner one day. Other than the customary hellos when one of us went in or out, we hardly ever spoke."

"Then you didn't socialize?"

"No. I asked Vivian a couple of times to come over for coffee, go shopping, you know, that sort of thing. She seemed so lonely. But she never accepted, although she looked like she might welcome the idea. I got the impression that somehow Paul wouldn't have approved," she added. "So after a while, I stopped trying."

It was obvious that Paul O'Neil was not on Laura's Man of the Year Award short list. Alix wondered why they had never reported the suspected abuse to the police and then guessed the answer to her own question. Alix suspected that, like many good people, they had probably not wanted to get involved in what they considered to be a family argument.

Yet her internal antenna had gone up. If Vivian O'Neil was battered like Eileen Murdoch, had she also sought help and joined a support group? And if so, which one?

"You know," Laura said, bringing Alix out of her reverie, "come to think of it, I haven't seen either Vivian or Jasmin, her little girl, for quite a while. I can't remember them ever being gone like that, just the two of them. Whenever they went somewhere, Paul was always with them."

"Do you have any idea where they might have gone?" Dave interjected as he saw the stunned look that had suddenly appeared on Alix's face.

Quite unexpectedly, Alix's mind had tripped on a startling thought and caught itself. Abuse? Rich Murdoch was dead. Abuse? Paul O'Neil was dead. And Steven Rathburn was also dead!

Madre de Dios! Alix thought. Wait a minute. Wait a goddam minute! Could it really be? Three dead men, all with perhaps one thing in common. Murdoch and O'Neil had abused their wives. Could it be that Meagan Rathburn had also been battered?

"No," Laura said she said in answer to Dave's question. "They kept to themselves and never came to the neighborhood's get-togethers. I don't know anything about their family or friends, and they never seemed to have company over."

So Vivian and her daughter had left sometime ago, Alix thought as she regained her composure. Why had they left and where had they gone? According to Laura, they weren't in the habit of taking trips by themselves to visit Grandma, Aunt Susan, or the cousins. Interesting that.

Still deep in thought, she almost missed Laura Wingate's next words.

"… and I noticed the porch light was off when we got back."

"I'm sorry, Mrs. Wingate, what did you say?" Alix asked.

"I remember the porch light being on at the O'Neil house when we left for the recital. When we got home, it had been turned off," Laura replied, looking at her curiously.

So Paul O'Neil *had* expected a visitor that night. As she had countless times before, Alix felt her pulse quicken. And as her thoughts telescoped in a domino effect like cars in a freeway crash, she was blinded by the truth. Bits of information fell into place, forming a perfect picture—the cheap red camisole in Meagan's bedroom with the torn bodice, the woman in red at the tavern. Had Meagan killed Rich Murdoch? Had she unconsciously picked a red dress to seduce him because her husband had bought her the garment to demean her, have her look like a whore when he abused her?

Now Alix had the motive for Steven Rathburn's murder she had hoped for. But why had it taken her so long to see what was before her eyes all this time? The seed of the theory that had sprouted from a corner of her mind was taking root and germinating with dazzling speed. It had to be the missing link she had been looking for all these weeks.

Alix thanked Laura Wingate, gave her one of her cards, and asked her to call if she remembered anything else. Suddenly, she could not wait to get out of there.

She saw the look in Dave's eyes and knew that he realized what was happening.

Like a bloodhound, Alix was on the scent once again.

* * *

Upon returning to the precinct, Alix asked Louise to get her the O'Neil file. After extracting the statement from Lee Edmonds and reading it a few times, she finally reached for the phone.

"Mr. Edmonds? Detective Mendez, Red Pine PD. When you spoke with Detective Barnes, you told him that Mr. O'Neil's family was away. Did you know they were gone? You didn't? I see. So how did you locate Mrs. O'Neil? Uh-huh. Oh, I see, the family's address book. Vivian's mother. You still have it? Good. Could you please give me her number in Calgary? No, no, just routine. I just need an answer to a couple of questions. Thanks for your help."

She had to talk to Vivian's mother to confirm what she already knew and what she suspected, and after identifying herself, she spoke in rapid, clipped sentences, listening intently and making notes on her yellow notepad. Then she called Vivian and added more notes to the yellow pad.

Half an hour later, fingers steepled under her chin, she thought for a long time about the facts the three conversations had revealed.

Everything dovetailed perfectly with the concept that had made its jack-in-the-box appearance at the Wingate home.

She had found a report about a family disturbance in the precinct's files involving the O'Neils, but she knew that Vivian was in Maine at the time of Paul's death. And now she also knew that the argument described in the police report was the reason for Vivian's and Jasmin's exodus.

Suddenly exhausted, she leaned back in her chair and closed her eyes. The investigations, coupled with the newly-discovered facts, were wearing her down, her mind full of jumbled thoughts, theories, and conjectures that she still could not prove but that she definitely couldn't ignore.

And then there was Lloyd. She could not put him off much longer. Although he was giving her plenty of time to make a decision, the question hung in the air between them whenever they were together, ironically enough, because of the very fact that they weren't discussing it.

Should she leave this place and focus on her marriage? Or should she tell him the truth—that to abandon her career would wrench her heart out? That she could not do it?

Sooner or later, she had to make a decision.

Love. Marriage. Commitment. Eons ago, they had been as far removed from her future as a trip to Saturn. She had been too busy, too committed to her career, too self-sufficient and independent. But even as she had tried to convince herself it was folly, she had fallen irrevocably, deliciously, helplessly in love.

She sighed. Marriage or career? It was all so complicated! And what if she was wrong about Meagan? And worse, what if she was right? But if her nascent theory had any validity, she planned to soon put it to the test.

The theory had emerged and taken shape as she and Dave drove back to the precinct from the Wingate home, and she had lovingly shaped it as an artist chisels a block of marble. Her legendary gut feeling told her she was on the right track. She could only hope that nothing she found in the file would create a major glitch.

She was so wrapped up in her thoughts that, though normally a conservative and safe driver, she drove right through a red light, eliciting a symphony of horns from other drivers and angry glances from pedestrians, some of whom felt compelled to shout at her unmarked car. She heard Dave chuckle at their choice of words—they were not terms of endearment. Then she spied the oncoming truck and saw Dave close his eyes and stiff-arm the car's console to brace himself for the inevitable collision.

Mortified, she gave him an apologetic smile. "Oops. Sorry about that," she told Dave, who appeared to be praying. She suspected that he was trying to quell the hammering of his heart and was undoubtedly never so glad that the precinct was right around the corner.

* * *

Alix's voice brimmed with excitement when she called Jon upon her return to the precinct. But she became evasive when he tried to elicit some details. He told her that he would come over after his last afternoon class.

Alix was not there when he arrived, so he waited impatiently in her office.

"Sorry I'm late," she told him, as she burst in a few minutes later. She offered him a cup of coffee, which he politely declined with a slight grimace that revealed that he, too, had been the target of Dave Barnes's coffee experiments. Tea was safer, so she fixed two big mugs of the *Constant Comment* they both liked.

"You look like something is bothering you. What's going on? Are you okay?" he asked.

"Yes. No. Not exactly," Alix replied. "I haven't been myself lately and haven't been sleeping worth a damn."

"Problems with the investigations?" he prodded.

"That, and at home, too," she said, avoiding his eyes and focusing instead on the little park just outside her office.

"You don't mean that you and Lloyd ... Alix, your marriage is one of the few that I know is rock solid! I can't imagine you guys having a problem. Why, you never even argue!" he said, looking stunned.

"Oh, we argue, all right, just like all married couples. But this isn't an argument. It's something else, and I still haven't decided what to do about it, which is why I hadn't mentioned it before. But now is as good a time as any, I guess."

He waited for her to speak as she struggled for the right words, toyed with items on her desk, spilled her tea, and finally blurted, "Lloyd wants me to resign and give up law enforcement."

She did not need to elaborate. She felt sure that from her obvious distress, he could surmise the intensity of the feelings with which she was wrestling.

"What are you going to do?" he asked gently.

"I don't know," she said helplessly, feeling as she was about to tear up but unable to do anything about it. "Giving up my job would be damned hard, but I love Lloyd, Jon. I'd do anything to make him happy."

"Alix, you need to give this a lot of thought," he told her, getting to his feet and putting an arm around her shoulders. "I know how you feel about your marriage, but I also know how much you love your job and how good you are at it. You've got to ask yourself if you won't resent Lloyd later if you give it all up, and how this will impact your relationship. I know you'll make the right decision, my friend, but let me know if there's anything I can do. Remember, I'm only a phone call away."

Her expression softened as she blinked away the tears and looked at him. She went to the window. Her heart was full as she realized how much she appreciated his kind concern and support right now when she needed it most. His friendship meant so much to her, but never more than now.

"I appreciate that, Jon," she said. "But to be honest with you, I really haven't had time to think it through, yet I can't avoid it forever. It isn't fair to Lloyd."

Her mood suddenly changed, and she was all business again. Now her face reflected excitement combined with a touch of sadness. She realized the magnitude of what she was about to say, knowing the impact it would have on him, but there was no gilding the lily.

Well, she thought, here goes nothing.

"Considering the theory I came up with," she went on, "maybe

I'll soon be able to wrap things up. I spoke with a woman by the name of Laura Wingate today, Jon, and she told me some things that threw a brand new light on the investigations. In fact, the more I thought about it, the more sense my theory made. And it was confirmed by the three phone conversations I had afterwards.

I must warn you," she went on. "You're not going to like it, but you need to know, Jon. A while ago, I talked to an old gentleman who lives a few doors down from the Murdoch house. He saw a car pulling away from the curb around the time of the murder. He couldn't identify either the car or the driver and said only that it was a small, dark automobile and that he thought it was foreign made."

"Yes, I know all that, Alix," he said. "You mentioned it earlier."

"Yes, but it meant little at the time," she told him. "Mr. Brown also said that the car drove about a block without headlights. I know this will sound nuts to you, but somehow I *knew* the murderer was behind the wheel and that it was a woman, probably our mysterious Jen.

"And then," she went on, bumping into a chair as she began to pace, "I reviewed the file and found a call made by a Mrs. Wingate. Mrs. Wingate is a neighbor of Paul O'Neil, the guy who was found dead in his house, so I called and talked to her."

She went on to tell him what Laura Wingate had told her. Then, placing both hands on her desk, she leaned forward.

"Don't you see?" she said, speaking faster now as her excitement grew. "Two cars fitting pretty much the same description were seen, once at the scene of a murder and once at the scene of what appears to be a natural death. Okay, I'll grant you it wasn't much, but then Mrs. Wingate also said that Paul O'Neil abused his wife."

Jon nodded but said nothing, motioning her to go on with a wave of his hand.

"Then I spoke with Lee Edmonds, O'Neil's partner who found the body," she continued, looking at Jon to see if he was following her. She decided that he was since he had not interrupted her narrative.

"And he referred me to Mrs. Henderson, Vivian O'Neil's mother," Alix went on, "and finally, I talked to Vivian who confirmed that she was abused. And I learned some other interesting things, too. That Mrs. O'Neil and her child were running from her husband after spending a couple of weeks in a shelter."

Why was Jon so silent, she wondered? Did he suspect where she was going with this? What was he thinking?

"So I thought to myself, what do we have here?" she said, her speech quickening as if trying to catch up with her thoughts. "Two battered wives who attended the same support group—I know, I checked. One of the husbands is murdered. The other dies home alone, ostensibly of respiratory failure. Aside from that, the men had nothing in common. Murdoch was a blue-collar worker, O'Neil a professional. But I'll stake my life against those two deaths as being coincidental."

Still Jon said nothing. What in the hell is going on behind this blank façade? It wasn't like him to remain silent for so long when he had always been too ready to ask questions. But not this time. Not today.

"I don't believe O'Neil died of respiratory failure, Jon. Not for a second," she went on as her pacing picked up speed. "At least, not without help. I think the same woman who killed Murdoch also murdered him. Laura Wingate caught a glimpse of the driver as the car went around the corner. She thinks it might have been a woman wearing a scarf. And Vince Hagstrom says he, too, saw a woman wearing a scarf leaving the area the night Murdoch was killed."

She finally turned toward him. Her expression was purposeful now. "So if my assumption that O'Neil was murdered is correct, then this brings me to the conclusion that the links weren't the men but the women. The women, Jon! Eileen Murdoch and Vivian O'Neil. Our killer is clever, make no mistake about that. The O'Neil murder—and again, I am sure now that he didn't die a natural death—was beautifully planned and executed, and disguised to look like respiratory failure. We're up against someone who's not only intelligent, but also extremely motivated. And that's what led up to my final conclusion."

And still Jon did not speak, but the expression she saw reflected on his face was one of infinite sadness, as comprehension finally seemed to dawn on him.

Alix's voice became thoughtful. "I was almost sure after Murdoch was murdered, that the killer was female. And I told Lloyd that I sensed strong emotions at work behind the killing. Fury, rage, whatever, I didn't know.

"As you know," she added, "female serial killers are pretty rare, and we don't know much about them—Martha Beck, Aileen Wuornos, and a few others. But even then, this woman doesn't fit the mold."

She sat down next to him, her eyes reflecting only compassion now, knowing the distress her next words were going to cause him, yet knowing she could no longer postpone the inevitable.

"Someone loaned Vivian O'Neil the money to get away from her husband, Jon. Someone who wanted to make sure the field was clear for what she had in mind and make certain Vivian wouldn't be blamed. Someone who facilitated the support group both Eileen Murdoch and Vivian attended. Someone smart enough to kill twice and cover her tracks. Someone who would go to any length to protect the women she counsels."

She stopped, pausing for effect like an actress about to make an entrance. "Meagan Rathburn killed those two men. I'd stake my career on it."

She had expected astonishment, denial, shock. Yet Jon displayed none of those emotions, and she felt curiously disappointed. She had not realized until now how important it was to her that he see all this as she saw it. It was not enough for him to grant that the possibility existed that she might be right. He had to be as convinced of it as she was. And yet …

But when Alix saw the look in his eyes, she thought that perhaps she had won him over after all. She sensed that he was thinking about everything she had told him, and from her past experience during their long working association, she felt sure that he was doing so with his usual impartiality and fairness. And she also believed that the fears, which she now suspected he had carefully hidden from her so far, had become reality. But perhaps this was just wishful thinking on her part.

"You're saying that she killed these men because of what happened to their wives?" he finally asked in a tremulous voice.

"That's exactly what I'm saying."

"Did anyone see her at the O'Neil house before his death?"

"I'm about to check that out, along with some other ideas I have," she replied.

She put her hand on his arm, realizing how difficult all this was for him to accept, yet she felt that it was important for him to have the whole story.

"I'm sorry, my friend, but it's the only thing that makes sense."

Despite her euphoria, his stricken face sobered her. It was difficult to add water to an already-full pot, but there was no way to soften the impact of what she knew to be the truth. "There's something else, Jon. Now I also know she killed her husband."

"Alix, for God's sake, not that old chestnut again!" he exploded. "You looked for a motive and couldn't find one. You tried to break her alibi and couldn't do that either. Give it up, Alix. Meagan didn't kill Steven, even assuming she killed the others."

She looked at him long and hard, unmoved by his anger. "Are you trying to convince me or yourself, Jon?" she said quietly. "She does have a motive because I believe in my gut that, like the other wives, Meagan was battered. Steven probably did it once too often, and she finally killed him."

She stopped to give him time to absorb her words. "Everyone, including you, told me how well the Rathburns got along, how devoted they were to each other, how solicitous he was of her, and it blinded me to the possibility of domestic violence as a motive. It never entered my mind until what I heard today made me realize it was the only possible one.

"And once it became a possibility," she went on, "I started to do some checking into the Rathburn's background before they came to Red Pine. I found an old lady in San Francisco, a Mrs. Collingwood, who used to live next door to them. She remembers hearing Steven yelling at his wife and, on several occasions, seeing Meagan bruised and seemingly in pain. She was sure Steven hit her, but Mrs. Collingwood is old and lives alone, and she was afraid of Steven, so she said nothing."

As she looked at Jon's face, she saw the conflicting emotions and the slow, gradual acceptance of what she had told him. She knew how difficult this must be for him.

She knew how intelligent and rational Jon was. Therefore, she believed that, down deep, he might have sensed that Steven's possessiveness was something other than love, and that abuse would certainly give Meagan a motive powerful enough to kill.

"What are you going to do, Alix?" he finally asked her. "There is still the matter of her alibi."

"I'm going to break it, Jon. I'm going to pick every detail apart again. I'm going to prove that I'm right, once and for all, if it's the last thing I do. And then I'm going to arrest her."

She felt good now, really good. She was on her way to the finish line at last. But, as elation and a sense of triumph filled her, she saw Jon suddenly spring to his feet and rush out of her office, leaving Alix to stare at his departing back.

After recovering from her surprise, she buzzed Dave Barnes. "Since we believed O'Neil died of a heart attack, the guys didn't follow the usual investigation procedures, right? Meaning that no one vacuumed the scene?" she asked him.

"Of course not! What for?"

"I want you to send the lab rats to the O'Neil place right away and see what they come up with. I want them to go over everything with a fine toothcomb and treat the area as if it were a crime scene. Then I want the stuff to go to Sally Moore in the lab pronto. I'll call her and tell her what I'm looking for."

He looked at her, perplexed. "You're the boss, but are you going to tell me what's going on or has this suddenly become top secret?" he said, sounding hurt.

"I always knew it was going to take a *deus ex machina* to solve this case, Dave, and I think we just got it."

"Say what? Look, boss, it's bad enough you chatter at me in Spanish already. Now you wanna throw Latin in, too? My days with the Jesuits are long behind me."

"An intervention from the gods, Dave," she said, shooting him a devilish smile. "I don't think Paul O'Neil died of natural causes and I believe Meagan Rathburn killed him, just as she killed Rich

Murdoch."

"Feel like sharing the details with me?" he said, eyes wide.

"Soon, Dave, soon, I promise. I still have a few more things to check out."

"Okay," he said, lifting his arms in surrender, "I'm on my way."

She leaned back in her chair after he had gone, mind churning, as finally she reached for a pencil and called the lab.

"Sally," she told the lab supervisor. "Dave Barnes will be down soon with some evidence the guys are going to be collecting shortly. I'd like you to go through the stuff personally, if you don't mind, and see if you can find some hairs, especially long, dark brown ones."

"Sure, Alix, no problem, but is this a priority or can it wait? We're swamped over here," Sally said plaintively.

"Yes, it's urgent, Sally, and if you do it, I promise you a date with Jorge, my gorgeous, wealthy cousin whom you met last year at my house. He's coming for a visit in the next month. What do you say?"

"Done," Sally said promptly. "But only if you make it two dates."

Impatience consumed Alix until the team returned, taking the evidence vacuum to the property room where each item collected was tagged before being delivered to Sally.

And then she waited. And waited. It seemed as though all she ever did was wait. She knew that Dave, who had haunted her office all day, sensed how tensed she was but true to form he, too, had waited, although his eyes held a silent accusation.

But Alix refused to feel guilty. To tell him too much too soon might jinx the whole operation.

"Alix, no long brown hairs, sorry," Sally said when she finally called back later that afternoon. "We found some short brown and black hairs, which came from the bathroom and bedroom, and lots of cat hair. But I checked out some short, blonde hairs that apparently came from the living room and …"

Alix heard the hesitation in Sally's voice. "Blonde hairs? Where exactly did they come from?" she asked.

"The seat of one of the armchairs. And there's something peculiar about them"

Alix white-knuckled the phone. "What?"

"They're human hair, all right, but they are not from a person. They have no roots. They're from a wig made with human hair."

Alix leaned back in her chair and closed her eyes, letting out a huge sigh of relief. Suddenly, she felt as if a weight had lifted from her chest. Now if she could only prove the second part of her theory …

"Sally," she said, lowering her voice. "I'm going to run to the property room and bring you other hairs taken from the Murdoch crime scene. I want you to run the same tests on them, and *rápido*, okay?"

"Gotcha!"

"Well?" Dave asked impatiently after rapping on her door and entering her office.

"I think we've just had a breakthrough. The evidence vacuum picked up some blonde hairs on one of the armchairs in the O'Neil's living room," she told him.

He gave her a vacant look. "That's supposed to mean something?"

"They came from a wig, Dave, a blonde, human hair wig. And I'm willing to bet my vintage T-Bird that some of the long brown hairs found at the scene of the Murdoch murder also came from a wig. Don't you see? O'Neil didn't die of a respiratory failure. He was murdered, Dave, murdered by the same person who killed Rich Murdoch and Steven Rathburn. Dr. Meagan Rathburn."

Dave looked at her in disbelief. So this is what she had been mulling over all this time and had refused to share with him? Although glad that she had finally confided in him, he was hurt and angry at her refusal to take him into her confidence.

"I don't know how she did it, how she managed to pass a murder off as a natural death, but she did it, all right," Alix continued. "I think she wore different wigs and drove the small dark car both times. I've asked Sally to check the hairs from the Murdoch house to see if she'll confirm my theory and am waiting to hear from her. And Dave, we've got to get Doc to perform another autopsy on

O'Neil and look for another cause of death."

"What specifically?"

"I don't know. Something other than respiratory failure."

"Jesus, it's a hell of a theory, boss," Dave said, shaking his head. "You did say you suspected Professor Rathburn, but I didn't take you seriously. Yet this might explain the footprint that Harrison found in the living room after they went to the O'Neil house the second time. You remember it, don't you?"

"What footprint? Why didn't I know about it?"

"It was in the report, Alix. Perhaps you overlooked it—a faint, muddy print of a small-size shoe the guys found in the living room near the armchair where the blond hairs were," he replied. "But what's Meagan Rathburn's motive? And why kill O'Neil and Murdoch? What's the connection?"

"Because both beat up their wives," Alix told him triumphantly, "and both women had left them or were in the process. Both were in the support group that Professor Rathburn led. And, by the way, she is the one who gave Mrs. O'Neil the money to get away. And a call I just made to an old lady in San Francisco proves that Steven Rathburn also beat up his wife, which means she probably killed him, too."

She paused for breath and looked at Dave who looked stunned and was shaking his head. "Call Vivian O'Neil, Dave. She may still be in town. Tell her that some new evidence has surfaced and that we need to perform another autopsy. In the meantime, I'll call Doc."

Dr. Gardner was out but returned her call within the hour.

"Doc, you've got to do a second autopsy on the respiratory failure victim," she said.

"Why? You got a problem with my findings?"

"Not with your findings, Doc, but what if I were to tell you there's something funny about that death, that I don't think he died of respiratory failure? Would you consider checking for other causes?"

"Sure, but what specifically?" the old ME asked.

"That's just it, I don't know. Anything that has symptoms that are similar to respiratory failure but caused by something man-made."

"Well," he said, "I can perform some tests on liver, spleen, hair, even eyeball fluid that would detect, say, a specific poison. Get me the body and I'll get right on it."

Half an hour later, she turned around to see Dave standing by her desk looking somber.

Her heart fell. "What now?" she asked, dreading the answer.

"Vivian O'Neil has left Red Pine," he told her. "I called Mrs. Edmonds, and she said she drove Vivian to the airport yesterday. She was going to see her parents in Canada, then fly back to Maine to rejoin her daughter."

She gave him a blank look. "So what's the problem? We can reach her by phone at her parents, can't we?"

Her heart constricted when she saw him shake his head. "No autopsy, Alix. According to Mrs. Edmonds, Paul O'Neil's body was cremated."

Alix furiously slapped the palm of her hand on her desk. So an autopsy was out, but she had not exhausted all the possibilities yet. She had come too far to give up now.

Reaching for the phone, she called Laura Wingate and asked her if she remembered seeing a woman with short blonde hair visiting the O'Neil home, particularly after Vivian and Jasmin had left town.

"No, I don't believe so," Laura said. "Like I told you, they had few visitors. Although I'm home most of the time, I don't make it a practice to check on my neighbors, but I think I would have noticed. Sorry, Detective, I don't remember seeing such a woman."

But there *was* such a woman. Alix was certain of it. And she was going to prove that the woman was Meagan.

* * *

Sally's enthusiasm oozed through the phone line. "Alix, I went over the brown hairs you brought down. Some belong to the deceased Mrs. Murdoch, who, I am told, had long, brown hair, but get this. Two of the other brown hairs, longer ones, also came from a human hair wig. Does this help?"

Alix leaned back in her chair. Relief, excitement, and pride filled her, her old self-confidence washing over her in rejuvenating waves. "Sally, I could kiss you," she exclaimed. "Thank you. Thank you so much!"

She could not stop smiling. Her suspicions were confirmed, and now she was positive that O'Neil had not died of natural causes and that the same woman, wearing two different wigs, had killed Rich Murdoch.

Meagan Rathburn.

But she was well aware that everything was still all guesses, conjectures, and circumstantial evidence.

She reached for the phone again. A pleasant contralto came on the line. "Margaret Woodruff, may I help you?"

"This is Detective Mendez, Red Pine Police Department, Ms. Woodruff. I understand you worked for Paul O'Neil?"

"Yes, I did. He was a great boss, and I'll miss him," the secretary said sadly.

"I need to see you and ask you a few questions."

"Of course. Is there something wrong?" Margaret asked.

"Just routine," Alix told her. "I'll be there in a few minutes."

Although she was anxious to speak with O'Neil's secretary, Alix took her time driving downtown, giving herself an opportunity to digest the latest information. A woman was doing the killing, no question about that. A woman wearing wigs who had already killed twice. No, three times, and she might strike yet again. A woman who might well be a respected professor. Was Meagan killing out of anger, revenge, or concern for the women to whom she was so devoted? Were these the emotions that made her blood boil? Had she killed her own husband in self-defense?

Margaret Woodruff was a short plump woman in her early fifties. She wore a tailored navy blue suit with a white silk blouse and an antique cameo at her throat. Her hazel eyes were thoughtful and alive with intelligence. Lovely gray hair, cut short in an attractive style, framed her face and softened its long, oval shape. Her office looked like her: efficient, uncluttered, functional.

"Ms. Woodruff," Alix said, "this is very important. You must know Paul O'Neil's friends and clients pretty well. I know this is a rather delicate question, but please bear with me. We know his wife and daughter were out of town when he died. Can you tell me the circumstances, and whether or not he was … inclined to date other women, particularly a woman with short blonde hair, around the time of his death? You needn't feel disloyal, your answers are really quite vital."

The secretary was clearly taken aback. "I don't think so, Detective," she said, frowning. "If he did, he was very discreet about it. He seemed quite fond of his wife and little girl, although I …" She stopped abruptly and looked ill at ease.

"Yes?" Alix said, smiling encouragingly.

"Well, first, I found out by accident that his family was gone and that he had hired a private detective to locate them. The man sent his bill here rather than to the house, and Mr. O'Neill was very upset about it and yanked it out of my hand. Another time, I heard him talking on the phone as I went into his office. He was speaking with the detective whose name was on the bill. His wife's name was mentioned, but he waved me out of the room so I wasn't able to hear more."

Alix nodded. This confirmed what Vivian's mother, and Vivian herself, had told her. "And what was the other thing?"

"Well, a couple of weeks before he died, Mr. O'Neil had a new client." Margaret Woodruff blushed. "I love nice clothes and jewelry, you see, and this woman wore a gorgeous and expensive-looking green suit, and when she paid her bill, I noticed she wore the most beautiful diamond solitaire I've ever seen."

Alix felt her pulse quicken. A solitaire. Meagan Rathburn had such a ring. She remembered seeing it the day of Steven's murder, sparkling brightly on Meagan's finger.

"Can you give me this woman's name and address?" she asked Margaret.

"Yes. If you'll wait just a minute, I'll get them for you." She soon returned with a slip of paper. "Here you are. Joan Campbell, and here are her address and phone number. The reason I mentioned her is that Mr. O'Neil seemed rather taken with her. Funny, I've never seen him look at a client quite that way before, but I can't say I blame him. She was a very attractive woman."

When Alix asked Margaret to describe the woman, the secretary told her that she had been about five foot three, a petite blonde with a great figure and blue eyes. When Alix inquired if the woman could have been wearing a wig, Margaret seemed startled but admitted that it might have been the case.

Mrs. Campbell, if that was who she was, had paid in cash and had not made another appointment. As for the purpose of the consultation, O'Neil had told Margaret that this client was getting a divorce and needed assistance with her financial affairs.

A perfect cover up, Alix thought, a client seeking financial advice. It would be easy to meet him alone on another occasion. But in his own home? The woman has guts, Alix thought with grudging admiration.

She thanked Margaret Woodruff, and as she left Paul O'Neil's office, the names repeated themselves in Alix's head like a drumbeat.

Jen. Joan Campbell. Meagan Rathburn. Whoever you are, whatever your reasons, I'm going to get you. It wasn't personal at first, but it is now, and I'm picking up the gauntlet.

She had uncovered Meagan's motive. Now all she had to do was shatter her alibi.

CHAPTER 24

The evening did not bode well. When Shawn arrived to pick her up for the party, Paige reminded him of her need to leave early, causing him to become as fractious as a three-year-old denied an ice cream cone. To get even, he had again pressed the issue of her moving in with him, and she had in turn become tense and defensive. Had she harbored any doubts about her decision to break off the relationship, none remained now. Yet she wasn't looking forward to telling him that tonight would be their last date.

Ten o'clock arrived, and Paige looked around for Shawn. They were silent during the first few minutes of the drive home from the party, but Paige knew it was just a matter of time before the inevitable showdown. She did not have to wait long.

"What the hell do you mean, embarrassing me like that in front of my friends?" Shawn snarled, letting the car swerve over the centerline. "You ought to know that when I party, I like to party. I don't need you whining about having homework to do."

Paige tensed. "I wasn't trying to embarrass you, Shawn, but we discussed this when I agreed to go to the party with you," she told him. "You knew I had to leave early, so it isn't like I sprang it on you."

"It makes me look bad, that's all. Like you're too good to

spend time with me and my friends. You want them to think I'm pussy whipped?"

"Shawn, I enjoy your friends very much, especially Donna, but I still have at least two hours of homework and …"

He seized on her words. "Yeah, I saw you talking with her. What did that gossipy little bitch say to you anyway? She was talking about me, right? She doesn't like me and the feeling is mutual."

"I thought she was really nice, and we talked about lots of things," she told him.

"Well, you'd better not listen to anything she says," he told her. "She likes to cause trouble. And by the way, I want a decision tonight about you moving in."

Here it was, the confrontation she had been dreading all evening. She took a deep breath and decided that honesty was the best policy, wishing belatedly that one of her classes had been in conflict management.

"Shawn," she said, "I've thought about it a lot, and I decided that it's best if we don't see each other for a while. I'm not comfortable moving in with you. It's too early in our relationship and I don't have the time to devote to you that I know you want. It's nothing personal. I really like you a lot and …"

"Like me?" he roared. "I thought you loved me. And you promised you'd move in with me!"

"I never promised," she said wearily. "I just said that I'd think about …"

"Well, you don't have to *think* anymore, okay?" he said, mimicking her. "I've got women waiting in line for a chance to go out with me. You always did think you were too good for me, you bitch!"

"That's ridiculous!" she said hotly. "I only wanted to make sure that …"

He did not let her finish. Livid with rage, he leaned over without slowing down and released her seat belt. "You don't want to be with me anymore? Fine, that's your problem!" he yelled as his fist connected with her jaw.

And without another word, he reached across her body,

opened the two-seater's passenger door, and shoved her out from the fast-moving vehicle.

Some split-second instinct told Paige to roll and cover her head with her arms.

The last thing she remembered was the sound of the car engine roaring away and the ground racing up to meet her.

* * *

Meagan was jolted into awareness by the phone. It was becoming increasingly difficult for her to fall asleep, and she had begun to rely heavily on sleeping pills in order to fall into a drugged, dreamless sleep. Now, disoriented, she forced herself to pick up the phone. The luminous numbers on her clock radio told her that it was eleven o'clock.

"'lo?" she whispered.

"Dr. Rathburn," a woman replied crisply, "this is the Red Pine Community Hospital Emergency Room. We have a young woman here, Paige Chatfield. She's badly hurt. We can't ask her about next of kin because she is unconscious, but your card was in her purse with a home number on it, and …"

"I'll be right there," Meagan interrupted, fully awake now.

She broke all speed records getting to the hospital, feeling as if her heart was about to fly out of her chest. Although she tried to control herself, she almost felt like her old self for the first time in weeks.

But at her first sight of Paige, she felt faint. Tubes protruded everywhere, and Paige's platinum hair was caked with blood. What she could see of the girl's face was covered with cuts, bruises, and abrasions. Her eyes were closed and her breathing shallow and labored.

Meagan immediately knew that whatever had happened to Paige had been caused by Shawn Connors. She just knew it, and dark rage burned inside of her. She was sure that animal had beaten her so brutally that she was barely recognizable.

The doctor who was standing by the bed said, "Her boyfriend brought her in and said that she fell from a moving car. It's too soon to tell, but it doesn't look good. She has multiple fractures and abrasions, a concussion, a broken arm, and she'll no doubt need extensive plastic surgery. But the worst damage is to her spinal cord. I'm not sure she'll ever walk again. I've called one of my colleagues in for consultation. He's one of the best neurosurgeons in the Pacific Northwest, but I'm less than optimistic. If she lives, and it's less than fifty-fifty right now, she may never walk again."

Meagan stood there looking at Paige's inert body. Paige, paralyzed for life, perhaps even dying? And all because of that miserable, vile creature who did not deserve to live? She felt herself unable to breathe, unable to think, unable to speak.

Without a word, she turned on her heels and left the hospital. She had a lot to do and almost no time to do it.

Time had finally run out for her, but not before she would exact revenge on Shawn Connors in a way he could not possibly imagine.

* * *

With shaking hands, Meagan dressed in a black turtleneck sweater, dark stirrup pants, ski cap, and dark sneakers, and tied her shoe laces only with considerable difficulty because of the blurring of her eyes and the unsteadiness of her hands. As with Rich Murdoch, she had shadowed Shawn Connors for a few days to study his routine. But, unlike the Murdoch scenario, she had little time to plan her move. Time was now a luxury she could no longer afford.

She had put her affairs in order a few days ago, and she had written and mailed out the crucial letter that was such a vital part of her plan. Phase One was in place. This would be the last, and perhaps the most important, of her missions, and she could leave nothing to chance.

She felt strangely detached now that she had decided on how to die, and she moved as if an alien force was controlling her body as she performed her daily chores: going to the university, teaching her classes, returning home, acting like a well-programmed robot waiting for its plug to be pulled, feeling nothing, wishing or hoping for nothing, functioning in a vacuum. And always so tired, so very tired!

But she had a job to do, and she must focus on it fully.

It took her only a short while to drive to Shawn's apartment. It was the same kind of night when Rich Murdoch had met his fate—dark, still, with rain hanging by its toes at the edge of the sky, ready to let go. Yet summer was near now, and she could feel its perfumed breath warming her face. She closed her eyes and caught the fragrance of the first roses of the season drifting through the night.

Ten o'clock. Shawn's apartment was dark, as was most of the complex. She guessed that the tenants were mostly working people who went to bed early. According to her research, Connors would be out on patrol until eleven o'clock, which gave her plenty of time to do what she had to do.

Unexpectedly, fog rolled in, clinging to her eyelashes and dampening the bit of hair that peeked from under the black ski cap. Although it reduced her vision even further, she knew that it would help conceal her presence. She went around the complex and discovered that each unit included a tiny patio, large enough for only a couple of chairs, each with its own gate.

Fortunately, Shawn's apartment was on the ground floor. Finding the patio adjacent to his apartment, she let herself in and discovered that the gate was well oiled and soundless.

The sliding glass door leading into the apartment was locked. From where she stood, she saw that a safety bar held the door in place. Now she would have to try the front door, a riskier proposition but her only chance since she did not want to break the glass door and leave telltale signs of her visit.

After closing the gate, she went around the building and unscrewed the porch light, pleased to note that the angle of each apartment was such that the front door was shielded by the intersection of the two walls, forming a protected area undetectable from either the street or another apartment.

Taking the credit card she'd brought with her, she slid it between the lock and the doorjamb and was inside in just a few seconds. She saw that the deadbolt was unlocked and wondered why Connors, so careful to put the safety bar in place on the sliding glass door, would forget to double-lock his front door.

Using her penlight, she looked around the apartment and found what she was looking for in the kitchen. Carefully wrapping her handkerchief around the item, she put it in the plastic bag she carried in her purse. She saw that the kitchen was small but well equipped with several state-of-the-art appliances and gadgets. Apparently Shawn Connors liked to cook, but she wasn't here to speculate about his culinary skills. She needed to get going.

As the familiar feeling of exhaustion overcame her, she paused for a few seconds and glanced at her watch. Ten thirty. Plenty of time to sneak back out undetected and go home.

She had worn the surgical gloves, and since she had not removed them, there was no need to take valuable minutes to wipe anything off. She locked the front door, screwed the light bulb back into its socket, and left without being observed. As she walked past the shrubs leading up to the entrance of the complex, she heard the roar of a motorcycle engine and saw a single headlight, approximately two blocks down the street, headed her way.

Connors was home early! A few minutes earlier and he would have caught her red-handed. But perhaps it was more than luck. She was destined to succeed in this mission. Nothing could stop her now, especially that idiot Connors. Little did he know he was about to play the lead in her newly written drama.

She quickly dodged behind a large oak tree, her slim, black-clad silhouette blending in with its trunk, fog surrounding her like thick cotton batting, and she held her breath as he passed within six feet without detecting her presence.

She realized that it had been a close call. Too close for comfort.

She waited until he had parked his motorcycle under the carport and gone inside before releasing the breath she hadn't realized she was holding and hurrying toward the Toyota that awaited her around the corner.

* * *

"Jesus, Jon! You mean you had your own suspicions and you didn't share them with me? What were you waiting for, the Second Coming?" Alix exclaimed.

"I'm sorry, Alix, I really am," he said. "I haven't slept for two nights, thinking about this. The signs were all there, but I guess I didn't interpret their significance. Probably didn't want to. And besides, I couldn't prove it. I still can't, but it's all so clear now. Meagan's obviously worn out, exhausted, like she's at the end of her rope. And her appearance! She, who's always looked like a fashion plate, now looks like death warmed over. Her makeup is a mess. Her clothes are stained. When she speaks, she often stops in mid-sentence, obviously forgetting what she's going to say. And that haunted look in her eyes! She's got to be at the end of her rope, physically and emotionally."

He leaned back, the lack of sleep evident in the deep shadows under his sapphire eyes. "The stress of holding everything together, of killing without being detected while trying to lead a normal life must be tremendous," he added. "I've researched the subject extensively, read every book and article I could lay my hands on, even called a friend at the FBI's Behavioral Science Unit. All the signs point to a stress-related breakdown. Grief about Steven's death might have explained some things but not others."

Although Alix was thrilled that Jon had come around to her way of thinking, her glee was mixed with sadness as she saw his face and heard his voice, realizing how difficult all of this was for him. Knowing how deep his feelings were about trust and friendship, she felt sure that he felt betrayed by Meagan's failure to confide in him.

"I suspected for sometime there was more to her behavior than the tragedy," Jon continued, speaking quietly but convincingly, "and I'm sorry I didn't tell you any of this when we last met, but I couldn't. Yet, to quote Sir Arthur Conan Doyle, 'When you have eliminated the impossible, whatever remains, however improbable, must be the truth.' I saw it was the only thing that fit. I'm sorry I dashed out of your office like but I just couldn't ..."

He stopped, unable to continue.

"I wondered what was wrong," Alix told him. "You were so quiet, and when you bolted out of my office, I knew there had to be a damn good reason. We've known each other for too long, Jon. We've sparred and parried, spent hours rehashing every possibility, every clue. We've been a team working toward the same objective, often playing devil's advocate with each other, but this time, you weren't acting like yourself, and now I know why."

She paced energetically for a while. "So you agree with my theory that she was acting as avenging angel on behalf of the women?" she asked, dropping down in a chair next to him and upending a stack of files with her elbow.

"I can only guess," he replied. "What motivates women to kill? Pretty much the same as men. Love, money, greed, jealousy, and you eliminated all of those, which left only two that would incite someone like Meagan to murder: hatred and revenge. They're powerful forces, Alix, so in that respect, yes, I do agree with you."

"Good. Still, I find it difficult to visualize someone like her killing people. She must be crazy!" Alix exclaimed.

"She's not crazy, not in the way you mean," Jon replied soberly. "She's on a personal quest for some type of dark justice only she understands, and I sense that she doesn't care if she gets caught. She's given up on life."

"But why?"

"I don't know, Alix, I just don't know."

"Well, revenge's a powerful motive for someone like her who works so closely with the women," Alix said pensively. "Eileen's death might have been an accident, but Meagan probably didn't believe it. And the private detective Vivian's husband had hired was about to reveal his wife and daughter's whereabouts."

She picked up a pencil and did a spirited tattoo on her desk. "So she took it upon herself to avenge one and protect the other. By the way, I found out that Joan Campbell doesn't exist. The address and phone number she gave to O'Neil's secretary were phony."

He nodded wearily. "I understand now why she wouldn't talk to me. I would have urged her to turn herself in and seek help, and she knew it, so what was there to talk about? Obviously, she wouldn't have complied, and by telling me, I would have become an accomplice."

"But something's missing here, Jon," Alix said. "I think that she knows that a crime demands punishment. She's a criminologist, for God's sake! I also sense some basic rectitude in this woman, even if she's a killer. Mind you, I'm relating to her as a woman in this respect, not as a cop. I felt something in her from the beginning that evoked a certain amount of understanding on my part."

She leaned forward, looking intently at him. "Besides, we still have no proof, my friend. It all boils down to that. She may have had the means, the motive, and the opportunity, but we have nothing to tie her to the scene of the crimes, except the hair from the wigs, and I've got to prove they're hers. And if she's as smart as I think she is, she would have disposed of them long ago. And I can't prove yet that O'Neil was murdered, although I'm working on it. Truth is, everything I have is circumstantial."

"She must be mad," Jon said, almost as if he were speaking to himself. "Not crazy, but mad. Something happened to her mind. We have to save her from herself."

"There's only one way to prove it," Alix said slowly, staring out the window.

"Catch her in the act?"

"Precisely. There're a lot of abused women out there. What if something happens to push her to do it again? What if we watch her for a while and see what she does? Dave and I can do it without involving anyone else in the department. I want to make sure she has no idea I suspect her. And if and when she makes her move, we'll be there."

"Multiple killers typically follow a time frame, with time periods gradually getting shorter between killings, Alix, but this isn't the case here," Jon said. "She doesn't fit the profile; she isn't your typical random serial killer, and she seems to kill more 'on demand,' as it were, as a result of an action that requires a reaction on her part. Am I making any sense?"

"Yes," Alix said slowly. "Yes, I see what you're getting at. In other words, she kills only in certain situations, like suspecting that Murdoch beat his wife to death and knowing that O'Neil hired a detective and was closing in on his family, but she doesn't kill otherwise. Sort of a damage-control specialist. As if she thinks of herself as some sort of avenging angel..."

He nodded. "Yes, something like that."

She gave him a look filled with compassion. "I know how you feel, *amigo*. To suspect one of your colleagues is bad enough, but a friend, someone you care about ... She may well be insane, but I can't help but feel some grudging admiration. She's got a lot of chutzpah. I sure wish I knew how she faked O'Neil's respiratory failure. That was brilliant, and her planning was flawless. Her motivation must have been considerable to put herself in such jeopardy."

"Unless she has nothing to lose," he said darkly.

"What do you mean?"

"I don't know, exactly, but everything about her reveals a total lack of interest in life. I suspect she may be seriously ill."

Suddenly, he felt very frightened for Meagan.

* * *

"Officer Connors, this is Dr. Meagan Rathburn. I want to talk to you about something Paige told me at the hospital. Let's meet somewhere privately since I don't want to discuss it over the phone." Meagan's tone was curt, her voice as icy as a mountain brook.

Shawn was shaken to the core. He had almost convinced himself that Paige had been unconscious since the accident. But now, to discover that she had spoken with her professor ... He had to find out what the redheaded bitch knew, see if he could convince her to keep her mouth shut, bribe her if he had to.

He held little hope, though, remembering the icy contempt in her eyes, accepting the fact that he faced an awesome opponent.

For the first time, he realized he wasn't in control of the situation. That damned woman was, and he did not like it one bit. He'd meet her all right, he had no choice, and she knew it. And he knew she knew.

* * *

A rictus of hatred distorted Meagan's delicate features as she stared at the receiver she had just replaced in its cradle. She knew Shawn would take the bait and meet her. Telling him that Paige had told her something that he ought to know for his own good had been all that was needed. He had to come.

Rain was predicted for tonight. The ground would be wet, but then she had counted on it. It was all part of the plan.

Perfect.

She wondered if District Attorney Patrick Conwell had received her letter yet. The timing was critical. And now the pieces could fall into place.

Phase Two of her plan had been set in motion.

* * *

Alix looked up from the stack of papers on her desk to see Dave Barnes peering around her door. "There's a call for you," he told her. "It's Amber Norton, you know, the young woman we interviewed at the King's Arms Tavern after Murdoch's murder?"

"Yes, I remember. Put her on, Dave."

Amber sounded excited and pleased with herself. "Detective, something's been bothering me about the woman," she said. "You know, Jen? The gal in red? There was something in the back of my mind that was bugging me, but I couldn't for the life of me remember what it was."

"Yes?" Alix asked, excitement welling up. "What is it, Amber?"

"Well, I was at the bank the other day and saw a woman standing in line just ahead of me. She was looking up at the guy behind her she was talking to, and she had a way of holding her head tilted to one side, and that's when I remembered. Jen did the same kinda thing whenever she looked up at Rich to smile at him. I don't know if it means anything, but I just thought you oughta know."

"What did the woman look like?" Alix demanded.

"Very thin and pale, short, strawberry blonde hair, big green eyes, and beautifully dressed, except the clothes looked too big for her. Sure wish I could afford clothes like that!" Amber added, sighing wistfully.

Alix closed her eyes. Meagan! She clearly remembered the flirtatious way Meagan had of tilting her head to one side as she had looked up at Jon after Steven's murder. One more piece of the puzzle had fallen into place, eliminating any remaining doubts.

She was filled with the same euphoria she always felt when nearing the end of an investigation and closing in on a suspect. But it was still circumstantial, she reminded herself. It could be argued that there were other women with the same habit of tilting their heads. And Meagan Rathburn wasn't the only woman to own a beautiful diamond ring like the one Margaret Woodruff had described.

Rushing out of her office, she collided with Dave who accompanied her down the corridor while she told him about what Amber had related to her, as well as her conversations with Jon and Margaret Woodruff, about their suspicions, her conclusions, and her plan regarding the surveillance.

"I'll be damned!" Dave exclaimed. "So there's no doubt about it now? Are you and MacLean positive?"

"Yes, but the only sure fire way is to catch her in the act."

"You realize you're assuming she'll try again?"

"Sure, but I think she will."

"Who do you want on the surveillance team?"

"We're dealing with a very clever woman here, Dave," Alix said in measured tones. "I don't want to do anything to spook her. She must suspect nothing, so it'll have to be just you and me for the time being. I don't want anyone to know what we're doing except Louise, MacLean, and Chief Harrison, of course."

"Okay," he agreed. "I'll phone Pat and tell her to expect me home when she sees me. When do we start?"

Alix referred to the notes on her desk.

"I've checked on Professor Rathburn's schedule," she told him. "This is Wednesday. She has a full teaching load, including a three-hour evening class that ends at ten. I doubt if she'll try anything in broad daylight, so we'll watch her house and wait until she comes home."

Dave nodded. "MacLean must be pretty shook up about all this."

"Yes, he's having a tough time coming to grips with it," she said, sighing and feeling a fresh stab of pity for Jon as the haunted look in his eyes and the sadness in his face flashed before her eyes.

But we're on our way at last, she thought, and she found that she was more relieved than she could have thought possible to see the end of her quest within reach.

On her way home, Alix made one more stop to visit the university's auditorium, following a growing suspicion she had been hatching for the last few days. She was there for a long time, and when she came out, her cheeks were flushed with excitement and her yellow eyes looked almost black.

The last barrier had come tumbling down. She now knew how Meagan Rathburn had killed her husband and felt something akin to pity for the beautiful woman with the big green eyes. Yet she was smiling broadly as she watched two burly men carry heavy red velvet drapes from the auditorium, load them into a dry cleaning van, and drive away.

She must tell Jon about how she had just shattered Meagan's alibi despite the pain she was bound to cause him again.

* * *

Meagan was already waiting when she saw the single headlight from Shawn's motorcycle approaching. He stopped when he saw her standing by the picnic table and benches, almost hidden by the willows bordering the river. She was dressed in dark clothing with a cape and gloves and she seemed to fade in and out of focus as he tried to make out her shape against the background of the bushes and trees. He killed the engine and dismounted.

"What did Paige say?" he demanded without making any attempt at pleasantries.

"That you pushed her out the door, you son of a bitch," Meagan said, her rage and disgust pouring out. "And in case you haven't heard, you bastard, she may not live. Even if she comes out of her coma, she'll probably be paralyzed for the rest of her life."

She saw from the look on his face that he had not known. He couldn't be bothered to go to the hospital or call to find out how Paige was. What a heartless, inhumane monster he was!

"What do you want? Money?" he demanded

She gave him a look of utter contempt. "I don't need your money. All I need is to know that you're going to be punished for what you did."

"What do you mean? You're going to tell somebody about this?"

She heard the note of fear that had crept into his voice.

Great! Let him sweat it out. He doesn't deserve an explanation. All he deserves is to go to prison for the rest of his pathetic life.

"I already have," she told him. "The district attorney probably has my letter by now. And you can be sure that you'll get what's coming to you."

"You bitch!" He rapidly closed the distance between them and struck her with his clenched right fist, knocking her to the ground.

"Get out of here, Officer Connors," she told him, unsteadily getting to her feet. "I've said what I came here to say."

"That's it? Why couldn't you tell me over the phone? Why make me come down here?"

"Because you had to be here," she said enigmatically. And, turning her back to him, she stared at the river.

Swearing under his breath, he turned on his heels, and strode angrily toward his motorcycle. "I'll get even with you, you crazy bitch, if it's the last thing I do," he shouted.

After he left, Meagan raised her face to the stars peering out from under the heavy cloud cover that had brought the rain earlier like a child turning her face to the sun after a long winter. One large star winked back at her, but it was soon obscured by the fast-moving clouds.

She saw her life in bursts of fragmented images, like a kaleidoscope of random colors and shapes with no substance. She knew that Alix was closing in on her, but it didn't matter now. Nothing mattered now. Unknowingly, she returned the silent compliment Alix had paid her earlier, glad that her nemesis had been someone like Alix, and in the corner of what remained of her shattered mind, she sensed that Alix would understand.

It was difficult to remember what to do now. Oh, yes, the knife. The knife she would use to kill herself with. Spartans fell on their swords, didn't they? The ultimate bravery, but not reserved only for men. She had already done all a man could do, and more. And everyone would know. Everyone …

With infinite calm, she picked up the knife purloined from Shawn's kitchen with her gloved hand, placed the razor-sharp blade below her rib cage, and with all the strength she could muster, pushed the blade upward into her heart.

She fell without a sound.

CHAPTER 25

"What's going on, Alix?" District Attorney Pat Conwell demanded as he charged into Alix's office.

"Pat, I was expecting your visit, but I think I'd better start from the beginning," Alix replied. "Sorry if I didn't tell you everything earlier, but I had nothing concrete to go on, nothing to bring you, no actual proof in order to arrest Dr. Rathburn for the murder of her husband and the others. It was all circumstantial, so I decided to watch her in case she tried again. It's like this ..."

Conwell listened intently as she told him everything. "I see," he finally said. "This helps me make some sense of a letter I received from her today. It says that Paige Chatfield told her that Shawn Connors had pushed her out of his moving car. It wasn't an accident at all as he claimed, Alix. Dr. Rathburn suspected that Ms. Chatfield was going to end her relationship with Connors. She did, and he apparently lost his temper."

Alix shook her head. "This is getting stranger and stranger, Pat. What else did the letter say?"

This was indeed puzzling, she thought. Just as she was about to arrest Meagan, another development had surfaced. This damned case had more twists and turns than a corkscrew.

"It said that if I got the letter, it meant that she had confronted Connors with this information. He apparently threatened to kill her if she told anyone," Pat Conwell replied, "and if this letter reached me, it meant that she probably was already dead."

Alix tried hard to hide her astonishment. What did all this mean? Damned if she knew. A letter predicting Meagan's death at the hands of one of her officers?

Pat Conwell reached in his pocket and handed her a sealed envelope. "And she included this letter for you," he added, placing it on her desk.

I am going totally going mad, Alix thought. Why would she be receiving a letter from her suspect? She was beginning to feel like a character in Alice in Wonderland and wondered when the Mad Hatter was going to appear. This was beyond bizarre!

Her intercom rang. "What is it, Louise?" Alix said impatiently. "I thought I asked you to hold all my calls."

"I think you'll want to take this one," Louise said in a subdued tone. "Dr. Rathburn's body was just found near the river by an older couple walking their dog. The patrolman who radioed in identified her from the contents of her purse, which were scattered all over the ground. She's been stabbed to death."

Alix felt the blood drain from her face as she slowly hung up the phone and turned to face the district attorney. "We're too late, Pat," she told him.

Reaching for her intercom, she said, "I want an APB on Shawn Connors. Now! The charge's murder."

Then she picked up the phone and punched in Jon's home number.

* * *

When Alix and Pat Conwell arrived, the Crime Scene Unit was already there, and Dr. Gardner was kneeling next to Meagan's lifeless body. The scene had already been roped off with yellow police ribbons. Because the rain had stopped only recently, footprints, a cigarette butt, and narrow tire tracks were clearly apparent in the eerie light cast by the revolving dome lights of the police cars that were also flashing red shadows on the river. .

Meagan's car was parked in the small graveled lot about a hundred yards away. She lay next to her open purse from which its contents had spilled and scattered next to her. There was a heavy bruise on the left side of her face, but the cause of death was immediately apparent—the thin blade of a kitchen knife protruding from her chest. Her eyes were closed, her face peaceful. The moon aimed ghostly, silvery rays on the copper hair spread around her head, and it sparkled like a pillow of gold.

Even in death, she was beautiful.

"Death was probably instantaneous," Dr. Gardner told Alix and Pat Conwell as he rose slowly. "What a shame, such a beautiful young woman! Who could have done this? And what was she doing here alone this time of night?"

Alix turned to face Jon who had just arrived. Slowly walking over to the spot where Meagan lay, he stood and looked down at her. The scene was now illuminated by spotlights, and in their yellow glare, his face seemed bloodless as tears ran down his cheeks.

"Now we'll never know for sure, Alix," he said in a strangled voice. "Who did this? And why?"

"Shawn Connors, one of my officers," Alix said. She summarized briefly what she had learned from the district attorney.

"Perhaps there's more in the letter she wrote you," Conwell said.

"The letter!" Alix exclaimed. "I forgot all about it. It's back at the precinct on my desk."

"Alix, I am sure you won't mind if I tell Dan DeVoe about this, "Jon said. "I suspect he was in love with Meagan and he was as concerned about her as I was."

Alix nodded and then turned back to the Crime Scene Unit detectives. "Sweep this area for anything you can find and make casts of all tire tracks," she told them. "Most of them look fresh. And keep everybody out of here. I don't want this scene compromised."

She watched as she saw one of her detectives pick up a half-smoked cigarette lying on the ground and place it in an evidence envelope.

Alix knew that she would follow this case to its conclusion with all the dedication she could muster. There would be no mistakes, no slip-ups. And in the end, her suspicions about Meagan would be confirmed once and for all.

After everyone had left the crime scene, Alix, Pat Conwell, and Jon drove back to her office where the forgotten letter still lay on her desk. She unfolded it and started to read as Jon looked on.

Its poignancy took her breath away.

After what seemed like a long time, she finally looked up. "Jon, you have to hear this," she told him. "I know you're going to find it difficult, but you must know. You'll never have closure until you do."

"All right," he said in a low voice. "Go on."

And so she did. She read aloud that if Alix had received the letter, it meant that Meagan had not only been found out but that she was also dead at the hands of Connors who had sworn to kill her if she told anyone about Paige Chatfield's alleged accident.

"She says that she feels sure I won't have any trouble getting enough evidence to secure a well-deserved conviction for Connors if Ms. Chatfield dies, and for her own murder at his hands," Alix said.

She paused to look up at Jon who, face grim, nodded for her to continue.

"She confesses to killing her husband and all the others but makes no apologies for the murders."

She suddenly sat up in her black leather chair. "Jon, this explains a lot of things. She says here that a few months ago, she found out that she had contracted AIDS from her husband. She knew she had only a short time to live."

Despite herself, she felt tears running down her face. By the look on Jon's face, she realized that he, too, shared her anguish.

"So that's why she looked so ill," he said, almost to himself. "Please go on," he added.

Alix went on reading. "She says that no one ever knew about the abuse. Apparently, she was also abused by her father, but her mother never believed her, so it, too, remained a secret."

She looked directly at him. "Jon, I told you I was going to break her alibi. Well, I did, and her letter confirms it. She did go to the lecture the day she killed her husband, but she left early through a side door that had not been used for years.

Eyes bright, she said, "It all became crystal clear when I saw two men remove the velvet curtains from the auditorium and load them into a dry cleaning van. I noticed that the hinges of the door the curtains had concealed had been oiled recently and that the door opened noiselessly. The woman who had been sitting next to Meagan told me she had to leave early because her son was ill, and since no one else was sitting nearby, it was easy for Meagan to leave and return in less than twenty minutes. Enough time to drive home, kill her husband, and return to her seat unnoticed.

For a while, no one spoke.

"Why do you suppose she just didn't get a divorce, Alix?" Jon asked finally.

Alix could tell he was having a very hard time assimilating all this. She was having a pretty hard time taking it in herself.

"Because she says that her mother had brainwashed her into silence so as not to shame the family name," Alix responded. "I guess in their world, revealing the incest and her abuse was not an option."

Jon gave a slow nod. "I can see where those taboos would prevent her from seeking help or leaving Steven," he said. "But why didn't she come to me? Maybe I could have helped her. Talked to her. Something!" he said, his voice rising.

Alix realized that he was blaming himself, but instead of offering platitudes, she said, "Apparently, she tried to get help but was rebuffed, made to feel that it was all her fault. After that, she just gave up and let the madness overtake her. Which is probably when she started killing."

She tipped the envelope, letting a key and a small piece of paper fall out. "These apparently are the key and address of a storage unit where she says we'll find the wigs and other items sufficient to prove what she told me."

"I wonder if she felt any guilt," Jon said quietly, "but I suspect that she believed herself anointed by a higher power to avenge the women she felt obliged to protect. If she did feel any guilt, her madness and her illness would have persuaded her that she was doing the right thing."

Alix nodded quietly. She was a woman, and although she had never experienced what Meagan Rathburn had gone through, she could not help but feel empathy for her.

"You feel sorry for her, don't you?" Jon said quietly.

Alix nodded. "She was a woman in agony, Jon. Imagine her loneliness. I can't imagine anything sadder. For the first time in my career, I feel sorry for a killer. What a damned waste," she added angrily.

Her look became stern. "But she wasn't blameless, Jon. She became blind to life's possibilities and her madness led to her death. Her life could have been so different if she had only trusted someone."

"I know," he said sadly.

Alix sighed. "Well, it's the last piece of the puzzle, I suppose. I should have understood the significance of her statement that day at her house when she killed her husband. I blame myself for not being more perceptive."

"What statement?" he asked, puzzled.

"When we were asking her if she was all right. She almost went ballistic and said 'Everything's all right. It's got to be all right.' She must have meant that it was because he was dead and she had nothing more to fear."

"You were right from the beginning, your know, Alix," he said grimly, "And I'm sorry I didn't believe you. I guess I was too close to the situation and just couldn't accept it."

"Probably, but this is one time when I find no solace in it."

"She was a victim to the end, wasn't she?"

Alix could only nod silently, torn between her compassion for the victim who, ironically, was also a three-time killer, and her revulsion for the killer's deeds. She sighed and squared her shoulders, becoming the tough, efficient cop again. "But I suspect that she felt in control for the first time in her life, and it was her decision to commit premeditated murder, Jon. She was wrong to take the law into her own hands, regardless of her madness."

"I wonder what she means here when she writes that she would choose the form of payment society demands," she said, brow furrowed. "How does her murder accomplish that?"

"I don't know. I wonder, too," Jon replied.

Alix was in on the arrest. Connors did not go quietly. Meagan was a bitch, he said, and what had happened to Paige was an accident. They had been quarreling, and she had opened the car door and jumped out.

But when confronted with the evidence—his fingerprints on the knife, the motorcycle tracks at the park, his DNA on the cigarette butt found at the crime scene, he collapsed like a pricked balloon and went with them without resisting

Strangely enough, however, he seemed more confused than anything else. The last thing Alix heard him say as he was led off to be booked was, "I didn't do it. That woman was alive when I left her. I swear to God I didn't do it."

* * *

The verdict was unanimous as Shawn Connors was found guilty of the murder of Meagan Rathburn.

Meagan's ultimate quest for justice from the grave was now complete.

CHAPTER 26

As Alix was headed for the precinct a couple of days after Meagan's funeral, she drove by the cemetery and saw a man standing by her grave, head bent, as the unrelenting rain came down in sheets slanted by the east winds that had brought the summer storm. The wind whistled and moaned through the poplar trees planted around the small graveyard, whipping his raincoat around his legs while the rain drenched the pants of his dark blue suit. But he seemed oblivious to the unchained elements.

A lone hawk, a dark chevron against a darker sky, circled high above, his heart-wrenching, lonely cry carried down by the wind, adding the perfect note to the funereal scene below.

Curious, Alix stopped the car. She was close enough to see the man raise his eyes to the pewter sky and look at the bird, then back down to the mound of earth under which Meagan rested. She watched him as he knelt on the ground and with great care, tears running down his cheeks, he placed a bouquet of delicate tea roses on her grave.

The season for ruffled daffodils was long gone, but down deep, Dan DeVoe knew Meagan would be pleased anyway.

CHAPTER 27

"Alix, have you seen my glasses?"

"They're on your face, Lloyd," Jon, Margot, and Alix replied in unison.

The Mexican sun shone like a red-hot, polished copper disk in the cloudless Cancún sky. Alix retreated into the shade of the *palapa* and applied more lotion to her legs and face, knowing her complexion could turn lobster red in a matter of minutes. She looked at her husband and friends whose skins displayed varying shades of tan, envying them their coloring and knowing that her redhead's sensitive skin, so much like her mother's, was not so blessed.

"It's so great to finally be able to relax!" she said, leaning back in her chair. "This vacation couldn't have come too soon for me."

She stretched like a cat and reached for her sunglasses. "You've been awful quiet since we left home, Lloyd," she added. "You've got something on your mind, I can tell, so let's have it. Whatever it is, I can take it."

She paused and grinned. "Let me guess. You've decided to run away with that buxom brunette at the grocery store, the one you're always gawking at, and you don't know how to break it to me, right?"

He chuckled, shaking his head. "Alix, what would you say about my going back to teaching? I've been offered a part-time position in the political science department in the fall."

She beamed at him. "Lloyd, that's wonderful! So *that's* the big secret! And here I was trying to figure out how to tell you about my own news."

"What news?"

"I've asked Chief Harrison for a year's leave to give us a chance to go abroad. How about putting off the teaching job for a while so we can go to Europe for a few months? You know, do the museum thing in Italy, eat *gazpacho* in Spain, drink *citron pressè* at sidewalk cafes, mess around in a field of daisies in Provence and ..."

"Alix! Jon and Margot will hear you!"

"No big deal, *querido*. They'll just be jealous. And besides, since Jon's proposed and Margot accepted, they may even go with us!"

He grinned at his wife's irrepressible humor. "I'd love it. But Alix ..." he said uncertainly.

"Yes, I know what you're going to say. You really never expected me to quit my job, did you?"

He shook his head. "No, and I knew that even if you had agreed, I wouldn't have let you. I know how much your work means to you. I've been a selfish old grump and I'm sorry."

She leaned her head against his bare shoulder. "Have I told you lately how much I love you, you selfish old grump?"

"Not in the last half hour. But Alix ..."

"What?

"Would you really have given up your job for me with no regrets?"

"Yes, but not without regrets," she said honestly. "Our marriage comes first, but I would have gone kicking and screaming."

He looked at her lovingly. "Thanks, my dear, this means a lot to me."

She kissed him again and then turned to Jon who was applying sunscreen to Margot's back. "What did Meagan's mother say when you called her, Jon?"

Jon's expression darkened. "When I told her what had happened, how ill Meagan had been, and what she had been through, she said she no longer had a daughter and hung up on me. I wonder if subconsciously, Meagan killed to get back at her."

"Makes sense to me. You know, in a strange and twisted way, she made me look at myself. I realize now that, although murder is never justified, some people are driven to kill by inner forces that are often too difficult to ignore. She taught me understanding and, to a certain degree, compassion. Life must have been hell for her."

She rose on one elbow and faced him. "Do you believe Connors killed Meagan, Jon?"

He stared at her. "What are you talking about? With all that evidence, and Meagan's own letter, and his fingerprints on the knife, and the jury ..."

"That's just it. There was too much evidence. He was a seasoned police officer. Why didn't he get rid of the knife? And pick up the cigarette butt? And eliminate his tire tracks or use a vehicle other than his motorcycle? He wasn't stupid. He would have thought of those things if he was planning to murder her."

"Are you saying he was innocent?"

An enigmatic smile played upon her lips.

She and Jon had both been wrong. Meagan Rathburn had *not* been a victim to the end. She had reached out from the grave to exact justice, and in the end, she had won.

Just as she had planned.

LaVergne, TN USA
11 February 2011
216149LV00002B/16/P

9 781606 934067